THE CAULIFLOWER®

Nicola Barker was born in Ely in 1966 and spent part of her childhood in South Africa. She is the author of ten previous novels – including *Wide Open*, *Darkmans*, *The Yips* and *In the Approaches* – and two short story collections. She has been twice longlisted and once shortlisted for the Man Booker Prize, has won the IMPAC, the John Llewellyn Rhys and the Hawthornden Prizes, and was named one of *Granta*'s 20 Best Young British Writers in 2003. She lives and works in east London.

Also by Nicola Barker

Novels
Reversed Forecast
Small Holdings
Wide Open
Five Miles from Outer Hope
Behindlings
Clear
Darkmans
Burley Cross Postbox Theft
The Yips
In the Approaches

Short story collections
Love Your Enemies
Heading Inland

THE CAULIFLOWER®

Nicola Barker

WILLIAM HEINEMANN: LONDON

1 3 5 7 9 10 8 6 4 2

William Heinemann
20 Vauxhall Bridge Road
London SW1V 2SA

William Heinemann is part of the Penguin Random House group of companies
whose addresses can be found at global.penguinrandomhouse.com.

First published by William Heinemann in 2016

www.penguin.co.uk

A CIP catalogue record for this book is available from the British Library.

ISBN 9781785150661 (Hardback)
ISBN 9781785150654 (Trade Paperback)

Typeset in 13/16 pt Fournier MT
Jouve (UK), Milton Keynes
Printed and bound by Clays Ltd, St Ives plc

This small book is humbly and lovingly offered – like a freshly picked wild rose – at the feet of Shafilea Ahmed, Uzma Arshad, Mashael Albasman, Banaz Mahmod and the 5,000 other women worldwide who are killed, each year, for the sake of 'honour'.

Not one, not two, not three or four

Not one, not two, not three or four,
but through eighty-four hundred thousand vaginas have I come.
    I have come
through unlikely worlds,
     guzzled on
pleasure and pain.
    Whatever be
all previous lives,
    show me mercy
this one day,
     O lord
     white as jasmine.

(Akkamahadevi — twelfth-century Indian poetess)

Catch us the foxes,
The little foxes that spoil the
    vines,
For our vines have tender
    grapes . . .

Song of Solomon, Holy Bible, 2:15

The beautiful Rani Rashmoni is perpetually trapped inside the celluloid version of her own amazing and dramatic life. Of course every life has its mundane elements – even the Rani, beautiful as she is, powerful as she is, must use the bathroom and clean her teeth, snag her new sari with a slightly torn thumbnail, belch graciously with indigestion after politely consuming an over-fried rice ball prepared by a resentful cook at the house of her oldest yet most tedious friend – but Rani Rashmoni is, nevertheless, the star (the heroine) of her own movie.

How will it all end? we wonder. Temporarily disable that impatient index finger. We must strenuously resist the urge to fast-forward. Because everything we truly need to know about the Rani is already here, right in front of us, helpfully contained (deliciously condensed, like a sweet, biographical mango compote) within the nine modest words engraved in the official seal of her vast and sumptuous Bengali estate: 'Sri Rashmoni Das, longing for the Feet of Kali.'

Hmmm.

Her husband, the late Rajchandra Das – a wealthy businessman, landowner and philanthropist, twice widowed – first saw her as an exquisitely lovely but poor and low-caste village girl bathing in the confluence of three rivers thirty miles north of Calcutta. He instantly fell in love. She was nine years old.

That was then. But now? Where do we find the Rani today, at the very start of this story which longs to be a film, and eventually (in 1955) will be? We find her utterly abandoned and alone in her giant palace (the guards, servants and family have all fled at the Rani's firm insistence). Her poor heart is pounding wildly, her sword is unsheathed and she is bravely standing guard outside the family shrine room as a local garrison of vengeful British soldiers ransacks her home.

In one version of this story we find the Rani confronting these soldiers. In other versions her palace is so huge and labyrinthine (with over 300 rooms) that although the soldiers riot and pillage for many hours they never actually happen across the Rani (and her sword) as she boldly stands, arm raised, fierce and defiant, just like that extraordinary goddess Kali whose lotus feet she so highly venerates.

The Rani, like the goddess, has many arms. Although the Rani's limbs are chiefly metaphorical. And the two arms that she *does* possess – ending in a pair of soft, graceful yet surprisingly competent hands – aren't coloured a deep Kali-black, but have the seductive, milky hue of a creamy latte. The Rani is modest and humble and devout. The Rani is strictly bound by the laws of caste. The Rani is a loyal wife. The Rani is a mother of four girls. The Rani is a cunning businesswoman. The Rani is ruthless. The Rani has a close and lucrative relationship with the British rulers of Calcutta. The Rani is a thorn in the side of Calcutta's British rulers. The Rani is compassionate and charitable. The Rani always plays by the rules. The Rani invents her own rules.

The soldiers – when they are finally compelled to withdraw on the orders of their irate commanding officer (who has been alerted to these shocking events by the Rani's favourite son-in-law, Mathur) – have caused a huge amount of damage. The Rani wanders around the palace, appraising the mess, sword dragging behind her, relatively unperturbed. She cares little for material possessions. Only one thing shakes her equilibrium. They have slaughtered her collection of birds and animals. Worst of all, her favourite peacock, her darling beloved, who lies on the lawn, cruelly beheaded, magnificent tail partially unfurled in a shimmering sea of accusing eyes.

He is only four years older, but still I call him Uncle, and when I am with Uncle I have complete faith in him. I would die for Uncle. I have an indescribable attraction towards Uncle. It is painful to be parted from Uncle – even briefly. It was ever thus. And it is only when I leave his side – only then, when I am feeling sad and alone and utterly forlorn – that the doubts gradually begin to gnaw away at me. Perhaps I should never leave Uncle's side, and then the doubts will finally be dispelled? Mathur Baba repeatedly instructs me not to do so, *never* to leave Uncle (Uncle is a special case, Mathur Baba insists, a delicate flower, who must be supported and nurtured at all times – and who else may perform this task if not me, his ever-faithful nephew and helper Hridayram?). I have great sympathy and respect for Mathur Baba's views, but how can I always be with Uncle when I am constantly doing the work that Uncle cannot manage to do himself? Sometimes Uncle is unable to fulfil his duties in the temple and I must perform *arati* – the sacred worship – on his behalf. Sometimes Uncle sends me to the market for sweets (Uncle has an incredibly sweet tooth) or on sundry errands. Even so, I guard Uncle jealously. I am Uncle's shadow. But Uncle is slippery. He can be secretive. Uncle is not as other men.

The family jokes about how Uncle's mother, Chandradevi, gave him birth in the husking shed at Kamarpukur. The old blacksmith's daughter was acting midwife. She was sitting on a stool in the half-darkness briefly catching her breath and then suddenly she heard the baby cry out. She leapt forward to take her first good look at the child. But he was nowhere to be found! She and Chandradevi – who is by nature a simple creature – were completely mystified. They both felt their way blindly around the shed until poor Uncle was finally located hidden in the pit below the husking pedal. In many of our local Bengali folk songs the husking machine — the *dhenki* — is seen as a kind of phallic symbol. Uncle had fallen straight from one vagina into the deep, dark depths of another! Ah yes. Looking back on it now it seems only right and natural that Uncle should eventually become a great devotee — perhaps even the greatest ever devotee — of the Black Mother.

Every story flows from a million sources, but the story of
Rani Rashmoni (and therefore, by extension, the story of Sri
Ramakrishna – as yet unborn, but already floating like a plump
and perpetually smiling golden imp in the navy blue ether)
might easily be said to begin with a pinch of **salt**. Yes, *salt*.
Sodium chloride. That commonplace, everyday, intensely
mundane yet still precious and once much-contested mineral.
Salt. That most revolutionary of crystals.

If we cast our minds back we see this powerful yet curiously
delicate whitish-transparent grain generating ferment (ironically
salt is a preserve) worldwide throughout centuries. **Salt** is
serious – it's no laughing matter – didn't we once look on in
awe as the ancient Hebrews gravely made a Covenant of **Salt**
with their jealous God? And what of Christopher Columbus?
Didn't he voyage the world (leaving in his wake that ugly
colonial legacy – that despicable flotsam – of genocide, slavery
and plunder) financed, in the main, by Spanish **salt** production?

A mere sprinkling of years before the mother of the beautiful
Rani Rashmoni gave her birth (in 1793) we see **salt** riots
playing a central role in the American Revolution, the *'gabelle'*,
a much-loathed **salt** tax, spurring on the French Revolution a
few years later, and beyond that, flowing far off into the
future, we see the fragile, brown frame of Mahatma Gandhi
(a passionate adherent of the philosophy of Sri Ramakrishna)
dressed in his humble, white *dhoti* and leading 100,000
protesters to the sea – a critical moment in the heroic march
towards Indian independence – on his 240-mile **Salt** *Satyagraha*.

But the episode we are to briefly dwell upon here is not an
especially glorious one. It is little more than a mere technicality;
a brief donning of the cap to Pritaram Das, no less, father of
the Rani's husband, Rajchandra, who started off his meteoric

business career as a poor and humble clerk in a Calcutta **salt** distributing agency.

The story of Sri Ramakrishna started with **salt**. **Salt.** Although it's probably equally conceivable that it may have started with sugar, a granule to which Sri Ramakrishna was passionately attached (although he passionately eschewed all earthly attachments). Yes, it's probably equally conceivable that his story may have started with sugar. But it didn't actually start that way. Not this time. Not in this telling. Not here. Not with sugar. Not so far as we are aware. No. The story of Sri Ramakrishna started with **salt**.

Salt . . .

Or – if you feel the sudden urge to rotate it on your tongue in the form Ramakrishna himself would have used – '*lobon*'.

Just over the border in Bangladesh (which wouldn't exist until 1971) this same word '*lobon*' means 'nun'. And if we think of Calcutta (364 miles from the border) we often think of the free flow of people, of poverty, of refugees, and then our minds sometimes turn (a sharp incline, a small bounce, a quick jink) to Mother Teresa.

Salt.

Nun.

Mother.

Saint.

Ma.

Ah . . .

Sri Ramakrishna.

There are so many strange stories I could tell you about Uncle's
boyhood. In fact all the stories of Uncle's boyhood are very
curious. It would be difficult for me to recall a single story that
is not thus. Uncle was always the weft in the weave. He was
singular. Chandradevi tells how she was once holding the baby
Uncle in her arms as she was relaxing in the sunlight by a
window when she suddenly felt him grow very heavy on her
lap. Somewhat alarmed, she quickly lifted Uncle up and placed
him down on to a winnowing fan lying on the bed close by.
Moments later the fan began to crack, then the bed underneath
Uncle started to creak and complain . . . She tried to lift Uncle
but she could not. Uncle had become an extraordinary – an
unbearable – weight!

Chandradevi – and she is a simple soul, by nature – began
to wail. Nearby villagers ran into the house to try and aid
her but she could not be calmed until a ghost-charmer was
summoned. Only once he had sung a *mantra* to pacify the
spirits could she be persuaded to hold baby Uncle in her
arms again.

On a further occasion I have been told how she left Uncle
on the bed and turned around for a moment to perform some
minor chore or other and when she turned back again the top
half of the baby's body (Uncle could not have been more than
three months of age) was hidden inside the nearby bread oven.
The oven was cool and full of ashes. Uncle withdrew from the
oven and proceeded to roll around on the floor until he was
coated from head to toe in white ash (*ash* – the dust of
renunciation – Lord Shiva's habitual raiment). Chandradevi
simply could not understand how Uncle – still such a small
baby – had crawled into the oven, nor why he now suddenly
appeared so large to her as he rolled around. Again she began

wailing, inconsolable, until a local woman ran into the house and – apprehending the dreadful scene before her – scolded Chandradevi for her terrible neglect of the child.

On a further occasion Chandradevi had placed the baby Uncle under the mosquito net for a doze. She then went off to perform some small task, but when she returned a fully grown man was sitting under the net in Uncle's place. Chandradevi was dreadfully shocked and alarmed. She simply couldn't understand where her baby had gone. Again, the tears, the wails, the pitiful calls for assistance. But on this occasion it was Kshudiram, Uncle's father, who rushed to her aid. I am told that Kshudiram was always a profoundly devout and holy man. People accused him – just as they do Uncle – of being truthful to the point of mania. In fact he had lost his fifty-acre family estate in Derepur after a powerful but corrupt local landlord tried to force him to testify falsely in court against an innocent neighbour. When he refused, the landlord's wrath became focused upon Kshudiram himself, culminating in a second court case and the eventual loss of his entire inheritance. Kshudiram, his wife and his family (Uncle had a sister and two considerably older brothers) were only saved from complete destitution when a kind friend – Sukhlal Goswami of Kamarpukur – stepped in to help him with the offer of a group of huts on his property and a half-acre of fertile ground. Kshudiram accepted this gift most gratefully. He thanked his chosen deity Sri Rama for it and then – apparently without any bitterness or resentment – he dedicated himself still more heartily to a dignified *brahmin*'s life of quiet meditation, *japa*, pilgrimage and worship.

Every happening in Kshudiram's life was perceived by this devout and well-respected man as a sign from God. On apprehending his wife's distress at Uncle's transformation, for example, he calmly told her to collect herself, hold fast her counsel (to please avoid encouraging the villagers from idle gossip or unnecessary speculation) and simply accept the fact that these strange occurrences were a part of God's divine plan for their son. They were beyond mere human comprehension. Uncle was different. It was ever thus. He was golden. He was special. He was oddly blessed. Most important of all Uncle was ours. He was *ours*. He came from us.

Twenty-one years earlier

The streets of Calcutta are flooded with books. Piles of books from England and America. Books in incredible, immense, *inconceivable* quantities. A veritable infestation of books; a plague!

At every brief stop or blocked intersection people thrust them into carriages or through palanquin windows. Huge consignments of novels and philosophical tomes. Books about free will and independence and revolution. Every kind of book. Sometimes (it occasionally happens) a ship from England or America bound for Calcutta is wrecked at the Cape of Good Hope – the Cape of Storms – and the sandy African beaches are littered with novels. Thousands of novels in colourful mounds – in prodigious, literary heaps – in giant, fictional dunghills. And the savage wind blows across them (as the savage Cape wind invariably must). Their pages flip and tear and whip over and over and over and over. A million sentences. A billion well-turned phrases. All clamouring for attention. Read me! Read me! Read me! *Please.*

The gulls circle and then take fright – keening pitifully – at this awful, bright mess of fatally sodden torsos, this tragedy of broken spines, this terrible, deafening, flapping and beating of horribly disabled limbs.

'I don't mean literally a child,' pursued Mr Jarndyce, 'not a
child in years. He is grown up . . . but in simplicity, and
freshness, and enthusiasm, and a fine guileless inaptitude for
all worldly affairs, he is a perfect child . . .'
When we went downstairs we were presented to Mr Skimpole . . .
a little bright creature with a rather large head, but a delicate
face and a sweet voice, and there was a perfect charm in him.
All he said was so free from effort and spontaneous and was
said with such a captivating gaiety . . . 'I covet nothing,' said
Mr Skimpole . . . 'possession is nothing to me . . . It's
only you, the generous creatures, whom I envy . . . I envy you
your power of doing what you do . . . I don't feel any vulgar
gratitude to you. I almost feel as if YOU ought to feel grateful
to ME for giving you the opportunity of enjoying the luxury
of generosity . . . For anything I can tell, I may have come into
the world expressly for the purpose of increasing your stock
of happiness. I may have been born to be a benefactor to you
by sometimes giving you an opportunity of assisting me in
my little perplexities. Why should I regret my incapacity for
details and worldly affairs when it leads to such pleasant
consequences?'

Monday, 30 June 1884 at 4 p.m.

Sri Ramakrishna (*with a melodramatic sigh*): 'I used to *weep*, praying to the Divine Mother, "Oh Mother, destroy with Thy thunderbolt my inclination to reason!"'
Truth seeker (*patently surprised*): 'Then you too had an inclination to reason?'
Sri Ramakrishna (*nodding, regretful*): 'Yes, once.'
Truth seeker (*eagerly*): 'Then please assure us that we shall get rid of that inclination too! How did you get rid of yours?'
Sri Ramakrishna (*with an apparent loss of interest*): 'Oh . . . [*flaps hand, wearily*], somehow or other.'
Silence.

This is the story of an unlettered sage who spoke only in a rudimentary and colloquial Bengali – described by some commentators as a kind of abstruse haiku. A curiously effete village boy who stammered. Who didn't understand a word of English. Who went to school but wouldn't – yes, *wouldn't* – read. At a time when the world was ripe with a glossy new secularism – bursting at the seams with revolutionary ideas about science and knowledge and art and progress – this singular individual would tie his wearing-cloth around his hips with an expanse of fabric hanging down at the back to simulate a tail (and him a respectable *brahmin* – a temple priest), then leap – with beguiling agility – from tree branch to tree branch, pretending to be an ape. No, worse. Worse even than that. *Believing* himself to be an ape.

Eventually he would be called God. *Avatar. Paramahamsa.* He would be called the Great Swan.

This squealing, furtive, hyperactive, freely urinating beast is none other than Sri Ramakrishna.

Although some people call him Gadadhar Chatterjee. Or Uncle. Or Master. Or *guru* (which he loathes). And his real name, his actual name – the name you will rarely ever hear – is Shabhu Chandra.

1857, the Kali Temple, Dakshineswar (six miles north of Calcutta)

This is our story, because Uncle belongs to us. And it is colourful. And sometimes I don't quite understand where the joyous *kirtans* and ecstatic love poems of Ramprasad and Chaitanya – or the heroic stories of *The Mahabharata* and the *Puranas* – begin and the tales and mysteries of Uncle's life end. Everything is woven together in my mind – by the tongue of Uncle himself – and it cannot be unpicked, because I too am a part of it all, and if I try to dismantle it, thread by thread, I will lose myself, and I will lose Uncle, and although Uncle depends on me for everything, my hold on Uncle has never been a strong one. Uncle has an independent spirit. Uncle is single-minded but he is also simple and humble as a child.

Which of us may truly hope to understand Uncle? Ah, not one such as me.

We are a poor family. There has been much loss and hunger and tragedy. And sometimes we call on the gods for aid, and sometimes it feels as though the gods are calling on us in their turn. They are very close. They are breathing down our necks. They are speaking through us and they are writing our history. They prompt us from behind a dark curtain. Of course some of us hear them more clearly than others. They whisper mysteries into Uncle's ear. From behind a dark curtain, or . . . or hidden under a cloth in the manner of a photographer. Precisely so. A photographer takes your picture but the portrait he makes belongs to you. It is your own. It is yours. A perfect likeness. Simply in a more formal setting – the studio. And holding very still. And carefully posed. That is Uncle's past. It needs to be stage-managed and well-lit. I am Uncle's technician.

14

Although Uncle will not be managed and he will not be directed and he will not be exposed. Uncle will expose himself in his own good time. He is very particular in that way. He will not be controlled. He will not be pushed. He will never be rushed.

In the beginning was the word. And the word was Calcutta. And the word was a place. And people disagreed about the origin of the word. In 1690 a man called Job Charnock – a dour and morose administrator for the English East India Company – anglicised the name of one of the three small villages already established in this swampy, malarial and deeply inhospitable location (Kalikata), believing (and correctly) that it would one day become India's great colonial trading city.

Three hundred and eleven years later, in AD 2001, it was renamed Kolkata, in line with the Bengali pronunciation of the word. Some speculate that the name originally came from the Bengali root *kilkila* (or flat place). Others say that the area was known for its production of quicklime or *kolikata*. Still others argue that the word might have its origins in the conjoining of *khal* (or canal) and *kata* (meaning 'dug'). But the general consensus is that it means 'field of Kali'. Kalikata is Kali's place. Kali: the fearsome, fearless black goddess of destruction and creation – mistress of *shakti*, or primordial, cosmic energy; wife of dreadlocked, ash-covered Shiva, god of renunciation – whose devotees traditionally call her Ma.

In the beginning there was nothing. Then there was a sound. The hungry, howling aaaa of Maaaa: *Aaaaa* . . . That was something. And that sound, that something, was somehow – quite miraculously – sustained: Aaaaa-*uuuuu* . . . And then it concluded, in a throatily dynamic, busy-bee *hummmm*: Aaaaauuuu*mmmm*. Finally it stopped. Or did it stop? How could it? How could such deep, primordial hunger, such yearning, ever be truly satisfied?

This strange *Aum*, this sound, this process, is embedded and celebrated in the Hindu faith by dint of its mystical triumvirate – its holy trinity – of three gods: Brama (the creator), Vishnu (the preserver) and Shiva (the destroyer).

In the beginning there was a piece of land and a stretch of river. Then there were three villages. Then there was Job Charnock. And Job Charnock was a dour and morose administrator royally despised by virtually all his contemporaries.

In the beginning there was a man called Job Charnock, a dour and morose administrator, a jobsworth, a company man, who was feared and hated by his contemporaries because of his inflexible stance around issues of smuggling and corporate corruption (endemic in Anglo/Indian trading at that time). His contemporaries (all happily accustomed to the long-established tradition of receiving backhanders) had nothing good to say about him. He was a man of stern and unbending moral character. He was universally loathed.

In the beginning was the word and the word was Calcutta and in 2001 it became Kolkata. And in 2003 a Kolkata High Court ruled that long before Job Charnock (that colonial lickspittle, that dour and morose and intensely unpopular administrator) had sailed down the Hooghly, a 'highly civilised society' had already existed there, that it was a thriving religious hub, an 'important trading centre': Kalikatah. The court therefore ruled that Job Charnock's name be summarily removed from all official histories of the city. This great city. Kolkata.

In the beginning (if there ever was a beginning – was there ever a beginning?) there were three powerful forces: creation, preservation and destruction. Over millennia these three competing and often complementary powers or concepts were deftly sewn into an exquisite weave of ornate characters and stories in four of Hinduism's principal religious texts, the *Vedas*. The creator is Brahma, Vishnu is the preserver, and Shiva, the destroyer. Shiva has a wife. Her name is Kali (the feminine form of *kalam* – which means 'black', or *kala* which means 'time'). When fierce Kali died, Shiva became uncontrollable with grief and rage. He carried her corpse on his shoulders and performed a violent dervish dance of anger, smashing his feet down upon the earth. The other gods became concerned that unless Shiva could be persuaded to relinquish Kali's body he would destroy the world altogether, and so Vishnu took a blade and threw it at Kali's corpse which was then scattered in fifty-two chunks across the earth. The little toe of the right foot landed next to the great River Hooghly in Bengal and a temple was built there to mark the spot. This temple was – and is – Kalighat. This place was – and is – Kali-kata.

In the beginning was Job Charnock. And Job Charnock was named after the famous biblical character famed for being sent endless trials by Satan with God's permission, to test whether his love for God was truly sincere. Job is celebrated for his righteous suffering. Our Job – Mr Charnock (who suffered righteously) – was born in London although his family originally hailed from the north, from Lancashire. He was a loyal, highly valued employee of the English East India Company in Bengal. He was a moral man and a devout Christian. In 1663 he took a common-law wife – a Hindu widow, a *sati* – whom he was reputed to have snatched from her husband's funeral pyre. She was fifteen years old and he renamed her Maria. They had four children together. They all lived in Cal-Kal-Kali-cutta. One of the daughters, Mary, went on to marry Bengal's first president, Sir Charles Eyre. Job was devoted to Maria and they lived happily together for twenty-five years until her tragically premature death in 1688. A devastated Job built a garden house in the northern suburb of Barrackpore, Cal-Kal-Kali-cutta, in order to remain close to her grave, where, rumour had it, he slaughtered a cock on the date of her death in a Sufi ritual every year. Maria was buried as a Christian although Job Charnock was accused of

18

converting to Hinduism and his life story was later – with considerable bile and aplomb – employed as a cautionary tale of moral laxity and improbity. When Charnock died, Eyre, his powerful son-in-law, erected a monument in his honour – which made no mention of his beloved wife – constructed from a form of shimmering granite which in the year 1900, after briefly apprehending it, the famous geologist Thomas Henry Holland would christen 'Charnockite'.

In the beginning was the word, and the word was Cal-Kal-Kali-cutta, but there is no word, and the person who created the word is no person, only rock, and if there was a person he was a most loathed, mistrusted, morose and morally degenerate company administrator. So it's probably better that we waste no more of our precious time and energy thinking about him here.

What better place in the world for one such as Uncle to be born than deep in the bosom of the Chatterjee family? Both Kshudiram and Chandradevi had been blessed with many divine visions. Uncle's brother, Ramkumar, had special spiritual gifts and foretold his own wife's early death. Uncle's sister Katyayani was prone to erratic behaviours and was once possessed by a bad spirit which Kshudiram exorcised with a pilgrimage to Gaya to worship at the feet of Vishnu. Kshudiram's sister, Ramsila, would sometimes believe herself to be possessed by the spirit of the goddess Sitala (the disease goddess, the goddess of smallpox, who brings coolness to victims of fever). I was very afraid of Ramsila as a boy, but Uncle – only four years older – showed no fear of his aunt during her transformations. No, the young Uncle was not remotely afraid. Uncle was fascinated. Uncle calmly observed the reverence and awe with which Ramsila was treated in their humble Kamarpukur household during these special occurrences. He watched her intently. He studied her closely. One time he even quietly whispered in my ear, 'Ah, wouldn't it be just splendid if the spirit who now possesses my aunt would some day possess me?'

Uncle was set apart from the very beginning. I have often been told that he was a beautiful baby and a beautiful child, and when I look back on those early years that is very much what I too remember. He was always cherished and celebrated. Uncle was handsome and charming. His face was full like a shining moon. He was greatly loved and admired in the small village where he was raised. One village elder was so besotted by Uncle that he would even take the young Uncle out into the rice fields, hang scented garlands around his neck, then secretly feed and worship him there as an incarnation of the young Krishna. Village religion is a private religion. It is a householder's religion.

The Christians have one God and one way to worship him. We Hindus have a thousand gods and a thousand ways to worship them. The gods call to us – they speak to us – and whoever speaks the loudest or the most persuasively we respond to with a most profound sincerity. We make the best choices we can and then try to cultivate as deep a love as we can possibly muster.

Uncle was always an impressive actor and a mimic. He made everybody laugh with his delightful pranks. The village women constantly sought out the wonderful Gadai to sing and to dance for them. He was one of their very own. Throughout his life women have treated Uncle as a girl, and men have happily indulged their wives and their mothers and their daughters in this curious whim of theirs. Uncle is so sweet and so innocent. They have nothing to fear from him. Uncle could never pose any threat. The very thought of it is laughable! He is a child. Untarnished by the world. And for this very reason Uncle could go wherever he chose. No door was closed to Uncle. The womenfolk of Kamarpukur were all completely devoted to him. Even as he grew from a child into a young man he continued to possess a feminine quality that made him at once their confidant and their plaything. Nothing could be kept hidden from the young Uncle. He could not be curtailed.

There was one exception to this rule, however, in the shape of a successful trader by the name of Durgadas Pyne. Durgadas Pyne was as fond of Uncle as everybody else but he maintained a strict system of *purdah* in his home and would often brag to other villagers about how nobody in Kamarpukur had ever seen the women of his family. On one occasion he made this brag within Uncle's hearing and Uncle was greatly provoked by this statement. He immediately insisted that he could know and see everything that happened among the women in Kamarpukur, even those cloistered in Durgadas Pyne's household. Durgadas Pyne merely laughed at Uncle. He did not take this brash boy seriously.

A short while later, at sunset, an impoverished weaver-woman dressed in a filthy sari, veil and coarse ornaments arrived at Durgadas Pyne's home, her basket of wares tucked under her arm. She told Durgadas Pyne that she had come to the market at Kamarpukur to sell yarn but had been unexpectedly abandoned by her thoughtless companions. She then asked – in pitiful tones – if he might provide her with a shelter for the night. After a brief interrogation of her story Durgadas Pyne was satisfied by her tale and sent her to his women's apartments to be cared for there. The weaver-woman spent the entire evening with Durgadas Pyne's womenfolk, eating, laughing and engaging in gossip for many hours. She was finally distracted by the frantic calling of Rameswar Chatterjee in the street outside who was then searching for his missing brother Gadadhar. I think you can probably work out the end of this story. Suffice to say that Gadadhar had hoodwinked Durgadas Pyne and all the members of his family with this prank, and while at first Durgadas Pyne was very angry with Uncle, he soon saw the humour of the situation and commended the young man for his impressive disguise.

Of course this was not the first occasion on which Uncle had dressed as a woman. Often in the past his female companions had dressed him up in saris and ornaments – Uncle was their joy, their plaything – so that he might better act the part – and sing the delightful songs – of Radharani or Vrinda. In fact Uncle loved nothing more than to get dressed up and masquerade as a village woman walking to the tank to fetch water with a pitcher. His observation of all the special female habits and mannerisms was very close. He was utterly convincing as a woman in every way. To the closed-off western mind Uncle's pranks may appear shocking, but in these parts we think of such behaviour merely as Uncle's *lila* – his special play. We see in it a kind of innocent devotion, an expression of the *madhura bhava*, a sweet mood. There is no deceit in it. Play cannot be deceitful. Nor devotional love. Like Uncle himself it is simply joyous. It is completely harmless. It is utterly blissful.

America, the late 1950s, early 1960s (an anonymous transgender man speaks)

'I remember being alone on a farm with access to my landlady's wardrobe . . . wearing the pretty, old-fashioned dresses made me feel so happy . . . but after a couple of hours in them I was overcome with sadness and frustration. I wanted to be a woman so badly . . . but I saw no way to achieve my goals.

'I started to shout at the top of my lungs, "I am a woman! I am a woman!"'

'No one could hear me in the sprawling countryside but the cows and trees and sky . . . Then all at once I was flooded with the sweetest, most glorious feeling I have ever had. It seemed to pour out of my heart into my whole body . . . pure joy just kept bubbling up within me, without any effort on my part. I felt that this feeling was the presence of God. And I decided that it was a sign that God's grace was most available to me as a woman.'

In the following scene we find the Rani cheerfully contemplating the wider socio-political ramifications of her husband's tragic early death . . .

Ha! No, we don't. Of *course* we don't. The Rani (although she is no '*rani*' – no 'queen' – this is merely a fond nickname her mother applied to her which then stuck like ornate sugar-work to the end of a wooden spatula) lives within the asphyxiating vice of the present moment. Clever as she is, hallowed as she is, she still can't step outside it. The awesome 'power of the present' treads rudely on the back of the skirts of her sari.

But we can. We can step outside 1836. We can stretch the melted sugar of the Rani's life and analyse it from a distance (although ornate, decorative sugar-work is a western weakness. Let's replace it with an Indian sweet – *burfi*, a popular Bengali treat made of sugar and condensed milk. Let's push our clean thumbs and index fingers into the metal tray containing this sticky, cooling mixture – possibly flavoured with coconut or almond or pistachio – pinch it lightly and then pull the glorious, glutinous mess closer towards us).

The Rani hails from the lowly *sudra*, or servant class. Her immensely wealthy husband has just suddenly died from 'apoplexy' (which in modern parlance is a haemorrhage or a stroke) during a carriage ride. He is forty-nine years old. Reports tell us that when Rajchandra died the Rani lay groaning on the floor, stricken, for three full days without any food or drink. Then the formal grieving process began: she weighed herself and gave this exact amount to the *brahmins* (the spiritual caste) in silver coins (6,017 of them, in total); she distributed food and gifts to the poor.

It may legitimately cross our minds whether the Rani considered – even briefly – the tradition of *sati*, and what the implications might have been for her if this practice had not been summarily outlawed by India's British colonial rulers in 1829 (seven years before). Research tells us that *sati* was considered to be the ultimate act of honour and devotion by a pious wife (a sign of both insurmountable grief and spiritual renunciation). The goddess Sati, also known as Dakshayani, was the first incarnation of the goddess Parvati (who is also called Durga and, ah, Kali). She burned herself alive after her father, Daksha, publicly humiliated her beloved husband, Shiva.

In *sati* (first celebrated among the *kshatriya* or warrior caste, and later cautiously embraced throughout Indian society, although notably disapproved of by the *brahmins*) we see a fascinating cross-over (a meeting of minds) between the spiritual and the pugnaciously pragmatic. Many Indian faith traditions venerate acts of voluntary self-negation and renunciation above all others (especially for women. These impulses – to negate the self and sacrifice for family – are the natural duties of a good wife and mother, after all). But we also see the widow as a social inconvenience. The widow inherits property, but may only ever be perceived as a temporary custodian of it, since all money and goods are passed on to the husband's family upon her death. And good widows were – and still are – expected to live only half a life (an excuse for a life, a grovelling apology); the life of an ascetic; wearing only white, eating plain food, rejecting all social activities and sleeping on the ground on a thin, grass mat.

Sati, on the other hand, was a helpful foreshortening of this social and emotional purgatory. It was a key to salvation. Its power was vested in the belief that when a widow submits her living body as a burned offering on her husband's funeral pyre (although many were drowned or buried alive) she not only gets to purge herself of all her sins, but to save her husband's soul, her own and those of the following seven generations from the tortuous cycle of rebirth and death. Suicide is forbidden among Hindus but *sati* is not suicide, it is a cruel and clever semantic sidestepping of the rules, it is an act of exquisite piety. And when a widow kills herself, her husband's family – the main players in a story in which the widow is merely a bump in the road, a narrative impediment – may inherit sooner.

What is the Rani thinking as she stands and watches the priests take a lighted tinder to her much-adored Rajchandra's funeral pyre? She is a modest woman, and pious and loving, but she is fiercely intelligent. Is there a measure of social pressure? Statistics tell us that the practice of *sati* was much favoured in Bengal during the early part of the Rani's lifetime. The practice was especially keenly followed in the areas surrounding Calcutta – kali-cutta; Kali, who was Sati who was Dakshayani, had immolated herself voluntarily. But the Rani (not a Rani, but *our* Rani) does not offer herself. Imagine the eyes of the crowd upon her. What are they thinking? Do they judge her?

The writer Lata Mani (in her book *Contentious Traditions*) calls that 1829 law 'a founding moment in the history of women in modern India'. And the necessary consequences of this 'founding moment'? 'Women became the site on which tradition was debated.'

This is a debate still raging today.

So our Rani, who is not a queen but of low caste, must now negotiate (in 1836 for heaven's sake) a complex path between conformity and independence, piety and survival, tradition and modernity, happiness and disapproval. This is a tortuous route. But the Rani will walk it. And she will walk it bravely and lightly. And as she walks it she will throw out sparks of hope to women everywhere. Women then and women now. She will become emblematic of something intangible. Of female power, a power that may only exist – and does and *will* exist – if it remains charming, superficially submissive, unerringly polite and appropriately dressed. See the Rani's flitting eyes? Her sharp mind works feverishly behind her veil.

Only a woman such as this – inhabiting a contested space, a contested territory – may become the heroic midwife to India's newest messiah: a *guru* who will not be called a *guru*, a priest who will not follow tradition, a wise man who will not read or write or lecture or develop a philosophy or tolerate publicity. Everything here is contested. This is a liminal space, an air-bubble within history.

So please, *please*, let us mentally offer flowers at the feet of the Rani, right here, right now, in the hope of keeping her safe for her difficult journey.

Uncle cannot remember the exact date of his birth. He has lost the related documentation. But I believe it must have been on an extremely auspicious day. There was probably a full moon. And the stars in the blue heavens must have been specially aligned. If he had still possessed it, I wonder if Uncle's astronomical chart may have foretold the great shadow cast across his happy childhood by the sudden death of his beloved father, Kshidiram, when Uncle was but eight years of age. Kshidiram was celebrating a festival at my family home in Selampur with his favourite nephew Ramachandra when he was struck low by a virulent attack of dysentery. He never recovered. Three days later he died with God's name upon his lips. He was sixty-eight years of age. I remember very little of that gloomy time, but I know that his body was cremated by the river. Even today I recall the warmth of that great pyre on my innocent, young cheeks.

After Kshidiram's death Uncle spent increasing amounts of time at home with his mother, taking on many of the household duties – especially the worshipping of the family deities. I think it would be fair to say that Chandradevi did not react well to her husband's passing. She clung on to Uncle ever more ferociously. She was always a guileless woman. I would not go so far as to call her slow-witted. No. I would definitely not go so far as to call her that. She has a special kind of innocence which Uncle has partially inherited himself. But Uncle's innocence is of a wise kind. It is profound. It has many sides.

Certainly Uncle's contempt for education grew stronger than ever during this sad interlude. To Uncle, education was only for wage monkeys. For worldly fools. Uncle was a lofty *brahmin* like his father. Uncle was always disgusted by money and by arithmetic. On top of this, Uncle would never take anything at face value. He would always ask why. Uncle was contrary by nature. I am told that this wrongheaded tendency of Uncle's caused his father much heartache and concern during his life, and that when his father passed his brothers felt the burden of this same wilfulness fall heavily upon their own shoulders.

When Uncle wasn't with his mother and passing his days as the special pet of the women of the village, he was spending time with the holy men and *sadhus* at the halfway house on the road to the great pilgrimage destination of Puri which runs through Kamarpukur. Uncle was a precocious child and would engage in arguments with these men on obscure spiritual matters. The *sadhus* were charmed and amazed by his cleverness on such issues. Uncle has an incredible memory. He will hear a story but once and he will never forget it. Much of what Uncle knows of the *Gita* and the *Mahabharata* and the *Puranas* he has learned through hearing them read out loud or during performances of local religious dramas. Uncle has always been a great observer of things. When he watches a drama or a *kirtan* you will see his eyes fixed enquiringly upon the crowd as much as upon the actors. Uncle will see what makes people weep or gasp or smile and he will carefully tuck this information away in a corner of his mind. Uncle does not long to please people so much as to understand them. Because there is no calculation in Uncle. Oh no. Not a whit of it. Uncle will often attract a great deal of attention to himself, but he is not a natural exhibitionist. Uncle is not a crowd-pleaser by nature. He is simply possessed of a great abundance of natural charm, and a quite extraordinary openness.

In fact when Uncle was nine years old he was asked to play the part of Shiva in a village festival after the person who usually played this role was indisposed. Although a wonderful mimic and singer, Uncle did not at once take to this proposal because he felt that it might distract him from his own private worship of the god. But when it was explained to Uncle that to play the role of Shiva was to worship him, Uncle was mollified and finally agreed to the request. Of course everyone in the village was excited at the prospect of their beloved Gadai appearing in a big festival performance.

Imagine their mixed emotions, then, when Uncle finally appeared on stage holding Shivaji's trident – his skin whitened by ash, his soft, curly hair pulled into dreadlocks – and then just proceeded to stand there, silently, and do nothing. Not so much as a word would he utter. Their initial delight and awe on seeing the beautiful and cherished Gadai on stage in his costume was soon overtaken by feelings of disappointment and confusion because Gadai would not speak or sing for them. Instead Uncle just stood there, in a daze, a small smile playing around the corners of his sweet lips, and such a profusion of tears pouring from his half-hooded eyes that after only a short while the ash on his chest was as striped and streaked as Shivaji's habitual tiger-skin.

There was a great commotion among the villagers as they witnessed this strange spectacle. What were they to make of it? Some people became angry and jeered and shouted insults at Uncle. But he did not appear to be remotely concerned by this. Some people called desperately for calm. Others began to pray.

Eventually, after quite some time had passed, one of the village women climbed up on to the stage and silenced the crowd. She explained that the village women had seen this strange behaviour from Uncle before during an outing with the child to the shrine of the goddess Visalakshi in nearby Annur. On their walk to the shrine Uncle had suddenly – and with no prior warning – lost all external consciousness and had fallen to the ground. The women had been afraid that Uncle was suffering from some kind of fit and had shaken him and splashed him with water, but eventually the individual who was now addressing the crowd had arrived and recognised that Uncle was not ill but in an ecstatic trance. She had therefore instructed the other women to step back and chant with her the name of the goddess Visalakshi. This they did, and after a short while Uncle returned once again to full consciousness.

Uncle is highly sensitive and even as a small boy he had learned from the example of his parents to love God deeply. Everything that happened in his life Uncle saw as an opportunity to draw closer to his chosen deity. Uncle had an amazing talent for painting and sculpture. He would dig pieces of grey clay from the banks of the village tank and form small idols with it. I remember a wonderful sculpture of Shiva that Uncle made and then worshipped.

Uncle had a very focused mind. All Uncle's attention would be drawn to one point or idea or image and then he would become completely lost in its contemplation. Anything – even most curious things – might bring about this devotional state.

Unfortunately the play was ruined by Uncle. Try as they all might they could not awaken him. Uncle was too far gone. It was a fiasco. And many people were full of consternation. But Uncle did not care. There was no regret in Uncle.

From this time, indeed from the death of his father onwards, Uncle's character changed. He began to wonder at the way in which people in the village longed only for fun and for gossip and for songs. Life was fleeting! Why crave only pleasure when pleasure obscured the path to the Infinite? Uncle now became much more serious. He could not see the point in any active human pursuit if it did not lead directly to the goal of God. So Uncle withdrew more into himself. He would pass hours in worship at the family shrine or spend time alone, often at night – with only the rats and the jackals for company – at the local cremation ground.

I remember one occasion when a group of us boys were playing together in the paddy fields. Uncle had walked a short way ahead of us, deep in thought, perhaps tiring of our childish noise and games. He was strolling along the sharp ridge of a green field eating a handful of puffed rice from the knot in the corner of his wearing-cloth when he suddenly beheld the sky overtaken by a dark cloud. Uncle gazed up at this grey cloud with his habitual focus, and then suddenly a flock of white cranes flew in formation across the darkening heavens. It was a sight of such beauty that Uncle instantly lost all consciousness. And this is how we soon found him, utterly lifeless, his handful of rice scattered on the ground around him. I will never forget that terrible moment, that dreadful sight, so long as I shall live. I was only a child myself, younger than Uncle – perhaps six or eight years of age – but when I saw him thus my heart swelled in my chest and I felt such an intense love for Uncle. Uncle was so beautiful and so defenceless! I knew in that instant – even so young and so ignorant as I was – that my mission henceforth on this cruel earth was only to care for Uncle, to love Uncle, to guard him and to preserve him from all possible harm.

A passing observation . . .

Sri Ramakrishna had unusually long arms. His hands reached almost as far down as his knees.

Eight haiku

The boy looks skyward:
An infinite, grey vista –
A flapping of wings . . .

Newly formed black clouds –
Flock of white cranes in full flight –
The child gasps then swoons

Narcoleptic minds
Cannot distinguish between
Waking and dreaming

Sri Ramakrishna –
Who gave you this moniker?
What is your true name?

Stormy, dark heavens
Illumed by giant, white wings:
God is everywhere!

Might there be some way
To engage with the Divine
Without mania?

God enflames his heart
Everything that happens
Reflects that strange glow

Joy will sometimes lead
Sensitive dispositions
To oblivion

Sri Ramakrishna, on the spiritual perils of domestic pet ownership

Truth seeker (*somewhat disheartened*): 'Master, how *hard*
it is to raise the mind and spirit above worldly concerns!'
Sri Ramakrishna (*shrugging, resigned*): 'Ah yes. Even he who
has no one to call his own will connive to raise a cat and
thereby create attachment.'

An enquiry into the essential nature of farina pudding

The word *farina* means 'meal' or 'flour' in Latin. Farina pudding can sometimes also be called Cream of Wheat. It is generally served as a breakfast cereal in the west, and is composed from the germ or endosperm of the grain (which may be either wheat or, more often, semolina). It is carbohydrate-rich and is cooked by placing half a cup of the dry powder into a small saucepan, then adding a full cup of milk or milk and water combined, an optional pinch of **salt** and knob of *ghee* (or clarified butter). This mixture should be brought to the boil and then gently simmered for approximately ten minutes. It should be frequently stirred. It may be served with either cold milk, brown sugar, honey, butter or cinnamon. It is incredibly rich in natural iron and so is highly nutritious for vegetarians and invalids.

An additional haiku

He has such long arms!
Fingers almost to his knees –
Might this mean something?

A few short weeks after her husband's sudden death and the
Rani (who is not actually royalty) is being visited by Prince
Dwarakanath Tagore (who is almost royalty). The Rani is too
modest to speak with the Prince directly, so she is seated
behind a curtain while her favourite son-in-law, Mathur Nath
Biswas, acts as go-between. Mathur was married to the Rani's
third daughter, Karuna, who died in 1833, whereupon the
Rani – who had always found Mathur to be an excellent and
obliging aide both socially and in business – asked if he would
consider marrying her fourth daughter, Jagadamba, so that he
might continue to remain a member of their close-knit family.
Mathur promptly and politely obliged her.

The Prince and Mathur are both magnificently mustachioed.
The upper lip of Mathur – who has a heavy, square-set face,
small, kind eyes but a generous nose and voluptuous mouth – is
bedecked with a spectacular handlebar moustache. The Prince
is lean-faced and handsome. He has large, sharp, keen eyes and
his moustache is in the chevron style – densely covering his lip
and stretching down and out on both sides almost as far as the
corners of his lean jawbone.

In a fight to the death between these two fine examples
of facial furniture it is difficult to know who might be
the victor. Perhaps Mathur's waxed tips may give him the
edge. But the Prince's moustache is less frivolous, more
work-manlike. The Prince's moustache, and the Prince himself,
mean business.

We find ourselves fairly well-briefed on the physical and
emotional location of the Rani at this present moment in history
(behind a curtain, rich, vulnerable, newly widowed), but the
Prince's circumstances are harder to gauge. The Prince is in a
temporary state of flux. He is a zamindar by trade (a kind of

gentrified/landed tax collector), but this is only the tip of his entrepreneurial iceberg.

In the not-too-distant future Prince Dwarakanath Tagore will be widely celebrated – and with much justification – as one of the most talented, innovative and industrious Indian entrepreneurs of all time. He will found banks (in fact he's already founded one), he will sell opium to China, he will purchase India's first coal mine, he will be in on the ground floor at the establishment of Assam's burgeoning tea trade, he will run tug services between Calcutta and the mouth of the Hooghly, he will build giant sugar, silk and indigo factories. It should be noted that the Prince has a reputation for merciless efficiency. He is a ruthless business hawk who will happily grasp any troublesome adversary in his magnificent claw, contemplate them coolly and then calmly tear their heads off. His is not a *bad* reputation, as such, but it's certainly not a reputation to be trifled with.

Like the Rani, the Prince has succeeded in business through his pragmatic contacts with Britain, the British government and the East India Company. Also, like the Rani, he has, on occasion, been burned by these connections. In 1827 this burn was a **salt** burn: the Prince rootled out an invidious web of corruption in the **Salt** Revenue Department (where he was working, for a mere pittance, simply to forge business connections) and was spitefully counter-sued for his trouble.

How can we possibly hope to look deep into the heart of a man like Prince Dwarakanath Tagore, who lived and breathed and schemed (and made inconceivably huge amounts of money) almost 180 years ago? We can't. It's impossible. We can only make a series of cack-handed assumptions and then cheerfully forge our equally fatuous, clumsy and superficial deductions from them.

What we *do* know for certain is that the Prince's unsatisfactory involvement in the **Salt** Revenue Department

40

corruption farrago has left a bitter taste in his mouth (*sic*) and formed in him the powerful and completely logical urge to shake off (*sic*) his 'official', governmental connections and move forward in a more independent, free-ranging entrepreneurial capacity.

It can't be an accident (can it?) that only a year after this decision (in 1828), the Prince and his great friend Ram Mohun Roy (who was definitely the spiritual and ideological brains of the outfit) helped to found what would eventually become (after a series of complex transfigurations) one of the most important social and religious Hindu/quasi-protestant/monotheistic/western-influenced/semi-egalitarian/pro-educational/anti-caste/anti-idol movements in India, the Brahmo Samaj (or Society of God). This embryonic movement – little more than a tiny, fluttering heartbeat or pulse (think of it, if you like, as a kind of very early, cultural pacemaker) – will start what is generally known as the Bengali Renaissance, a neat porthole through which Modern India herself may eventually be glimpsed.

In one of the Samaj's future incarnations, under the leadership of Keshab Chandra Sen, it will become utterly instrumental – nay, *critical* – in bringing the soft, stuttering voice of Sri Ramakrishna *Paramahamsa* to the attention of the world.

Salt connects the Prince and the Rani – it lightly seasons them – but they do not know it. And eventually they shall both – one consciously, one inadvertently – give a helping hand to the childlike saint who will be God.

But this is all a long way off. For now, the present moment is treading on the back of the Rani's skirts, remember? And history is a buzzing mosquito that likes to hang – quite infuriatingly! – just in front of the stern nose of Prince Dwarakanath Tagore, distracting his attention and sometimes prompting him to irritably and scowlingly flap his hand.

So we know what connects these two individuals in the past (**salt**) and in the future (Sri Ramakrishna), but why exactly is the Prince visiting the Rani on this sweltering, pre-monsoon day (I've added this climactic detail myself – we have no idea of the season in which the visit was undertaken, although we can be pretty certain that if we are in Calcutta then the weather will be dreadful). Is it to help or to swindle her?

When we tune in to their halting exchange (stage-managed by Mathur) we can hear the Prince (who does not excel in small talk) expressing his condolences over the death of his former friend and business associate, Rajchandra, and then idly wondering (just by the by – cue the arrival of a small flying formation of several large and mean-looking Indian vultures) if the Rani is truly equipped to cope with the enormous responsibilities incumbent on a person in possession of a giant land/business portfolio. In plain English (or even in Bengali) this actually translates as: the Rani – a mere woman – has just inherited a vast estate and Prince Dwarakanath Tagore is strongly of the opinion that she needs to employ herself a competent manager to oversee it.

Mathur listens to the Prince's opinions with immense courtesy, twiddles his moustache, nods obligingly and then disappears between the flapping curtains. Ah, what might be the Rani's expression when he meets with it on the other side? Fearful? Flustered? Indignant? Let's settle on 'cynical with a touch of anxious'. Perhaps the dear Rani even goes so far as to indulge in a small eye-roll.

Mathur stands before her. 'The Prince helpfully suggests that you employ an efficient manager to take charge of your vast estate, madam.'

The Rani nods. 'Please thank the Prince for this excellent piece of advice, Mathur, but tell him that I am concerned that it may be difficult to find – at such short notice – someone reliable and completely trustworthy to fill this important role.'

Mathur nods. He pushes his way back between the curtains. 'Prince, the Rani thanks you for your most excellent advice,' he announces (another moustache twiddle), 'but is concerned that it might be difficult to find a suitably reliable and trustworthy individual at such short notice.'

The Prince receives this news in an attitude of detached thoughtfulness and then, after a suitable duration, cheerfully announces, 'Please be so good as to inform the Rani that – in the light of my great attachment to her former spouse, Rajchandra – I am more than happy to take on the prodigious responsibility of this Herculean task myself.'

Mathur's small eyes widen slightly. He nods his head and then quickly disappears between the curtains.

At this stage it may be fruitful to consider whether either partner involved in this polite exchange is actually able to hear the other without the benefit of Mathur's involvement. My guess is that they can (if only because this quadruples the comedy potential of the scene).

Let's imagine Mathur back behind the curtain again and coming to a halt in front of the Rani with (in the English colonial style), a small, officious click of his heels. 'Prince Dwarakanath Tagore has generously offered to place his own not-inconsiderable skills at your disposal, madam,' he informs her, his voice creaking slightly under the stress.

The Rani gently dabs a shell-pink silk handkerchief against her upper lip where a small line of perspiration has recently formed. She knows that it would be socially ruinous, not to mention utterly ungrateful, for a brand-new widow like herself to knock back such a munificent offer from an individual as well-connected and as powerful as the Prince. She slowly inhales and then turns to Mathur, a gentle smile playing around her lips. 'Please thank the Prince for his generous offer, Mathur,' she begins, her voice slightly louder now than it has been hitherto. 'I am deeply touched by it, and greatly flattered, but at the present moment I find it impossible to guess exactly how much money or property I am actually in possession of . . .' She pauses, judiciously, before delivering her killer blow: 'One of the few things I *am* aware of, however, is that my late husband, Rajchandra, recently loaned the Prince the sum of 200,000 rupees, and if I could get this money back it would be immensely helpful to me at this difficult time.'

Mathur's mouth drops open as he listens to the carefully chosen (and sweetly delivered) words of his indomitable mother-in-law. This is the *Prince* – the celebrated *brahmin*, Dwarakanath Tagore! Who in Bengal might dare to stand in opposition to his schemes?
The Rani gazes at Mathur calmly and evenly. She does not flinch.

After a short interval Mathur closes his mouth, draws a deep breath, and turns to make his way back through the curtains. He is flustered. Perhaps he walks into the fabric at the wrong point and is to be seen floundering helplessly for a few moments among heavy and asphyxiating folds of drapery. Eventually his exit is accomplished. He stands before the Prince, breathing heavily, his usually immaculate hair in a state of disarray.
'Prince Dwarakanath . . .' he starts off, haltingly, his cheeks reddening, 'the Rani is immensely—'

The Prince raises a curt hand to silence Mathur, but the gesture is extended into an irritable swipe at something infinitesimal – possibly a mosquito – that currently seems to be pestering him. 'Tell the Rani that I shall repay the money shortly,' he snaps. 'I will return first thing in the morning in order to discuss the most efficient means by which this may be achieved.'

He promptly takes his leave.

The following day Prince Dwarakanath Tagore returns and is obliged to tell the shuffling Mathur that he has no access to such a large amount of cash as things currently stand, but that he is happy to sign over a prime piece of property to the Rani which is worth an equivalent amount in value. Mathur disappears behind the curtain. He delivers the Prince's curt message to the smiling Rani.

The Rani – to Mathur's intense mortification – innocently wonders how much annual revenue this property might be expected to fetch and is duly informed (I think we can probably assume that the Prince just shouts the relevant figures directly at the drapery) that it usually amounts to approximately 36,000 rupees. The Rani smiles at this, and nods. She is satisfied. She sends Mathur out beyond the curtain with one final message for the Prince.

'The Rani says that she is only a humble and ignorant widow,' Mathur mutters, his eyes fixed on the exquisitely woven rug that lies passively under his feet, 'and her property is not large. Touched as she is by both your concern and your interest, she believes that it would be nothing short of an act of profound discourtesy on her part to expect someone as exalted and powerful as Prince Dwarakanath Tagore to lower himself to the management of her piddling affairs. It seems that she is now determined to depend solely upon the services of her sons-in-law and heirs.'

The Prince scowls ferociously. A short silence follows. A small cough may be heard from behind the curtain, the gentle shifting of a chair, several soft footfalls, the quiet opening and closing of a door.

The Prince remains standing with Mathur for a minute or so, both of them furiously resisting eye contact, then he suddenly expostulates and clamps an angry hand on to one side of his lean, tanned neck. It seems possible – nay probable, even – that history has just bitten him there.

August 1885, the Cossipore Garden House, north Calcutta

On the floor, by the bed, is a half-consumed bowl of farina
pudding. The visitor sits down, cross-legged, by the Great
Master's side and inadvertently knocks it with his knee.
He glances towards it and then sharply recoils. The milky
pudding – this congealed baby food – the only substance that
the Great Master has been capable of consuming for many
months now, is liberally splattered with not only numerous
thick, dark clots of blood, but also several ghoulish streaks of
stinking, yellow pus.

The visitor half retches and glances over towards the naked
and emaciated Master who – supported by a long bolster on his
bed – is lost deep in a trance. He has a magnificent garland of
flowers around his neck which almost manages to conceal the
great, suppurating, cancerous hole that now ominously pulsates
in the centre of his throat.

We poor Hindus must accept our station in life and simply
do the best we can under whatever circumstances we find
ourselves, no matter how difficult or unfair or hopeless they
may sometimes seem. We are not all born equal. It is God's
will – and the burden of *karma* – that we should enter the
world rich or poor, healthy or sick, loved or despised. We
must resign ourselves to these circumstances. What is the point
in fighting them? What good will it do us? There are always
clear boundaries in life that must never be crossed. Every
caste has its role and plays its part within the wider body of its
community. Where would we be without the warriors to defend
us, or the farmers and traders to feed us, or the labourers to do
all the hard work? Uncle always says that only humility and
renunciation and selflessness and devotion may bring us some
relief in this harsh life and perhaps help to improve our fortunes
during our next incarnation. Uncle despises ambition. Uncle
despises *my* ambition. He laughs at it all the time. 'Just look at
Hriday – so tall, handsome and strong, and so determined to
make the best of himself!' Uncle chuckles.

Uncle comes from a family of *brahmana*. We are *brahmins* – a
caste of priests and teachers – and we worship the Vedas. There
is only one God in our Vedic faith but he may be worshipped
in many different forms. The world of the *brahmin* is full of
rules and rituals, and one of the most important of these for a
brahmin boy is *uponayon*: the investment with a sacred thread.
Uncle was invested with his thread when he was eight or nine
years old, but even then, when Uncle was so young, he
managed to provide his family with an additional measure of
heartache and perplexity. Because, well, that is Uncle, after all.

The *upabeet*, as we like to call it in Bengal, is nothing more
than a simple cord made up of three separate strands that are

twisted into a single thread. It is pulled over the head and under one arm and so hangs across the chest. It must be worn at all times. The knot in the middle that ties the two ends together represents the formless Brahman or God who is the beginning and end and middle of all things.

There are many different meanings surrounding the sacred thread, not all of which I can recall, but one of them is that the first strand signifies the wearer's debt to his *guru* or teacher (the person who initiates him and teaches him how to recite the daily devotions or *sandhyavandanam*, which are the prayers and rituals we like to perform at dawn, at noon and at dusk). The second debt is to one's parents and ancestors. The third is to the learned *rishis* or scholars who have brought us knowledge and wisdom, although some of us believe that this debt is only to God who is wisdom itself. These are our three, chief debts and the sacred thread constantly serves to remind us of them.

Some like to think that the three strands also symbolise the three great *devis* or goddesses: Ma Saraswati who is the goddess of knowledge, Ma Lakshmi who is the goddess of riches, and Ma Parvati who is the goddess of strength. And sometimes we hope to remind ourselves with those three, humble strands of how purity is expected from all good *brahmin*s, first in thought, then in word and finally in deed.

The *uponayon* is a kind of rebirth. I am told that Christians are also born twice or even three times in their faith. And the Jews and the Mohammedans celebrate the journey of boyhood to manhood with a ritual whose name I have never learned.

Towards the end of the *uponayon* ceremony – after the boy has received his sacred word or *mantram* from his *guru*, which is known only to him and whose constant repetition in *japam* or prayer throughout his life will guard him from misfortune and bring him prosperity – the boy will be obliged to beg his food from a close member of his community. In fact he will then go on to beg for three days like a humble monk seeking alms. It is a great honour to be the first individual to offer alms to the newly initiated child, and, as we know all too well, Uncle was universally adored by the womenfolk of Kamarpukur and so many were eager to be afforded this special privilege. But one woman in particular was most devoted to Uncle – the old blacksmith's daughter, Dhani, who had helped Chandradevi at his birth. She had for a very long time indeed dreamed that Uncle would approach her first, receive her food, and then address her as Ma (as is the custom during this ritual). This was her greatest heart's desire. Uncle – who loved Dhani very much – immediately agreed to Dhani's fond request, and thought little more of it until his oldest brother, Ramkumar, had been made aware of their longstanding agreement and was deeply troubled by it.

Uncle was to become a *brahmin* and Dhani was of the blacksmith caste. The first person to offer alms was traditionally always of a similar caste to the boy to whom it was offered. Ramkumar told Uncle firmly that Dhani could not make the first offering. Uncle was to tell her that this was impossible.

You may imagine that Uncle might have regretfully obeyed his brother – and the traditions of this ancient custom – by telling Dhani the bad news. But no. Uncle dug in his heels and refused to disappoint his dear friend. Ramkumar insisted. Uncle resisted. A terrible scene was forthcoming! But still Uncle held his ground.

In the end a village elder well versed in the scriptures was consulted. Uncle presented his arguments before him. He said, 'Surely, in such a case, it is more important that the young initiate should keep his word and not indulge in untruthfulness than that the rules of caste should be upheld?'

After some deep consideration the elder agreed with Uncle's viewpoint, and humble Dhani was permitted to be the first to feed Uncle at his special ceremony.

So Uncle had his way. He is very clever in such matters. He has an intellect as sharp as a new blade. We should only be grateful that Uncle was drawn to an honourable life. Imagine what havoc such a keen and disruptive mind as Uncle's might have wrought on the world had it not been completely God-centred?

I tell you this story of Uncle's *uponayon* – which may seem slight and insignificant to some – only because of a complete turnaround in the views of Uncle (and, indeed, the views of his brother) with regard to the rules of caste and the partaking of food cooked by a *sudra* shortly after his arrival at the beautiful Dakshineswar Kali Temple (when Uncle was around nineteen years of age).

I would never dare to call Uncle a turncoat or a hypocrite, but my, how things may change in only a few years! Yet who am I to pretend to understand the mysterious workings of Uncle's mind? It would be foolish for one such as Hridayram to even try. I must simply regard this as another perplexing example of Uncle's mysterious *lila* – the most fascinating and beguiling and magical divine play of my strange and singular Uncle Gadadhar.

Late at night in Sri Ramakrishna's room at the Dakshineswar Kali Temple, August 1884

The boy was lying on a mat on the north-eastern veranda of the Master's room, struggling to fall asleep. Sri Ramakrishna himself rarely ever slept more than a couple of hours a night. The rest of the time he would pace around, restlessly, or climb up on to the roof, muttering to himself, chanting God's names, singing, or clapping his hands, or talking emphatically with an invisible someone, always moving, always walking, frantically walking, back and forth, back and forth, back and forth. Was this devotion or madness? Joy or distraction?

The boy was exhausted after a full and inspirational day of spiritual teaching, prayer and song. He was only young and not wise in the ways of the world, but it seemed to him that after dark, once all the crowds had finally dispersed, the Master would become mysteriously transformed; everything comforting and familiar about him – everything he thought he knew and understood – quite magically dematerialising. His mother had warned him: 'What?! You went to visit that crazy *brahmin*? Are you mad?! Don't you know what they say about him? That he has destroyed the minds of 350 young men?!'

The boy frowned at the memory. He rolled gently on to his side – into the foetal position, his arms crossed against his chest – feeling hungry and perplexed. Minutes passed. He yawned and lowered his knees a little, then suddenly, without warning, the Master came barrelling outside on to the balcony and commenced pacing – like a thing possessed – around and around the mat where he lay. He could hear the Master's bare feet slapping against the polished concrete floor, his voice whispering and wheedling, hoarse and cajoling. He could see, through his lashes, the Master's hands frantically wringing, '*Mother! Mother! Mother! Mother!*'

The boy froze and held his breath. Could this be it? Finally? Was this it? The thing he'd heard so much about? The thing that he'd been waiting for? The thing that he'd been dreaming of?

He scrunched his eyes shut, terrified.

Was this it? At long last? Was this to be the night that he was blessed?

Ah, the things the Rani has seen! The things the Rani has done! She has been attacked by thugs on stilts in the bug-infested swamps of the Sunderbans, she has resurfaced the road to Puri for faithful pilgrims to walk upon, she has donated generously to the Imperial Library, she has constructed bathing *ghats* for the needy and dug ponds for the parched, she has opened a home for the dying in Nimtala, she has been a powerful patron of wrestlers and weightlifters, she has bought the fishing rights for a segment of the Ganga from the British government and then blocked it, with chains, because the big ships were – *ahem* – 'frightening the little fish', she has been hilariously and outrageously and adorably litigious. But most important of all, she has built a giant temple on the banks of the Ganga, at Dakshineswar, after the terrible goddess Kali appeared to her in a dream and told her that she must. It's a long story. But before we get around to that . . .

Chained up the great and holy Ganga?!
(Although some still doggedly maintain that she actually blocked the sacred river with thousands of bamboo canes.)

Two stories of the Rani's legendary verve, cunning and spunk neatly intertwine here – like a couple of temple cats, one black, one white (let's call them Yin and Yang), winding their way around the legs of the temple cook. The first involves an English gentleman neighbour of the Rani who complained to the authorities after she hired a group of musicians to process – with her family priests – early in the morning, to the sacred Ganga, to perform a ritual there in anticipation of the great Durga festival (or *puja*). She was cautioned by the authorities and promptly responded by hiring twice as many musicians to process (joyously! Cacophonously!) the following day. At dawn. Obviously. The furious neighbour sued and the Rani was fined.

The Rani – who was intensely law-abiding – paid her fine, but was incensed that the government (the heathens!) had acted against a religious observance during one of the most important holy celebrations of the Hindu spiritual calendar.

Revenge, as we shall soon discover, is an intemperate dish generally best accompanied by a mouthwatering selection of chutneys, pickles and a cooling *raita*. The Rani promptly put up barricades at either end of Babu Road from Jan Bazar to Babu Ghat. No traffic could pass through. The authorities complained, but the Rani calmly informed them, by letter, that she owned the road and could therefore do with it exactly as she pleased. And she did. The road remained shut, the people rioted (in support of the Rani, a series of ecstatic songs and limericks were penned in her honour), until she was grudgingly reimbursed the value of her fine. Then she opened Babu Road again, without a murmur.

But these high jinks were merely a small prelude – a brief warm-up – a colourful aside. The Rani's main symphony had yet to be played. Some time later the government (this tune's composer) imposed a crippling fishing tax on the impoverished fishermen of the holy Ganga. The fishermen appealed to numerous individuals in positions of power to come to their aid (they needed a conductor), but nobody would take up their proffered baton, not, at least, until they approached the dear Rani. The Rani picked up their baton readily but she handled it furtively and proceeded with great stealth – no officious tapping on the music stand here to draw attention to herself! Instead she quietly took up the lease of the fishing rights on the great river between Ghusuri and Metiabruz, then told all the fishermen in that area to barricade the river and fish to their hearts' content, tax-free. This they did, and gladly. All commercial shipping was promptly brought to a standstill.

Just imagine the scene: the terrible honking and parping of indignant sea captains, a tangled chaos of boats and ships and tugs, bobbing about, either end, unable to reach their ports or drop off their cargoes.

The government summonsed the Rani, demanding that she remove her barricades *post-haste*. The Rani replied (let's imagine a swishing of saris, a jangling of bangles) that the giant steamboats had been disturbing her fish, making them dash about and rendering them incapable of laying any eggs which meant, in due course, that the poor fishermen had been struggling to net any kind of livable catch.

Once again, the government was obliged to concede (dammit!) that the Rani had the law on her side. They refunded her the money for her lease and rescinded the loathed tax.
Job done!

Ah, the Rani. Is it any wonder that they composed songs about her, renamed Babu Road after her, built an imposing statue of her, put her lovely face on a stamp?

What happens when Sri Ramakrishna quietly asks you to open your mouth, circa 1883?

You spit out your tongue —
He'll scratch a *mantram* on it
In ancient Sanskrit

Remember those dreadful thugs? In the swampy Sunderbans, raising merry hell on their pesky stilts? During the course of the mugging (shots were fired, a thief was wounded) the Rani discovered that this terrible, legendary and much-feared band of brigands had only resorted to their vicious trade because of an awful paucity of legitimate local work options. The land in question (it transpires) was part of the vast property handed over to the Rani by Prince Dwarakanath Tagore (remember?) to settle his outstanding debt. So the Rani promptly sat down and brainstormed with the thieves, thrashed out a few ideas, drew up a business plan, reached deep into her coffers and helped them to establish a series of incredibly successful fisheries which utterly transformed the local economy – and the impoverished local community – for ever and ever and ever, Amen.

God bless the Rani! Let's throw our hats into the air – *en masse.*
Can we try that again, please, on the count of three (it's the sound man's fault – he'd nipped off for a quick fag)? OK, one . . . two . . .

Hair! Make-up! Repair the Rani's *chignon*! Apply some powder to that beloved chin! It's *hot* down here! Deepen her blush! Redden her sweet lips! Prepare our star for her next big close-up . . .

Because in the not-too-distant future our beloved Rani will be slapped in the face while worshipping Ma Kali in the temple that she built herself by a lowly – and seemingly demented – temple priest (*gasp!*).
Any ideas who? Go on. Go *on*. Take a guess.

Once again, we ask . . .

Sri Ramakrishna –
Who gave you this moniker?
What is your true name?

1878. The grandmother of a woman who will eventually become one of Sri Ramakrishna's most devout female disciples (Yogin Ma) asks a stranger in the Dakshineswar Temple garden for directions . . .

Yogin Ma's grandmother (*having just alighted from a barge into the exquisite and fragrant temple gardens and happening across a man gathering armfuls of red hibiscus in a plain white wearing-cloth and shiny black slippers or 'scuffs', whom she presumes to be a gardener*): 'Excuse me, sir, I have come here to see Ramakrishna *Paramahamsa*. Can you please direct me to his room?'

Sri Ramakrishna (*gazing at Yogin Ma's grandmother, blankly*): 'Pardon?'

Yogin Ma's grandmother (*slightly irritable*): 'The *Paramahamsa*. Ramakrishna. I have read several articles about him in the papers by the Brahmo's Keshab Chandra Sen. I wish to meet with him and see what I make of him.'

Sri Ramakrishna (*with contempt*): 'Argh. What do I know about him? Some people call him *Paramahamsa* . . . [*shrugs*] . . . others call him "young priest", and still others call him Gadadhar Chatterjee [*turns away, boredly*] . . . Please ask someone else to direct you to him.'

(*Yogin Ma's grandmother scowls, disgruntled, then goes for a stroll around the grand temple and its gardens, promptly abandoning all interest in this so-called God-man.*)

In 1886, a few months before Sri Ramakrishna's death, on being told that a famous holy man of Ghazipur has a photographic image of him hung on his wall . . .
(haiku to be read in a hoarse whisper):

Sri Ramakrishna
Points to his shrunken torso:
'Just a pillow-case!'

Twelve slightly impertinent questions about Ma Kali:

1) Why on earth is she spitting out her tongue like that?

2) She appears to be resting her foot on the chest of a prostrated, pale-skinned man. Who is he? Is he dead? Has she killed him?

3) Hang on a second . . . is she . . . is she *stark naked*?

4) She looks rather tipsy! Is she drunk?

5) Is that a necklace of human skulls around her neck?

6) Is my mind playing tricks on me or is she actually wearing some kind of . . . of weird *skirt* made out of severed human arms?

7) Is she black?

8) Why is her hair such a dreadful mess?

9) How can people *love* this horrible creature? Aren't they afraid of her? Isn't it merely a love born of fear?

10) Do people honestly worship her in cremation grounds?

11) Why is she surrounded by howling, blood-smattered jackals? Are they her familiars?

12) Is it true that Hindus actually *feed* their statues of Kali, and dress them up, and moisturise them, and dab them with perfume, and cool them with fans, and put them to bed in the afternoon for a quick snooze?

1857, the Dakshineswar Kali Temple (six miles north of Calcutta)

Rotting food everywhere, Uncle says, everywhere you looked. Of course I was not yet serving Uncle at this time, but Uncle has told me many things about the very early days of the Dakshineswar Kali Temple. There was so much food, Uncle says – spicy curries and steaming breads and delicious sweets and tempting side dishes – all prepared by the clever *brahmin* cooks, but nobody wanted to come to eat it. Not at first. Not even the poor and the starving. Instead, Uncle says, the temple authorities were obliged to feed it to the sacred cows, or to the flocks of geese, or to the wild cats and dogs that scavenged within the temple walls, or to the raucous crows who filled the trees in huge flocks, or – as a final resort – to throw it into the great River Ganga for the fish and the giant eels to argue over.

All because the Rani – who had built this beautiful temple for a tremendous amount of money, Uncle says – was a *sudra* and a *sudra* is not permitted to offer cooked food to the deities (only a *brahmin* may perform this special service). It is a law of caste. But the Rani had built her temple and she wanted to offer cooked food there for the poor, the *sadhu*s and the pilgrims to eat.

Perhaps some people find it difficult to comprehend why it is that we Hindus offer food to our deities? Well, our faith is a humble one and much of our religious observance takes place in our homes. Our gods are like members of our extended family and we treat them as such – with love and with reverence. If a god visited your home would you not water him and feed him and show him every kind of hospitality?

We Hindus like to call the food offered to our deities *prasad*. If it has been offered to the deities then naturally it is blessed by them – it is pure and purified – and so when we eat what they leave behind it is a holy act (in larger temples the offered food is added – once the deities have partaken of it – to giant cauldrons of other food and the blessings from the *prasad* infiltrate the whole so that many people may eat and then benefit). Uncle tells me that Christians also enjoy *prasad*, but that in their faith the food is plain bread and the water is wine, and when they consume it they believe that they are eating the body and the blood of Jesus the Christ. Uncle never lies so I must believe that this is true, no matter how much my nature rebels against it.

Long before the temple was opened, Uncle says, there was great opposition from the pandits to the idea of a *sudra* – even a rich, much-respected and devout one like the Rani – offering cooked food in a place of worship. She had been desperate to find a way to sidestep these caste rules. There had been many consultations, Uncle says. She had asked many opinions. She had sought much advice. But no respectable pandit would countenance the idea, Uncle says. Not, at least, until she happened across a *brahmin* by the name of Ramkumar Chatterjee who was then running a struggling Sanskrit school in Calcutta (and living with his young brother, Gadadhar, who was adding to their mean kitty by conducting private worship in people's homes). Ramkumar responded to a letter that the Rani had sent him by saying that according to his understanding of the scriptures he saw no good reason why the Rani might not offer cooked food in her new temple so long as she made a formal gift of the temple property to a *brahmin* and allowed him to oversee the installation of the deities and the cooking of the food to be offered therein.

The Rani was ecstatic, Uncle says, when she received his advice and so proceeded accordingly. The temple was formally signed over to her family *guru* and when it was opened she invited the *brahmin* whose advice had been so helpful to her to officiate over the installation of the image of Kali and to stay on as a priest until another could be found.

Unlike his older brother, Uncle was very contented with his life working as a household priest in Calcutta. His employers were always charmed by his intense devotion and made a great fuss of him, Uncle says. They gave him free rein. Some priests will just go through the motions, but definitely not Uncle. Uncle's love of God spills from his every pore and flows through his every vein. And he sings so sweetly, and dances so beautifully. He is so handsome and so innocent. Who can fail but to be bewitched by him?

I believe I may already have hinted earlier that Uncle had become much more strict in his adherence to the rules of caste since his boyhood misadventures. Uncle was now nineteen. His family was still very concerned for his mental well-being. Uncle had a profound contempt for all worldly things – 'for woman and for gold'. The love of God was his only interest. And when Ramkumar gave his advice to the Rani, Uncle was not entirely happy with it. Uncle was a wet blanket. Uncle was very concerned at the idea of a *sudra* serving cooked food – even under his brother's strict provisos. My, how things had changed! Now Ramkumar was playing fast and loose with the laws of caste and Uncle was trying and failing to make him conform to a more conservative way of thinking.

Surely God works in mysterious ways! Perhaps we are all destined to make our own mistakes and then to suffer the indignity of living through them again and again in the mistakes of those closest to us?

So Ramkumar installed the beautiful, black basalt image of Kali in the Dakshineswar Temple and then stayed on as priest. There was much celebration and feasting. Considerable amounts of money were spent, Uncle says, and many precious gifts handed out to pandits and pilgrims. Ramkumar – true to his word – accepted the cooked *prasad* from the temple. But when Uncle attended the grand festivities he refused to eat the food, preferring to receive uncooked provisions from the temple store and then make his own private dining arrangements. Uncle is stubborn. And as soon as the deity was installed he returned to Calcutta, by foot, fully expecting that his brother would follow on shortly after.

But Uncle was wrong. He waited and waited for Ramkumar's return, yet Ramkumar never came. Another priest could not be found to officiate at the Kali shrine and so the Rani respectfully asked Ramkumar to stay on. Which he did. Ramkumar believed that the Dakshineswar Kali Temple was a good environment for Uncle, a place where he might prosper, find new opportunities and move forward with his life.

It would take some considerable amount of time before pilgrims and visitors felt ready to accept the cooked food at the Dakshineswar Kali Temple, Uncle says. People are naturally suspicious and also stuck in their ways. The Rani had thrown money at the problem but life teaches us that money will not buy you everything. Uncle suspected that it may have bought the Rani the services of his brother and this thought made him very unhappy. But after a few weeks of living on his own he was obliged to cave in and move to the Kali Temple to be with Ramkumar. His brother was much older and Uncle loved him very dearly – almost like a father – although God teaches us that all human attachments will ultimately end in tragedy. They are impermanent. They are a part of the bewitching illusion of *maya*. They are fleeting and unreal. Because only the love of God, as Uncle never tires of telling us, is completely real, after all.

*If you were a little Indian swift (**Cypselus-affinis**) dashing around catching insects in the newly opened Dakshineswar Kali Temple grounds circa 1855, what great delights might you espy with your tiny, beady and perpetually darting swifty eye?*

Well, let's get one thing straight right off the bat: cute and charming as this idea undoubtedly is, an Indian swift is not remotely interested in aesthetics or in architecture. All objects – no matter how grand or ornate – are merely objects to a swift, just abstract shapes, and are only of interest insofar as he/she can avoid them, eat them, shit on them or construct a nest upon them. Swifts – unlike swallows – do not tend to perch. The Indian swift has funny little feet that aren't shaped as other birds' are. The claws are powerful (designed for hanging on to things) but the individual toes are splayed out, not unlike a gecko's, and this makes it more tricky for them to both hop around and/or stand about. They live on the wing. In fact the only time an Indian swift stops (either its shrill screaming or its acrobatic flying) is when it enters its nest (which is made of mud, feathers and copious quantities of sticky swift spit).

Perhaps rather than relying on the little swift's eye and limited brain-capacity (not to mention its fractured swift thoughts of '*safe . . . DANGER . . . left, right, SWOOP, avoid, quick, BIG, empty, light,* **dark***, hungry, mosquito . . .*' etc.) we should attach a tiny camera to our *circa* 1855 Indian swift's compact torso and proceed gingerly on that basis. Let's catch one. Go and fetch your butterfly net. This shouldn't be too difficult because the *circa* 1855 Indian swift is quite silly and highly accident-prone . . .

Excellent! In the blink of an eye the job is done. A miraculously tough but tiny and portable technology is deftly applied, suspended (on a modern twine as flexible, light and strong as a spider's silk) so as to hang at the bird's throat, just under its beak. You will observe that we have even coordinated it with the *circa* 1855 Indian swift's greenish-black plumage, and if you look especially close (with the aid of a magnifying glass, perhaps) you will see our tiny Cauliflower® logo exquisitely painted just below the camera's lens, which – in its entirety – is only the size of a large pin-head. The whole piece of kit is, in fact, lighter in weight and smaller in diameter than a mid-sized, blood-bloated tick.

Right. Let's toss him up into the air and see what he can find out for us . . . *whoosh!* Fly, little swift, fly!

Ah, he's momentarily spooked and so is heading straight for the holy Ganga. Technically speaking this is actually the River Hooghly which is a large, tidal tributary of the Ganga but is considered equivalently holy and sacred (because it originates at the same source and contains the same water). You will observe *two* (count them!) bathing *ghats*. A *ghat* is a series of twelve shallow steps (both of these are constructed from a lovely, red brick) leading down directly into the river so that pilgrims and visitors can remove their clothing and bathe in the holy Ganga water (an act that is believed to purify the soul and wash away one's sins).

Oh dear. Are the high-pitched screams of the *circa* 1855 swift bothering you at all? Perhaps I might . . . yes . . . just turn the volume down a little . . . uh . . . good . . . that's better.

At the top of the main *ghat* is a large, open portico or *chandni*, a place where the many bathers can find shade, undress, get dried, oil their bodies and chat. You will see . . . *whoooh* . . . (as the swift quickly jinks under the *chandni*) . . . that some women bathers leave their saris to dry in the warm, large, tiled courtyard which lies beyond, creating a dizzying patchwork-quilt of explosive colour. The tiles in this grand central courtyard area often get so hot that barefooted pilgrims are liable to singe their soles on them and the temple authorities spread out grass mats to prevent . . . uh . . .

If we could just . . .

The swift has doubled back on itself in pursuit of a midge . . .
but this is good. Yes. It allows us to see that on either side of the
chandni, facing the water, are a grand line of twelve individual,
white, ornate, double-red-dome-roofed Shiva temples (six either
side). Each of these contains its own natural stone *lingam*. Shiva,
Lord of Destruction (although it should always be borne in
mind that destruction is an essential/inherent part of the
creative process, too) is traditionally depicted and worshipped
by Hindus in an abstract form. Possibly these objects (these
lingam) are held to represent a phallus or a pillar or a sacrificial
post. Whatever their origin, they are generally worshipped with
simple offerings of bael leaves and milk.

Ah, there you go . . . we're now actually *inside* one of the . . .
oops . . . An irate temple guard is running around trying to hit the
swift with a giant fan . . . He'd certainly better . . . *ouch* . . .
the tiny camera just got a bit of a *thwack* and then the swift
flew straight into the . . . *oooh* . . . that isn't . . . that wasn't . . .
go-aan, me lad! . . . another quick . . . *yup* . . . and we're out!

Phew! Although the camera is slightly wonky now . . .
uh . . . just tip your head to one side if you will . . . yes . . . the
circa 1855 swift is heading at pretty much full pelt (if you press
the green button on your remote you'll see a small reading of
his current speed) towards the dramatically red flowering
oleander which stands close to the water's edge, and just beyond
it, the two huge and quite magnificent palms.

He's just . . . he's gradually . . . there's quite a bit of wind
from the river at this altitude and it seems to be making the
slightly damaged camera vibrate rather rapidly . . . *wooooah-
wooooah-wooooah-wooooah* . . . I'm going to turn the volume down
completely because I'm finding that noise strangely disturbing.
It's something of a teeth rattler.

In truth, I rather regret not fastening the camera (which has
actually taken up over 76 per cent of this book's total budget)

to something a little more sedentary — a sparrow, perhaps, or a cat . . . although . . . *woooop!* Here we go . . . we're back inside the main courtyard . . . to your left is the large, flat-roofed, many-arched white and red Radhakanta Temple which contains images of Krishna and Radha (the great lovers) . . . if you get a chance to peer through the . . . no . . . we've moved on. The floors (I'm reliably informed) are marble, and there are chandeliers covered in sackcloth to prevent . . .

Now *that's* the *Natmandir* or theatre hall . . . It's on the other side of the . . . the Kali Temple compound and it . . . it echoes the Radhanka Temple architecturally with all the . . . you know . . . the grand flourishes: a series of majestic pillars supporting a flat roof, the smart white and red finish . . . but if you just . . . quick! While you have the chance . . . in the far right-hand corner of the screen you can see the magnificent wedding cake form of the nine-spired Kali Temple which stands on its high platform accessible via a grand flight of stairs. It's in the . . . you probably can't see from this angle — we're suddenly flying up rather close — but it's in the traditional Bengal style and rises to a height of over thirty metres . . .

Oh. We've nipped around the back. Up ahead is the big tank (or reservoir) with its plate-washing *ghat* . . . this is basically the business end of the structure. If we'd had a chance to get a better . . . if we'd . . . because the courtyard of the Kali Temple is fenced in on three sides by a neatly balconied rectangular wall of offices and kitchens and guest rooms and temple stores . . . in fact . . . just to the right of this vast tank you can get a fleeting glimpse of a big pile of construction materials. The Rani started building in 1847 so it's taken her almost eight years thus far and there's still plenty to . . .

Oh. These are the orchards. This really is a prodigious plot, almost twenty acres, in total, and was originally the site of an ancient — but long abandoned — Muslim cemetery. In fact if we could . . . if we could just fly a little higher for a moment (we can't – we aren't – forgive my mordant laugh/groan) you'd see that the whole thing is in the shape of a giant tortoise shell (lower on the edges, higher at the centre), which is considered highly auspicious to the . . .

Another orchard. Everything newly planted and incredibly lush. To the right (or the east) are the imposing main entrance gates, although we probably won't get a chance to . . . to the left . . . ah . . . the *kuthi* . . . can you . . . ? No. Well, it's the beautiful mansion the Rani had built for when she and her family are in residence. It will mainly be used to house important guests and host lavish events. Although for many years Sri Ramakrishna himself will inhabit a big room on the ground floor to the western corner of . . .

Two more tanks . . . yes . . . one is the goose tank . . . We're heading north, no south . . . you'll see the tiny compass rotating crazily at the base of the screen . . . I'm not sure if . . . Oh! Yes. And this is actually quite a significant area in the Ramakrishna story . . . that's . . . to the top left . . . that's the ancient bael tree (or vilwa) in the dense, forested area or 'wilderness', at the northern boundary of the compound, where Ramakrishna first removed his sacred thread (much to his poor nephew Hriday's abundant horror) while meditating, alone, at night, and where . . . if you look – sharp right! Very quickly – you will see the Government Magazine just beyond the boundary with its affable Sikh guards whom Ramakrishna became very friendly with during the course of . . . and the . . .

Oh . . . oh no. Oh dear. Please, ladies, gentlemen, avert your eyes. We've jinked into the pine grove which is used principally for defecation. That's . . . oh dear . . . oh no . . . uh . . . oh goodness gracious me . . . that's just . . . There are a fair number of little insects in the vicinity and so the *circa* 1855 swift is rather drawn to . . . uh . . .

Ah! We're now rapidly approaching an area where – in the not-too-distant future – Ramakrishna will experience some of the most important moments in his *sadhana* (or spiritual journey). Peel your eyes! To the left! Quick! Quick! That's the site of Ramakrishna's small, thatched meditation hut and just beyond it he will (in 1868, after a pilgrimage to Vrindavan) plant his famous *panchavati*. He will collect some dust in that most holy city – the site of the ancient forest where Krishna spent his happiest childhood days – and scatter it here, in this spot. The word *panchavati* refers to the forest home of Rama (seventh *avatar* of Vishnu), but in plain English, it is a small grove of five trees: the banyan, the pipal, the amlaki, the ashoka and the bael, and is considered to be a perfect, peaceful, shady venue for spiritual pursuits.

Oh. To the right. That's the other *ghat* . . . the second *ghat*, the Bakultala *ghat* which is very close to Ramakrishna's corner *kuthi* room, and also close to the northern *nahabat* or music tower (there are two: one situated on the northern and the other on the southern side of the main courtyard. They play holy music there during various phases of the day's worship). Ramakrishna's mother, Chandradevi, and then later on his wife, Sarada Devi (aka the Holy Mother – yes, he did marry, and the union was blissful but unconsummated) would live for many years (in considerable discomfort, I imagine) in the tiny storeroom at the base of the northern *nahabat*.

Um . . . There seems to be something . . . I don't really like to mention it, but you may have noticed a certain amount of . . . of break-up in the visual transmission? Some kind of dark . . . black . . . a shadow, almost, in the top right-hand corner of the . . . ? I'm just hoping against hope that if we continue moving forward for a couple more seconds we may actually get to fly past the small room just beyond the northern *nahabat* which is situated at the end of the northern wall of kitchens/stores/offices etc . . . with its wonderful south-eastern veranda looking directly into the main temple compound, and its other north-eastern one with views of the gardens, the *kuthi* and the

71

nahabat, not to mention its grand, semicircular porch to the fore which looks straight across the holy Ganga ... This was to be Sri Ramakrishna's second main residence during his long stay at Dakshineswar. It's now open to the public in its original state, virtually untouched – although they upgraded the floors, which is a great shame – and a site of pilgrimage for many thousands, nay millions, of loyal devotees from all across the ...

No. Nope. Sorry about that. The swift has suddenly doubled back and is rapidly returning to the *panchavati*. If you glance to the left you'll be able to feast your senses upon the furthest reaches of the extensive and perfectly heavenly flower gardens which the Rani has planted to run along the river banks either side of the main *ghat* and the *chandni*, and which fill the humid air with the heady perfumes of rose, hibiscus and Arabian jasmine. Just close your eyes for a second and imagine inhaling the intoxicating perfume of ...

Ouch!

Thwack!

Crunch!

Eh?! What the ... ?! I think we may ... it ... it seems like ... We were heading our way back to the *panchavati*, minding our own business, when that persistent black shadow that has been dogging us for ... for quite some time now suddenly grew darker ... more intense, and then ... then it appeared to collide with ... to tangle with ... Brace yourselves! I'm going to turn the audio back up again to try and identify what on earth might be ...

Gracious me! What a dreadful ... ! I think that's the ground. And I think that's a claw. And a giant beak. Just jabbing and jabbing at ... And the sounds! And the *blood*! And the feathers! Those heart-rending *squeaks* ... And in the distance a deafening and victorious caw-caw-cawing ... But how could ... ? Why would ... ?

I'm going to quickly mute the ... If you're of a sensitive

disposition I suggest you turn away for a second, because from what I can tell a murderous crow seems to have . . . it seems to be . . . they will sometimes . . . if they're hungry . . . or simply for the sport . . . or maybe because it caught a quick glimpse of something fascinating and reflective at the *circa* 1855 swift's throat as it flew . . .

Hang on . . . *what* . . . *?!* See that?! The shadow has lifted, very suddenly, and if you look to the left of the screen . . . Is that . . . ? Is that a man approaching, at speed, holding a home-made catapult . . . ? Am I correct in deducing that he seems to have shot a pellet from this primitive contraption towards the crow while it busied itself tormenting the . . . and now he's running to the spot . . . barefoot? That's his toe. Do you see his toe? I'm going to turn the volume up again . . . Yes, *yes*, I know the picture keeps cutting in and cutting out. But you must see the man, surely? A young man, skinny, with a pretty, golden complexion and a moon-shaped face, peering down at our wounded, our fatally injured – our poor, dead *circa* 1855 swift (RIP). He looks very concerned. That's his . . . that's his index finger, gently poking at the bird . . .

I'm not sure if he's noticed the . . . has he spotted the camera? Tiny as it is? Do you see his eye gazing straight at us? He is picking us up. He is holding us in his hand! Yes, the camera keeps cutting in and cutting out and . . . yes . . . yes . . . the swift is dead. But that's not . . . Just . . . just quiet down your wailing, please – over there, at the back – because if I've not completely lost the plot – and I don't *think* I've completely lost the plot – the hand that now holds us . . . the camera . . . the swift . . . belongs to none other than a nineteen-year-old (although we can't be sure that's his precise age) Gadhadar Chatterjee (if that *is* actually his real name), who will eventually become . . . who will eventually be hailed as . . .

Ahhh. Do you see the tenderness in those brown eyes? Such beautiful eyes! Such intelligent eyes! Fringed with such an abundance of luscious lashes! There remain very few images of him . . . very few . . . just three or four . . . and those only from when he's way, way older . . . but to see this boy . . . this little Krishna, this artless Mowgli, and to sit in his warm hand, like this, to lie in his revered palm . . .

He is inspecting us, very closely. He is looking deep into our souls. Do you feel that? Do you? The sheer intensity of his gaze? And there is such . . . such sadness in those eyes, and then . . . then there is such resignation, and then there is . . . there is laughter. *Laughter?* Of course. Do you see his lips moving? 'This is her play,' he murmurs, as if to comfort himself. 'This is the play of the Divine Mother.' (He speaks in his rural Bengali dialect – but no stammer – not a *hint* of a stammer!)

Ah. Such extraordinary detachment! Such exquisite fatalism! Yes. This is the *lila* of the Divine Mother. He thinks that this (the *circa* 1855 swift's violent death – and, who knows? *Us?* The camera?) is her play. This is her divine sport. *We* are her play.

And who's to say that we aren't? Eh?

I'm just . . . urgh . . . the words have dried up. I'm rendered inarticulate. I mean if you don't quite appreciate how significant this moment is . . . how rare, how *precious*, then I can only . . . Although (in your defence) I suppose you've clambered a little tardily on to this speeding, spiritual train, haven't you? You're a fraction green. Feeling slightly travel-sick. Somewhat unprepared.

And I'm a . . . I'm sorry if I'm not proving entirely capable of rising to the . . . I'm just a little bit . . . a little bit overwhelmed by it all . . . flustered . . . Just to be . . . to be held by the hand of . . . well of . . . of *God*. To be held by this hand . . . but before everything . . . at the start of that great journey . . . years, even *decades*, before it would all coalesce into . . .

Oh my, oh my, oh my.

Hup! Eh? Hang on! What now? We seem to be . . . we're

suddenly moving towards the . . . very rapidly . . . we're . . .
Good heavens! Is he . . . ? Are we being . . . ? Is he planning
to . . . ? Is he tossing us into the . . . ? Throwing us into
the holy Ganga? Into the river? Giving us a sacred burial?
Before we've even had a chance to retrieve the technology?!
Is he . . . ?

Plop!

Aaargh! Into the water . . . but we're supposed to be . . .
We're meant to be waterproofed at . . . at . . . at . . . at some
level? Aren't we?

Have we become detached from the *circa* 1855 recently
deceased swift? Are we alone? Are we sinking? If you press
the yellow button on your remote you'll be able to see how . . .
tell exactly how . . . how *deep* . . .

Oooh. It's very murky down here . . . Did he do that on
purpose? Just throw us . . . ? Did he not understand . . . not
recognise . . . ? Did he not *want* us to be a part of . . . to see
his . . . to bear witness to his . . . to his phenomenal . . . ?

Is that a . . . a GIANT CATFISH? Swimming towards
us? NO! NO! *NO!* Please don't! *Please* don't! *AAAARGH!*
It *swallowed* us! We've been swallowed by a giant catfish!
And this is . . . this is its throat . . . and now this is its upper
intestine. I'm not sure if we can . . . the signal . . . I'm not sure
if it will . . . if it will carry on for too . . . for too much . . . for
too . . . for too . . . for . . .

Hmmm. Seventy-six per cent of the total budget up in smoke. The
Cauliflower® is now officially in ruins. Seventy-six per cent!
And that's from a total budget of . . . uh . . . *um* . . . of nothing.
So how much does that add up to, exactly? You do the maths.

What?! In pounds sterling?!

Oh! Oh thank goodness! In rupees . . .

In 1856 Gadhadar Chatterjee, who will one day become Sri Ramakrishna (although we don't know quite how), is perched, stark naked, on the steps of the main ghat at the Dakshineswar Kali Temple holding a fistful of dirt in one hand and a fistful of coins in his other, repeating, under his breath, with an extraordinary level of concentration and intensity, seemingly ad infinitum:

'Rupee is dirt, dirt is rupee. Rupee is dirt, dirt is rupee. Rupee is dirt, dirt is rupee . . .'

In the not-too-distant future, such will be Sri Ramakrishna's profound abhorrence for money that even the slightest *touch* of a coin to his sensitive fingertips will leave unsightly singe-marks on his delicate skin. So powerful will become his state of divine non-attachment that he will prove incapable of engaging in financial transactions of *any* kind. He will not spend money. He will not save money. He will not use money. He will own nothing. *Nothing.* Other people – devotees, helpers, generous benefactors – will now need to support his every whim.

Of course this is an immense blessing. Because the privilege of supporting a great saint financially is an honour of almost inconceivable magnitude.

Imagine the joy of purchasing a prayer mat for Muhammad, a bathing cloth for Buddha, or a sandal for Jesus. Imagine the simple joy of service *as* worship.

March 1885, early afternoon. The cynical brother of a disciple enquires

Cynical brother (*in the hope of provoking the saint into a show of ego*): 'Sir, what do I call you, please? What is your name?'
Sri Ramakrishna (*smiling, while gently massaging the cynical brother's back*): 'Names? Do we have names? [*waving his hand genially*] Hey! Hey you! Hello! If you call me like this then I will know that I am being called.'

While engaged in conversation with a new devotee, Sri Ramakrishna falls momentarily silent (apparently lost in deep spiritual contemplation) and then suddenly, perking up, he exclaims:

'It's both sweet and sour,
Made with lemons and it fizzes.
Bring some next time, please.'

Ah. Lemonade. The *Paramahamsa* wants *lemonade*.

Spring 1857 at the Dakshineswar Kali Temple (six miles north of Calcutta)

Uncle says it is almost impossible to eliminate the ego completely. He is very fond of using the example of a bowl that has been used for the purpose of storing chopped onions. Even when all the onions have been removed, Uncle says, no matter how carefully you clean out that bowl, some trace of the smell will always remain. The ego is like that. You think it is gone but something always stays behind. A slight smell or a taint. And it will pop up and startle you when you least expect it to.

Of course extremely holy men after years of intense austerity and renunciation can sometimes reach a state which we Hindus call *nirvikalpa samadhi*. If, during a divine vision, you finally get to see Brahman – or God – face to face, then your body will not manage to survive the experience. After only a short while you will be dead. It is as though the ego is burned away by the light of God and then the body shrivels up like an empty seed pod. Spiritual pursuits are very good for your soul, but they can certainly be harmful to your health.

Look at Uncle. Who can deny that Uncle is blessed? That he is special? Uncle can bring such joy to people. He is full of love. There is an intensity and an honesty and a childlike innocence. There is an intoxicating attraction. I have heard people call it a charisma. Uncle could live a charmed life. And all the Chatterjees and the Mukkerjees could live this life right alongside Uncle. But there is a perversity in Uncle. And this is his longing for God, which is almost like a sickness. It is very nearly a madness.

Just one year after the inauguration of the Kali Temple Uncle's beloved brother, Ramkumar, tragically passed away. Thank God I was here with Uncle to offer him support through this difficult time. How would he have managed otherwise?

Ramkumar was Uncle's rock. He was one of the few people to whom Uncle showed any deference. So then, when Ramkumar died, Uncle lost all hope. Uncle's world turned black. He felt such bleakness – such a disaffection with all worldly interests and pursuits, as if there were nothing of any value left for him on this whole, broad earth. Poor Uncle suffered most dreadfully.

Before his early death, Ramkumar had been involved in many conversations with the Rani's son-in-law, Mathur Baba, on the subject of Uncle. Mathur Baba had noticed Uncle around the place and had been charmed and captivated by his obviously spiritual nature. It is hard not to be struck by Uncle's natural intelligence and his simplicity and his deep sincerity. Uncle has a kind of perfection. How might one possibly hope to explain it? It is simply his very essence.

Ramkumar had slowly persuaded Uncle over many months (inch by gradual inch) to help him with the Kali worship. But the rituals of Kali worship are very onerous and complicated. So Ramkumar made Uncle receive some formal training from an experienced *guru*. Uncle raised no particular objections to this process. And things went ahead swimmingly, or so it seemed, until during the initiation ritual the *guru* leaned forward and whispered Kali's holy *mantram* into Uncle's ear and Uncle unleashed a most dreadful cry – a cry so loud and so terrible as to strike pity and fear into the very hardest of human hearts – and then fell into an impenetrable trance. We were all greatly perplexed. What new mischief was this? But after a short while Ramkumar just slowly shook his head and laughed. Because when did dear Uncle ever do anything by halves?

At around this time an upsetting incident took place at the Dakshineswar Kali Temple. One afternoon, after worship, the head priest in the Radhakanta Temple slipped while carrying the image of Krishna and Krishna's foot was broken in the fall. The priest was promptly dismissed. Damage to an image is considered highly inauspicious. It might attract very bad luck.

And this image was one to which the Rani was especially attached. There was much debate about what to do next. Many pandits suggested that the Rani retire the image and replace it with another. But the Rani was very fond of the image and this thought distressed her. One day Mathur Baba approached Uncle and asked him his opinion on the matter. Of course Uncle – young and insignificant as he then was – took this question in his stride. Nothing intimidates Uncle! He merely thought hard for a second and then he said, 'If the Rani's son-in-law fell down and broke his foot would the Rani then abandon him? Of course not. She would carefully tend to him until he was recovered. The Rani should treat the image of Krishna with the same level of compassion. She should fix the image and then return it to the temple.'

You may remember that Uncle had a great talent from his childhood with clay and sculpture. He volunteered to fix the image himself using clay from the banks of the holy Ganga, and he did so with considerable skill.

The Rani was delighted. Uncle had effortlessly solved all her problems. One cannot deny that Uncle had much spiritual authority for one still so young. Nobody could ignore it. And so both Mathur Baba and the Rani felt that Uncle should be persuaded to take a more active role in the life of the temple thereafter. Mathur Baba asked Ramkumar if Uncle might now be willing to act as priest in the Radhakanta Temple. Uncle accepted the offer (after much huffing and puffing) only because the burden of worship was not too heavy there. Alas, Ramkumar's health soon began to decline until it became increasingly difficult for him to continue in the demanding worship of Ma Kali. Mathur Baba and Ramkumar decided that the best thing would naturally be for Uncle to now move to the main temple and for Ramkumar to take on Uncle's lighter duties.

Well, you might think that Uncle would be delighted by this unexpected promotion. But quite the opposite! Uncle was horrified.

He had no desire to spend his time tied to the routines of the Kali worship. Uncle was a free spirit. He could not be expected to conform to certain traditional ways of doing things. And he did not want the responsibility of looking after the goddess's expensive jewellery, either. Uncle had a terror of such things.

Even though Mathur Baba (a powerful and influential man) showed Uncle (a poor village boy of no formal education) so much favour and deference in offering him this promotion, Uncle responded to these great kindnesses by claiming that he lacked the knowledge of the scriptures needed for such an exalted role, and when Mathur Baba insisted that this was of no importance (Uncle's spiritual qualities were of far more significance than mere book learning, he said) Uncle commenced avoiding Mathur Baba like the plague! If Uncle caught so much as a whiff of Mathur Baba in the vicinity he would instantly scurry off. You can only imagine how much consternation this caused both myself and Ramkumar! Uncle is extremely perverse! It was only when I myself promised to assist Uncle in all his duties and to take full responsibility for the jewellery and precious items in the Kali Temple that Uncle was finally persuaded to relent.

Uncle is perfectly unmanageable! Who might compel him into anything? A wild stallion may be tamed, but who may tame Uncle?

Ah. Even as I ask this question I am quietly prompted with a response. Ma Kali, that is who. It is Ma Kali who will tame Uncle. And yet Uncle's gradually developing devotion to the goddess would express itself in yet still more displays of shocking perversity! Oh, the trials Uncle would put us all through! The shame and the confusion and the heartbreak! Who can understand Uncle? Not me. Uncle is truly beyond my comprehension. But I love Uncle more than the very breath that fills my lungs. Even though I doubt him, and I doubt him and I doubt him. Even so. I love him.

Twelve attempted answers to the twelve slightly impertinent questions about Ma Kali

1) The main monotheistic faiths cleave to the idea that there is one God who is good. All evil comes from another place, a different place. In the Christian tradition, this place is the devil. Muslims call him *Shaitan*. But the Hindus yearn to transcend what they call the 'pair of opposites', e.g. good/bad, love/hate, attraction/repulsion. They believe that it is necessary to do this if you are to journey beyond the limited world of the ego and its attachments, beyond the cage of relativism. To the Hindu, God is beyond 'opposites', beyond good and evil. Often the example of fire is used to illustrate this idea. We use fire to warm ourselves and to cook, but fire may also hurt us and destroy our homes. So fire transcends good and bad. The human mind, the ego, will *call* fire good or bad according to the context. But fire is neither good nor bad. It is simply fire. And it *burns*.

2) Kali is a creative, dynamic, destructive force who is both good *and* bad. She is *Dakshina* Kali (the loving Kali who grants boons and blessings) and she is *Smashan* Kali (the terrible, terrifying form, who destroys). *Smashan* Kali is traditionally worshipped in cremation grounds. These are places of ash and decay, burned bones, bad smells and jackals.

In the west it could be argued that we sublimate this special 'spiritual mood' into our phases of simmering teenage angst, or when we read books about vampires and ghosts, or watch horror films, or when we dye our hair black and become goths and listen to Joy Division or Marilyn Manson. When we celebrate Halloween, even. It's the same fundamental impulse, and a curious irony, too, that a sense of comfort/release is sometimes felt when we actively go out of our way to embrace the sweet and sticky black treacle of darkness.

Kali's famous cremation ground is a location in which it is suddenly rather easy to renounce the body and the ego (a bleak and despairing place – how can we possibly evade the truth of death and decomposition here?), but it is also, and equally importantly, a place where we may master something even more powerful than our ego (or our attraction to life and the living), and that's our deep-seated fears and aversions. Our aversions are even more difficult to eliminate and overcome than our natural human weakness for cheap thrills and attractions. A true saint feels neither attraction *nor* repulsion *nor* fear.

3) People happily and readily love Kali in both her main forms (in fact she has countless forms – there is a custom-built Kali for all occasions) because even though she may *appear* to both bless us/nourish us and/or kill us/destroy us, she actually does neither. Our world is just a kind of transitory dream, an illusion. We exist on a relative plane. The Hindus call this earthly realm *maya*. And what takes place here is only divine play – a game. Life and death are inconsequential. To move beyond *maya* you must consciously stop playing the game, then Kali may spare you and free your soul to unite with God, with Brahman, who is the ultimate reality, in a place and state of incontrovertible truth and infinite bliss.

Life is illusion. It is *maya*. Kali is the puppet-master. We are the puppets. She may stoop and cut our strings if she feels the sudden impulse. But take nothing for granted here. She is perplexingly coquettish and a creature of strange whims.

4) Kali spits out her tongue not as a gesture of defiance, but as an expression of embarrassment or coyness because she has

(during the course of an orgy of vengeance and destruction) accidentally stepped on to the prostrate body of her beloved husband, Shiva (Shiva, who is not dead, just deathly pale and smeared in the white ash of renunciation, has lain in front of his wife to try and curtail her inexhaustible wrath). Kali is fierce, but confused. On a purely symbolic level, Kali's tongue is red and represents *rajas* or activity, but this tongue is held between her white teeth, and white is the colour of *sattva* or purity and spirituality. Her passion is restrained by purity, or, in other words, by God.

5) The fifty skulls that Ma Kali wears around her neck represent the fifty letters of the ancient Sanskrit alphabet. Kali creates worlds and she creates words. The ancient concept of the *logos* is contained here and originates here (long before St John thought of it or wrote about it in his exquisite gospel), nestled in the musky bosom of the Black Mother.

6) Kali's name comes from the word *kala*, or 'time'. Time consumes everything. Kali is black because she *is* time, and she has destroyed everything. She is a giant vacuum, an endless, dark void. She is inscrutable. The ignorant devotee can only really see her from a distance. She is similar to the night sky. Draw up close and (like God, or Brahman, who is ultimately formless) she will simply disappear.

pouf!

7) Kali's hair is in disarray because she is wild. She is an all-singing, dervish-dancing, ecstatically stomping, bloody-sword-wielding Beyoncé Knowles. She sings to her own crazy tune. She is utterly unfettered. She is fearless. She is free.

8) Kali's priests at the temple may dress her image in priceless saris and cover her with precious scents and expensive jewellery – this is how they honour her, it is all a part of their divine service – but Kali herself may never be dressed. She may never be curtailed. Can you dress a storm? Can you bejewel the wind? For this reason Kali is called Digambari: she who is naked.

9) Kali cannot exist without Shiva, her husband, but Shiva (who, as he lies flat and pale at her feet, represents the blinding light of infinite consciousness) cannot manifest his destructive power without his wife, Kali. Creation and destruction are an endless cycle. One cannot exist without the other. They are two opposites, eternally conjoined. This is an eternal love affair.

10) The girdle of arms around Kali's waist represents work or action. The arms symbolise her creative energy. They also represent – at some level – the pointlessness of all human endeavour. Everything we build will ultimately be destroyed. Nothing we do may last for ever.

11) Kali provides a source of delirious bliss to her devotees (Kali herself reels about, drunkenly, high on this blissful intoxication, but also, perhaps, on blood-lust after slaughtering copious demons) through the physical mechanism of what Hindus call the *kundalini*.

Kali's energy is sourced at the base of the human spine. It extends down to a point just below the anus and then rises up to the crown of the head, travelling through the heart, the base of the throat and the point between your eyes at the top of your nose, en route. Her power writhes and vibrates like a snake through this channel. But it is a dangerous, overwhelming and ecstatic energy to release, and very difficult to control once you have. Play with it at your peril, girls and boys.

12) Illustrious Ma Kali, Mother of the Universe, your blissful power, it seems, is infinite. But how may our pens hope to describe this infinity without promptly running out of ink? How may your great bliss be expressed by our mean and paltry descriptions of it? How may the dreadful fire of your ecstasy be controlled within our fleshy torsos? How, how, *how* may the creatress of all words (of language) be clumsily manacled by their petty meanings?

How indeed?

Sri Ramakrishna on truth:

Always speak the truth –
The tusks of an elephant
Can't be retracted.

Winter 1857 at the Dakshineswar Kali Temple (six miles north of Calcutta)

Uncle has gone completely mad. And who am I? Who is Hridayram Mukhopadhyay – still so young and strong and full of promise, tall and handsome, once his dear mother's greatest hope? Who is he? Yes! The servant of a madman! And is not the servant of a madman a madman also? Ah! How can this stain not stick?

I am Uncle's shadow, his keeper, his watchman, his guard. I am tied to Uncle by the clinging vines of love. And I live in a state of dreadful doubt and confusion. I live in profound uncertainty. I am sick with worry and anxiety. Not unlike poor Uncle himself.

Poor Uncle hardly sleeps! I carry his towel and water pot to the pine grove at 3 a.m. when Uncle answers the call of nature. I say nothing. I am fearful. And then on to the *ghat* where Uncle washes himself. I say nothing. I am fearful. And then he sits and I carefully smear his emaciated body with oil. Still saying nothing. Still fearful.

But this is a good day. On a bad day Uncle will not clean himself. Uncle will roll in the dirt on the banks of the Ganga, hour after hour, howling and weeping. He has a tantrum. He calls for Ma Kali like a child bleating for its mother. He cries with such yearning that the crowds form around him. 'Isn't this the young temple priest?' they ask. 'Has his mother just died?'

What can I say? How do I explain to them? Uncle suffers so dreadfully. Because Uncle has such a longing to see the Mother and she will not appear to him. Ma Kali eludes Uncle. Uncle's charms will not work on her. And Uncle cannot stand it.

He spends all his days in prayer and in worship and in *japa*. He will not eat. Like an angry child, a spoiled child, Uncle is

fractious. He will not rest. He grinds his teeth. He whimpers
and wrings his hands.

And I am fractious too. I must guard Uncle. At night – if I
close my eyes for just a second – he disappears and I must then
go out and find him. Where is he? Where has Uncle gone?
Uncle? Where are you? *Uncle! Uncle!* Come back!
Oh why oh why must Uncle play such games?

I am so tired. I am worn down with Uncle. I must cover for
him at the temple, but every moment as I perform the *arati* – as
I wave burning camphor before Ma Kali or offer her choice
morsels of food – I am thinking only of Uncle. Where is he?
What might Uncle be doing? What scandal might now be
unfolding and I, Hriday, faithful Hridayram, am not there to
extinguish the flames?

Uncle has taken to wandering alone in the jungle at night.
His bare feet sliced and pricked by spiky plants. Surrounded
by a halo of biting insects. Stalked by wild animals. I am too
afraid to follow him there. It's as though Uncle is in a trance.
He is lovelorn. Since Ramkumar died Uncle cares for nothing
but God. But God eludes him. So Uncle yearns. Uncle is
hungry for God. He thirsts for God's nipple. His chapped lips
open and close but often now he is too tired to wail.

Uncle is so thin. He cannot eat. He cannot keep his
wearing-cloth upon him. It falls off. He does not care. He
walks around naked, his chest stained a dark red. I do not
know why. And the wind! Uncle has dreadful wind! Uncle
is flatulent! Whenever he does appear at the temple – filthy,
like a madman – he dances and sings (the strangest songs! The
wildest dances!) before Ma Kali and he flatulates with every
step. The temple administrators are astonished by Uncle's
displays. And the visitors. The pilgrims. They ask, 'Who is this
lunatic! What is he doing here?' They stare at him in revulsion
and horror and fear. It is dreadful! And I am with Uncle. I am
Uncle's nephew. They laugh at me behind my back. I hear

them! I hear them laughing! But never to my face. I am tall and strong. I will defend our honour even through all my crippling doubt. I will defend Uncle's honour with my life. Or else my fists. But what am I defending? What has Uncle left us with?

Man is a simple creature. And for the most part the formless Brahman is beyond his foolish comprehension. How are we to worship him, then, without using the familiar examples of our daily lives? When we Hindus worship the divine we find many different ways to adore him. We call this worship *bhakti*. Sometimes we like to worship him as his servant. He is our master. Sometimes he is our divine spouse, our lover. Sometimes God is our mother or our father and we throw out our arms for comfort and worship him, moaning, like a child. Or else God is our dearest friend, our great strength and companion through every earthly trial.

Uncle was Ma Kali's neglected suckling. He moaned and moaned but she would not comfort him. Her dark nipples were full of milk but she would not feed him so much as a single, blessed drop. Uncle could not rest without her comfort. I was always full of doubt. But now Uncle, too, became doubtful. Questions. So many questions. 'Is the Mother real?' he would ask. 'Am I going mad?' he would ask. 'If Mother is real then why will she not appear to me?' he would ask. 'Where is Mother?' he would ask, striking his chest. 'Mother! Mother! Hridayram! Why does she still hide from me?' he would ask. 'What have I done wrong, Hriday? Tell me! Tell me! Tell me!'

I could not answer. I could only stare. Fear had silenced my tongue. But I could still hear. I could still listen. And what I heard made me yet more fearful. Because there were many complaints about Uncle. The temple guards, the other priests, the administrators, the cooks. They all complained about Uncle. First there were simply mutterings, but then they grew louder. Soon it was a roar. It was only a matter of time until such a great racket must reach the ears of Mathur Baba and the Rani. Then we would be ruined.

One night, when Uncle rose, in secret, and wandered, sobbing, into the jungle, I steeled my nerve and I followed him there. I needed to know where Uncle was going. After a while I saw him pause in a small clearing under a sacred vilwa tree. I was some distance away. I was too afraid to draw closer. I saw Uncle calmly remove his wearing-cloth and sit down. And then I saw something truly dreadful. I saw Uncle remove his sacred thread and place it on the ground beside him. What to do? How to respond? I bent over and I picked up a small stone and I threw it at Uncle. Then I picked up another stone, and then another. Soon stones of all sizes were raining down on Uncle. Uncle was deep in meditation, but eventually his eyes flew open and he beheld his nephew.

'What are you doing, Hriday?' he called.

'You have removed your sacred thread, Uncle,' I called back. 'What are you thinking, Uncle? This is too much, now, too much! This is not acceptable, Uncle!'

(Was this not the same man who on grounds of caste had refused to eat the temple *prasad*? And now to remove the very symbol of his proud *brahmin* inheritance?!)

Uncle shrugged. 'To see God one must be free of all earthly ties, Hriday, even ties of caste. My *brahmanical* thread is a source of status and pride. To see the Mother clearly during meditation I must toss aside such fetters.'

I shook my head at Uncle. Then I cast down the remaining stones. What more could I say? What more could I do? I was truly at my wits' end with Uncle. How might I reason with Uncle when Uncle always had an answer to every question I might think to ask him? Uncle has always been possessed of a devilish logic.

A few days later and Uncle was performing the *arati* in front of the goddess. I was preparing lunch for Uncle, something very plain (Uncle was plagued by terrible indigestion. He constantly complained of a burning sensation in his chest), when suddenly a temple gardener – who has always held a soft spot for Uncle – came running across the main courtyard calling out my name. I sprang up. 'Is it Uncle?' I demanded. This poor man could hardly catch his breath. 'I was delivering garlands to Ma Kali,' he panted, 'and Gadai was causing a great commotion in the temple. He was shouting at the goddess. "What more can I do, Mother?" he was screaming. "What more can I give you, Mother?" Then his eyes suddenly turned towards the ceremonial sword that is hung on the temple wall. "I shall give you my life!" he cried, and then, before any person could stop him, he had grabbed this sword from its mount, unsheathed it, raised his arm with a bloodcurdling cry of "Mother!" quite as if to stab himself with it, and then collapsed into a heap on the temple floor. We have tried our hardest to revive him but nothing seems to be working. There is almost no pulse. And no signs of life. He is very deeply unconscious.'

We ran the length of the veranda together and then entered the Kali Temple through the back entrance. Outside, the crowds of visitors and pilgrims stood many deep, craning their necks to see what was happening. And there we found Uncle Gadai, lying at the feet of Ma Kali, naked (Uncle's wearing-cloth abandoned), cushioned by a bed of flower offerings, deathly pale, a living Shiva, the unsheathed sword close by. The temple administrator was already in attendance. 'What new madness is this?!' he demanded. 'Your Uncle has finally taken leave of his senses!'

We kneeled down and gazed at Uncle. A small crowd had formed around him. An elderly woman, a widow, had somehow slipped past the guards and entered the temple sanctum and was stroking Uncle's forehead with the hem of her white sari. 'How beautiful this boy is!' she whispered, quite utterly beguiled by

Uncle. 'In all my many years I swear that I have never seen a face as sweet and as radiant as his. Look! Look! See how he smiles!'

Uncle was indeed smiling. He wore a blissful expression. His young face which had recently looked so thin and careworn was now transformed. It was difficult for all the people clustered around Uncle – even the temple administrator – not to sense the bewitching atmosphere of deep spiritual peace that Uncle now exuded.

It was very warm and close. The fragrance of sweet camphor and crushed flowers was overwhelming. Many eyes turned from Uncle's glowing face towards the image of Kali that towered above us all. There was a brief silence (who can guess why?) and then a bright shaft of light passed from the shining basalt eyes of the black goddess on to the naked boy with the moon face who lay offered – as if dead – before her. Perhaps this light was reflected from the blade of the ceremonial sword which a guard had now retrieved and was placing back into its sheath? Who can say? But there was an audible gasp. 'The image has awakened!' someone shouted. 'This boy has awakened the goddess!' cried another.
And then the widow began to clap her hands together, to rock and to chant: *Ma, oh Ma, Ma go Ma! Jai Kali! Jai Kali Ma!* This cry was caught up by the ecstatic crowd as Uncle was lifted, still unconscious, and held aloft, pale and glowing, light as a feather. It continued, and at great volume, for many hours after Uncle had been carried back to his quarters. Not one of us spoke in the sanctum aside from the widow, however. Not one of us clapped and chanted. We were silent. We were perplexed. We were full of confusion and of awe.

1857. Gadhadar Chatterjee sighs and groans:

The great hands of God
Are squeezing my restless heart
Like a wet towel!

Aaaaaaargh!

It hurts! It hurts!

1885. Three years after a brief meeting with Navagopal Ghosh and his wife (in which Sri Ramakrishna tells Navagopal to find God through singing kirtan daily), the Master suddenly thinks of them and asks a mutual acquaintance to tell them to come and see him again. They visit, astonished that he has remembered them, then Navagopal (who has faithfully chanted kirtan every day since) and his wife, Nistarini, host a party for the Master. Many dishes are served to the Master, but as Nistarini presents him with his favourite dessert (sandesh – a sweet, moist fudge made of cottage cheese) she is overwhelmed by a powerful urge . . .

Sri Ramakrishna (*gazing at Nistarini intently, amused*): 'What? You wish to feed me this sweet with your own hands?'
Nistarini (*astonished and embarrassed that the Master has read her thoughts, lowering her eyes, modestly*): 'Yes, I would like to, very much.'

Sri Ramakrishna nods, then smiles, then opens his mouth. Nistarini picks up a small piece of the sweet and prepares to feed the Master with it – in much the same way as one might make an offering of sweets to the image of a deity. She lifts her eyes and gazes into his open mouth then gasps, appalled. Inside the Master's throat she sees the head of a giant snake, jaws agape, waiting to receive the offering. This serpent-like creature she recognises as the Master's *kundalini*. She rapidly withdraws her hand, stops feeding the Master and retreats. The Master slowly and quietly feeds himself, then kindly offers what remains on the plate back to the terrified Nistarini to be distributed as *prasad* among her many guests.

1885. Sri Ramakrishna meets a former devotee after a long interval. The former devotee admits that he has stopped visiting the guru because some of his newer devotees are now proclaiming him as the new messiah. Sri Ramakrishna just laughs, points to his throat and croaks:

They think I am God –
But their God has throat cancer . . .
What fools they must be!

*A potted version of the crazy, stand-up comedy life of one of
Sri Ramakrishna's most loyal and eccentric devotees: Durga
Charan Nag*

Durga Charan Nag, 1846–99 (better known as Nag
Mahashay – or Great Souled One), was training as a
homeopathic doctor when he first visited Sri Ramakrishna at
the Dakshineswar Kali Temple and Sri Ramakrishna became
his *guru* (although Sri Ramakrishna would not tolerate the use
of this word, obviously). He was one of Sri Ramakrishna's
householder disciples. These were men and women who were
totally dedicated to God but who were nonetheless obliged to
support the burden of wives, husbands and families. This meant
that they were tied to material concerns (running homes,
earning wages, etc.) and so could not fulfil their ultimate dream
of giving up all worldly obligations to become itinerant monks.

Nag Mahashay celebrated a kind of faith called *urjhita bhakti*
(or exuberant devotion) and had been this way from his early
childhood. It was a state of mind completely natural to him. He
would only talk about spiritual matters. If anyone spoke in Nag
Mahashay's company on issues that were not spiritual he would
instantly change the subject.

Nag Mahashay was so unbelievably humble that he would
never contradict another person or speak a harsh word against
anyone. A notable occasion on which he broke this rule (a show
of irritation or loss of temper was contrary to the will of God,
which is *love*, after all) resulted in him picking up a large stone
and beating himself over the head with it until copious amounts
of blood were drawn.

Nag Mahashay had been forced – by a strict and demanding
father – to marry, even though this was against all his
inclinations. His first wife died, and then his father forced him
to marry again. His second wife was spiritually inclined and

highly forbearing. Nonetheless, the young Nag Mahashay often made a habit of sleeping outside their home perched on a low tree branch so as to avoid jeopardising his sexual virtue.

Nag Mahashay lived by the holy maxim that 'He who has controlled his tongue has controlled everything.'
He never applied sugar or **salt** to his food in case it might excite his palate into desiring more.

Nag Mahashay could not bear to hear Sri Ramakrishna challenged or criticised. On one occasion he was present when a wealthy denizen of Calcutta was insulting Sri Ramakrishna. He gently asked the individual to desist. This approach did not work. The insults continued. So Nag Mahashay ripped a shoe off the man's foot and beat him with it, frenziedly, until he fled.

Girish Chandra Ghosh, the great Bengali playwright, once, out of love and pity, presented Nag Mahashay with a blanket even though he knew that Nag Mahashay was too full of the spirit of renunciation and humility to accept gifts. Nag Mahashay accepted the gift so as not to insult Girish, promptly placing it, neatly folded, upon his head. A while later, a mutual acquaintance of Nag Mahashay and Girish went to visit Nag Mahashay in his humble village home. Throughout their meeting Nag Mahashay kept the blanket gift of Girish's balanced on his head. It transpired that Nag Mahashay had felt unable to remove the blanket from his head since his first having taken receipt of it. Girish was then obliged to invent some subtle ruse whereby he might take the gift back again without offending Nag Mahashay. There is little doubt that Girish's literary skills will have played a helpful role in successfully resolving this curious escapade.

Nag Mahashay's spiritual worldview meant that he had an inordinate respect and empathy for all other creatures, including plants. He would feel their hunger and their thirst. Although agonisingly poor, he would buy live catches of fish from fishermen and then release them back into the wild. A group of European hunters once came to Nag Mahashay's village to hunt birds. Nag Mahashay asked them to stop but they did not understand his native tongue. So Nag Mahashay – alone and unarmed – attacked them, singlehandedly relieved them of all their rifles, and promptly absconded with them.

Nag Mahashay would never kill an insect and was especially protective of ants. On one occasion a dangerous cobra entered the courtyard of his home. He spoke to it gently and then accompanied it back to the jungle. On another occasion he was washing his feet when a water snake violently bit his toe. Nag Mahashay refused to withdraw his foot, just left it where it was and muttered, 'He means no harm. He has simply mistaken my toe for his food.'

Towards the end of his life, although often suffering from extreme ill health, if anyone visited his home Nag Mahashay would instantly invite them to stay and give up his meagre bed. He would offer his hospitality so humbly that people would generally feel compelled to accept it. Nag Mahashay and his wife would then sleep on the kitchen floor. On one such occasion a feral cat jumped on to Nag Mahashay's head and clawed his eye as he was sleeping. His eye was badly scratched, but instead of being enraged he happily exclaimed, 'God visited me in the form of a cat to punish me for my bad *karma*! This is truly the grace of God!'

When a young devotee visited Nag Mahashay's home during the monsoon season and Nag Mahashay realised that they had no dry firewood to prepare him a warm meal, he took up an axe and commenced cutting down one of the supporting poles of his cottage so that he might burn it as fuel. On being asked to desist he exclaimed, 'What kind of a person would I be if I could not give up my attachment to this humble cottage for someone who has visited me in such terrible conditions?'

When the Holy Mother (Ramakrishna's wife or 'spiritual consort') gave Nag Mahashay a piece of mango to eat, instead of placing it into his mouth he delightedly rubbed it all over his head. The Holy Mother was then obliged to feed him what little then remained, calmly but firmly, by hand.

Such was Nag Mahashay's sensitivity to all life that he refused to cut back the large clumps of bamboo that were persistently growing through the walls of his home. He'd say, 'How can I destroy something which I have not the power to create?'

Nag Mahashay would never let others serve him. If he paid for a river crossing he would always insist on taking the oars himself. On one occasion, when the roof of his cottage was collapsing, his wife took the opportunity of hiring a thatcher while he was away, knowing that while present, Nag Mahashay would refuse the service of others. Unfortunately he returned home early and became so distressed at the sight of the roofer – hitting his own head, repeatedly – that the roofer was obliged to climb down from the roof where he was then fanned by Nag Mahashay, served tobacco, paid in full and sent away.

During Ekadashi (or the eleventh day of the moon, an excellent time for fasting) Nag Mahashay went to visit Sri Ramakrishna but would not eat. To get around this Sri Ramakrishna touched the food to sanctify it so that Nag Mahashay could eat it in the form of *prasad*. Such was Nag Mahashay's devotional fervour, though, that he not only ate the food but he promptly – much to everyone's profound consternation – consumed the palm leaf plate on which it was served.

The thatched roof of a close neighbour's home once caught on fire and the flames threatened to engulf Nag Mahashay's cottage, too. Other villagers were frantically trying to locate and quench the flying sparks, but Nag Mahashay merely stood calmly by and watched. When his wife ran inside to try and save a few of their meagre possessions, Nag Mahashay roundly chastised her. 'What is this?! The great Brahma, god of fire, has come to visit us and instead of worshipping him you think only of worldly possessions? Shame on you!' He then yelled, 'Victory to Sri Ramakrishna!' and danced, exultantly, around and around the courtyard.

Like – as they say – attracts like.
Diamond cuts diamond.
Victory to Durga Charan Nag! Victory to Sri Ramakrishna!

(*Nag Mashahay now rapidly exits, stage left, pursued by a tiger.*)

1860, Sri Ramakrishna earnestly entreats:

Oh please, Ma Kali,
Find a rich benefactor
To fund all my needs!

Winter 1858, the Dakshineswar Kali Temple (six miles north of Calcutta)

Uncle will never tell me what he sees during his many trances. Because I, Hridayram, am insignificant I suppose. And I ask Uncle all the wrong questions. I am ignorant in such matters. I irritate Uncle. Uncle insists that mystical experiences and visions cannot be described in words. Language both cheapens and tarnishes them. And these things are very precious to Uncle. They are his great secret.

What I can say for certain, though, is that after Uncle's deep trance following his exploits with the ceremonial sword in the Kali Temple, he found himself unable to perform even the most basic of tasks for many weeks. Because Uncle was drunk on spiritual bliss. He could not walk in a straight line. And what few rules still remained in his mind concerning the *arati* Uncle now completely abandoned.

I tended to Uncle as though he were a baby. I cleaned Uncle and I fed him. I patted Uncle's back when he had indigestion. And Uncle burped. I took over most of Uncle's worship at the Kali Temple. Uncle was a full-time job.

Mathur Baba had been informed about the incident with the sword and he often came to the temple to visit Uncle. He was infatuated by Uncle. He would sit at the back of the shrine room and watch Uncle singing, hour after hour, to the goddess. Uncle wooed the goddess with the holy songs of Chaitanya. Uncle would have lengthy conversations with the goddess. Uncle was flirtatious. Uncle was often full of mischief and girlish sass. He would touch the offerings to his own head and hands and feet and then offer them to the goddess with a coy giggle. Uncle would dance and jiggle around. Uncle would feed the goddess bits of food. He would say, 'Will you take this lovely bit of *Luchi*, Ma? No? Not until I eat some

104

myself? You want me to try it for you, Ma? Like this? Do you see? I am eating it, Ma. It is delicious! Are you happy now, Ma? Will you eat some now, Ma?'

Uncle was guest of honour at a wonderful party to which only Uncle had been invited. There was only one invitation. Ma Kali was the host. And Hridayram? He was peeping into Uncle's strange new world through a dirty window from the dark street outside. Uncle was within. Hridayram was without.

After the incident with the sword, Uncle had become aware of great waves of divine consciousness which he saw pervading the entire universe. He found them intoxicating. He would dance around in them and sing. He began to see God in all things. And he began to see all things as God.

On one occasion during *arati* I witnessed Uncle feeding the goddess's food offering to one of the temple cats. The cat had just entered the shrine room, mewing. 'Ma, you must eat,' Uncle gushed, following the cat around on his knees. 'Ma! Ma! Please, try a little!'

People were astonished! This behaviour was nothing short of sacrilegious! Many complaints were made. It was a scandal of inconceivable proportions. Mathur Baba and the Rani were called. But Mathur was not in the slightest bit concerned. 'Your Uncle is awakening the goddess,' he said. 'Let him worship her exactly as he chooses. Do you not sense the atmosphere in the temple now? It is extraordinary! I have never felt anything like it before.'

And Mathur Baba was right. There was an excitement. It is most difficult to describe it. Like an unscratched itch. A nagging anxiety, a restlessness. Akin to the feeling one sometimes gets before the monsoon breaks.

And Uncle was also restless. He would argue with the goddess. 'But Ma, I am not a man of letters. I have not read the scriptures. How am I to do what is being asked of me here?'

Then he would be quiet for a while, as if listening. 'Well, please tell me everything I must say, Ma. And tell me everything that I must do. It should all come from you, Ma. Because I have nothing, Ma. I am nothing. Just a humble village boy.'

Uncle had been blessed by many extraordinary spiritual visions, but still he was not satisfied. On some days his confidence would falter and he would turn to me for comfort. 'I am afraid, Hriday,' he would say. 'Of course I long to feel the presence of the goddess at all times, but often when I meditate I hear locks turning and feel manacles fastening, one by one, first around my feet, then around my legs, then my hips . . . Eventually I am completely imprisoned inside my own body and the goddess alone has the key. But she will not release me until she is ready. She makes me stay there for many hours, Hriday, in terrible bondage. Until my bones feel like they must surely snap! She frightens me, Hriday. But this is just her divine play and I must submit to it, Hriday, like an obliging child submits to its parent. I must submit to it because I love her more than life itself.'

Uncle's first phase of perpetual bliss lasted for many weeks but eventually it faded. And Uncle began to miss the feeling and to hunger for it once again. Uncle was addicted to the goddess. He could not sleep. He thought about her constantly. He called for her. But there was fear in his voice now as well as longing. Uncle was so brave. He could not eat. His chest was always burning, always red. He could not digest his food. Uncle thought he was going mad.

Sometimes as we sat together talking in the evenings he would suddenly raise a hand and hush me. 'Do you hear that?' he would whisper. But I could hear nothing. 'Do you hear that?' he would repeat. 'Do you hear the jangle of the bells on the goddess's anklets? Do you hear her, Hriday? Walking up and down the veranda? Climbing the stairs? Going up on to the roof? Ah . . . *Silence! Listen!* Ma is standing up there under the stars and gazing out at the holy Ganga!'

Through my contacts at the temple I managed to employ the services of a doctor. He came to see Uncle and he was greatly perturbed by what he found. He felt that Uncle needed a rest. He was concerned for Uncle's physical and mental well-being.

But who may tell Uncle anything? I spoke many times to Mathur Baba, saying that I felt Uncle needed to get away from the temple for a time (the atmosphere in the temple was not healthy for Uncle). Yet Mathur Baba was so intoxicated by Uncle that he would not listen.

Often Uncle would spend hours in the Rani's flower gardens collecting flowers to make garlands for the goddess. And as he carefully cut and arranged the flowers he would be laughing and talking all the while. But there was nobody there. Uncle was talking to himself. At other times he would fall to the ground without warning and wail in agony. He would rub his cheeks against stones and thorns without so much as a second thought. His face was constantly bloody and bruised. His cheeks would stream with endless tears. Such was Uncle's confusion and yearning.

Of course things eventually came to a head as I knew that they must. The Rani had come to visit the temple. She was eager to witness Uncle perform the *arati*. But Uncle was very tired and sluggish that day. I was concerned that the worship might be too much for Uncle. But the Rani wanted to see Uncle and Uncle is so obliging and he would not disappoint her. He went to the temple and he began the worship. But Uncle was jumpy and fractious, like a child. So he appealed to the goddess. He danced for her, and he sang.

It would be impossible for anybody who has not heard the delightful voice of Uncle to understand how sweet and charming it truly is. He tugs on one's very heartstrings. Uncle sings with such love and longing and intensity. It can make the hair on one's arms stand erect. Uncle's voice is so unforgettable.

And Uncle was singing to the goddess. He was singing his heart out to the goddess. And the Rani was seated just a few steps behind him, in the temple sanctum, on a mat, her eyes closed, in prayer, when suddenly Uncle interrupted his song, and he turned, and his face was contorted with rage. And the source of this rage was none other than the Rani herself, the founder of the temple, one of the richest and most pious women in Calcutta, who was praying quietly there. But Uncle seemed oblivious of these facts. In four short steps he made his way over to where the Rani sat, and quickly, without warning, Uncle drew back his hand and he slapped the Rani, violently, across her cheek.

All hell then broke loose! In seconds Uncle was grabbed by the guards and by members of the Rani's entourage. 'How dare you!' Uncle screamed at the Rani. 'How dare you think such things in the presence of the Mother!'

The Rani was startled. Her eyes had flown open. She had raised a hand to her smarting cheek. She gazed at Uncle, perfectly astonished. And then she nodded her head, curtly. 'Release him!' she said. 'Let the worship continue.' At first people were hesitant to release Uncle. The temple administrator (who already despised Uncle) was burning with fury on the Rani's behalf and he started to protest. 'What the boy said is true,' the Rani calmly interrupted him. 'I should have been immersed in prayer, but my mind was preoccupied with a legal case I am fighting. This was an insult to the goddess and I have been duly reprimanded. Let the *arati* continue.'
So Uncle was unhanded and he finished the worship.

The Rani bore this great, public insult without flinching! She truly is a most remarkable woman. But afterwards several conversations were had about Uncle. Mathur Baba and the Rani were most concerned that an excess of abstinence might have turned Uncle's mind. Uncle was exhausted. And after *arati* one evening Uncle stood before Mathur Baba and he firmly announced, 'Tonight the goddess has finally agreed to accept Hriday's service in the temple in exchange for my own.'

Of course Mathur Baba understood that it would be difficult for me to continue looking after Uncle while also conducting the time-consuming Kali worship, so he gave permission for me to send for our cousin Haladhari. Haladhari is a devotee of Vishnu and well-versed in the scriptures but is not in favour of animal sacrifice. Even so he felt happy to take on the *shakti* worship. But on his arrival, just like Uncle before him, he firmly refused to accept the *prasad* prepared in the temple kitchens. Mathur Baba remonstrated with him, saying, 'Gadai and Hriday both now accept the temple food, will you not accept it?' But Haladhari insisted on preparing his own food and Mathur Baba finally consented to it. Everything proceeded smoothly for a few weeks under these new arrangements, but after about a month, during the Shyama *Puja*, where live animals were to be sacrificed, the goddess suddenly appeared to Haladhari in her terrible form and told him that his conduct of the service was lukewarm. She was angered by it. And to punish him she said that his son would die. Shortly after, he received news of his beloved son's death.

Haladhari told Uncle what had happened and I was then obliged to take on the Kali worship in his place.

I am in awe of the goddess. I am quite afraid of her. But Uncle said with his own mouth – did he not? – that the goddess would accept my service in exchange for his own. So I therefore imagine that the goddess must appreciate my service in some small way. I have no desire to offend her. But I am not like Uncle nor even Haladhari. I am not overburdened with devotion. And I have never seen a holy vision. The goddess has never granted me with any special boon. Uncle emphatically disagrees. Uncle says that he himself is the goddess's special boon to me. Uncle is my gift – that when I serve Uncle I serve the goddess. And I do love to serve Uncle. Even through all our many hardships.

Mathur Baba has been so good to us. He has employed an eminent Ayurvedic physician, Gangaprasad Sen, to look after Uncle. We have been provided with endless powdery concoctions and potions and creams. Mathur Baba regularly sends Uncle expensive bottles of Syrup of Candy to try and dispel his dreadful flatulence. In time, when Mathur Baba inherits the Rani's estate, I hope that he may become Uncle's most generous benefactor. And mine too. If we keep in his good graces. Because where would we be without Mathur Baba's good graces? Truly. *Truly.* I hate to imagine where. I only know in my heart of hearts that wherever it was, however poor and lonely and dreadful, Uncle and I must needs be there together. Because the goddess wishes it so.

1865. A terrified Sri Ramakrishna, at a critical juncture in his gruelling, twelve-year-long sadhana (or spiritual journey), is initiated – at the Dakshineswar Kali Temple (six miles north of Calcutta), by a mysterious, orange-robed woman – into the sixty-four bizarre and often dangerous disciplines of Tantra

1.

March 1865: on the careful instructions of this mysterious, orange-robed woman, an anxious Sri Ramakrishna helps to construct a meditation platform in the *panchavati* which rests upon the five skulls of five different species, one of which is human.

2.

June 1865 (or sometime thereabouts), the mysterious orange-robed woman presents Sri Ramakrishna with a beautiful young girl and asks him to worship her as the *devi* (or goddess). Sri Ramakrishna does exactly as she requests:

Mysterious woman: 'Good. And now that the worship is completed, will you please sit on this girl's lap and chant with your prayer beads?'

Sri Ramakrishna (*weeping*): 'But I have pledged myself completely to the Divine Mother! Would you honestly tempt me thus?!'

Mysterious woman (*pointing, unmoved*): 'Go. Sit.'

A still-snivelling Sri Ramakrishna inhales deeply, turns his thoughts to Ma Kali, then sits on the girl's lap, starts chanting and instantly becomes lost in a trance.

Some considerable time after, he becomes aware of being shaken into consciousness . . .

Sri Ramakrishna: 'Eh?!'

Mysterious woman: 'My child! Enough! Have pity! The discipline is now completed! This poor, long-suffering girl has terrible cramps!'

3.

July 1865 (or some time thereabouts), Sri Ramakrishna is
taken to a private house, seated comfortably on a mat,
and then, following an intense period of prayer and meditation,
the aforementioned mysterious, orange-robed woman leads a
naked couple into the room. They lie down together on a bed
and proceed to make love. Sri Ramakrishna watches them
writhe and groan and cavort with complete equanimity:
Mysterious woman (*mildly interested*): 'Pray, what do you see
here before you, my child?'
Sri Ramakrishna (*smiling*): 'All is beautiful! All is holy! I see
nothing before me, *nothing*, but the blissful sport of the Divine
Mother!'
The mysterious orange-clad woman nods, satisfied, as Sri
Ramakrishna enters a state of deep ecstasy.

4.

August 1865 (or some time thereabouts), the mysterious,
orange-robed woman offers a quaking Sri Ramakrishna a small
chunk of rotting human flesh which has just been offered in
tarpana (i.e. to the deity), and asks him to touch it with his
tongue:
Sri Ramakrishna (*wincing, aghast*): 'Can it be done?'
Mysterious woman (*matter-of-factly*): 'Of course, my child.
Look . . .'
She puts the rotting human flesh into her own mouth, pauses,
then calmly withdraws it again.
Mysterious woman: 'How else, pray tell, are we to conquer our
weak and pathetic human aversions?'
Sri Ramakrishna closes his eyes, visualises Ma Kali in her
terrible form and then, chanting – 'Mother! Mother!
Mother! Mother!' – he enters a light trance, opens his
mouth, and the flesh is placed on to his tongue with no
trace of aversion.

5.

11 September 1865 (or some time thereabouts), Sri Ramakrishna
enters into a state of uncontrollable ecstasy at the sight of
inebriated revellers outside an overcrowded tavern.
p.s. This is not – officially speaking – a part of the Tantric
sadhana.

6.

12 September 1865 (or some time thereabouts), Sri
Ramakrishna enters into a state of uncontrollable ecstasy
at the sexual union of two stray dogs.
p.s. Nor is this.

7.

15 September 1865 (or some time thereabouts), Sri
Ramakrishna enters into a state of uncontrollable ecstasy
at the sight of a poor prostitute plying her trade on Calcutta's
filthy streets.
p.s. This neither.

8.

21 September 1865 (or some time thereabouts), Certain quite
random words – because of their sub- or *un*conscious
connection with the divine – will henceforth act as linguistic
trip-wires and cause Sri Ramakrishna to fall into an immediate
and uncontrollable state of ecstasy at any – and every – given
moment.

Ooops! There he goes! He's just fallen into another trance. You
take his head, will you? And I'll grab his . . .

Circa 1882, Sri Ramakrishna offers some practical advice to his householder devotees:

Live like the mudfish —
Even though it dwells in filth
Its skin stays spotless.

The Rani's dream(s), 1847

Of course (as with most things in life) it's simply a question of finding the right angle . . . And yet no matter which angle we attempt to film it from, the actress playing the Rani still seems to find the scene of her 'assault' deeply troublesome. She has been slapped so many times now (albeit simply in pretence. This is all sleight of hand . . . *well*, there may've been the occasional slip, the actor who plays Ramakrishna being a trenchant realist/naturalist/drama queen/bitch – and who'd have it any other way?) that we no longer need to apply blusher to her precious cheek, but are obliged to cover over the marks – obscure them! – with copious quantities of heavy make-up.

The actress is losing heart. We try to remind her of her subject's lofty morals and profound spirituality. But still she harbours resentment. She's been hired to play the Rani, hasn't she? A queen? So how can she be expected to simply submit to such appalling treatment without struggling to bring a twinkle of feminist fire – nay *ire* – into it?

Oh dear. She's such a modern creature. Between takes she's been poring over Rudyard Kipling's *City of Dreadful Night* (for Calcuttan background, for *atmosphere* – it's her first film and she's annoyingly keen) and as a consequence she's now livid with Kipling, too (which is doing precious little to improve the quality of her, *ahem*, 'performance'). She is righteously indignant. She was hoping for another *Jungle Book*, where all the rough edges (man's and nature's) are neatly and sweetly tidied up. But this no-frills Kipling's a bust!

She is currently pondering the chapter in which R K (while on his tour of Calcutta's more terrifying districts with the local police force – all jolly chaps) encounters a white prostitute (of Eurasian stock), mother of nine and widow of an English soldier. This woman is called Mrs D, and she stands in her cheap doorway on her filthy street with her shameless eyes boring into Kipling's lily-white (Union-Jack-enrobed) heart. Her grimy hovel – which is littered (Kipling haughtily imagines) with cheap paintings of the saints and badly engineered statuettes of the Virgin Mary – rings with the echo of her saucy tongue and her lilting and curiously affecting laugh (this laugh – no whorish cackle – even Kipling admits, has markers of true gentility in it). Mrs D is certainly to be judged and found wanting by the colonial Rudyard (as all things Calcuttan surely must be).

The actress longs to inhabit Mrs D and wrest back her humanity from Kipling's sneering gaze.
'Oh, he sees how hard I am, all right,' Mrs D (aka the actress) improvises, adopting a fetching southern Irish accent. 'A slut, a potential murderess . . . [*They said I'd poisoned my husband by putting something into his drinking water . . . !* p. 74], but even so far as I am from God,' she persists, hands clasped, cheeks streaking with righteous tears, 'I feel that I am suddenly held close, gripped tight – by the contempt in his eyes – to the black heart of the goddess. I am *here*. I am *hers*. So completely fallen and yet so warmly embraced within this strange world of reeking filth and death and darkness . . .' (*Bravo! Rousing rounds of applause!*)

But this is not our scene! We tell her, panicked. The light outside is swiftly fading. We must get our take. The actor playing Ramakrishna (our star! Our Great Hope!) is already in a fearful bait. His slapping hand is suffering from twinges of RSI. We dare not offend him any further. He's been dieting for months now to get down to the requisite size (featherweight!) and is already up in arms about playing his nude scenes after an especially vicious bout of food poisoning (his local chippie must take the blame; a tepid saveloy of questionable origin – we're filming all interiors, for financial reasons, in an adapted mansion in London's leafy Kensal Green).

Perhaps if we screen what we have accumulated so far —
everything in the can — backwards, we may lessen the impact
of what is yet to come? Perhaps the actors will be mollified if
they can see where they've been, where they've travelled from?

Watch the film rewinding. Look! The Rani is unslapped and
then deep in prayer, and then leaving the temple and then
talking with her lawyers. The tape rewinds faster and faster
until. Ah! Stop! *Stop!* Play it! We're in 1847 and we see the
Rani asleep in bed. Her rest is fitful, as all rest in her great city
must be (because of the heat, humidity, the bugs). She has been
planning a six-month pilgrimage to Varanasi, the city of light.
But there is no train. And the roads are treacherous. So she is
sailing there by boat . . . along the child Hooghly and the
Mother Ganga, following these great and holy rivers in the
strong conviction that every pitch and bob of her valiant craft
will resound in her head, her heart, like a prayer.

It's the night before she leaves and there are twenty-five
boats in her convoy: three for her daughters, one for her doctor,
one for the washerman . . . One contains four cows, and
another is stuffed full of their fodder. Imagine the preparation!
Well, you don't have to imagine it — we can rewind the tape
further and you will see . . . but how expedient! There's the
fleet of boats (the *grab*, the *brig*, the *pansi*, the *katra*, the
fealchara, the *hola*, the *sloop*, all painstakingly recreated in our
Thames-side studios based on the watery etchings of François
Balthazar Solvyns) being gradually *un*-loaded. Because during
her sleep on the night prior to her departure the Rani is visited
by Ma Kali (in some accounts the Rani is already onboard and
adrift; it's her first night on the water and she is passing the
very spot — Dakshineswar — where her Kali Temple will be
built) who tells her that there is NO NEED for her to head off
on this pilgrimage. Instead she is to use the money put aside for
her trip to build Ma a temple on the banks of the Ganga. The
goddess will graciously accept her devotions there.

Cynics may pooh-pooh the dream. Cynics may think that there were other reasons – an attack of toothache, a legal problem, the prospect of a big business deal – for this last-minute cancellation, but we believe in the dream. If we explore the Rani's dream (the Rani dreams in black and white! How curious!) we can see the goddess and hear her speak. The goddess is HUGE and seems to be operated by stop-motion model animation (the Rani is so ahead of her time – even as she sleeps!). Look beyond the light and you can almost see the shadowy figures of Don Chaffey and Ray Harryhausen, in conference. This is a re-make, no, a *pre*-make of 1963's *Jason and the Argonauts* . . . Listen . . . There's even a rousing theme tune written by Bernard Herrmann!

Oh dear. But the Rani's daughters are all packed up and ready to go and really, *really* looking forward to their trip . . . And the doctor . . . Even the cows! I'm sorry. I'm really sorry. But the Rani has had a dream (*kindly insert communal, Munch-style silent scream here*). In fact she has had *two* dreams: the first to go on a great pilgrimage (this is a waking dream, a yen); the second telling her not to go and to use the money to buy some land instead and build a temple there.

We have inspected all minor details of the actual dream (our experts are compiling a lengthy and highly informative dossier) and we are still unable to confirm (at this early stage) that the goddess actually mentions the serving of *cooked* food at her new temple. Cynics (ah, you're back again!) may think that this was all simply a matter of social status not spiritual necessity/divine intervention and hence contrary, in principle, to Hinduism's adherence to the rules of caste, and, worse still, the spirit of resignation/renunciation/destruction of the ego etc. which jointly underpins its most essential tenets. But we choose to see this as simply another dream of the Rani's – another waking dream. A deep desire (or 'earnest desire' as the Ramakrishna Movement would have it). An inexplicable urge. And therefore an expression of her profound spiritual devotion – her modest need to serve as best she can – not an undermining of it.

It's also important to bear in mind that if the Rani *hadn't* had this dream (the cooked food aspiration) then she could've hired any number of priests to serve in her temple. But she *did* have it, which meant casting around for the one specialist, the one expert, the one (quite frankly pretty minor) pandit who would feel inclined to find some kind of working compromise to fulfil it. This was Sri Ramakrishna's brother, who had engaged with this tricky problem before, remember? (Gadai's sacred thread ceremony?) Hmmm.

When you play it backwards it suddenly all seems . . . well, so bizarre and incidental as to be divinely inspired. But the cynics (hello, y'all!) see something else. They see a group of individuals who have been naturally inclined, obliged, even forced, to compromise (sidestepping the restrictive rules of sex, gender, race and caste). They see brash modernity posing as (but signally undermining) the vital traditions of sincere devotion. How could these special someones – these social and spiritual and (yup) *political* trailblazers – *not* be drawn together? Is this destiny or rather just plain (even bare-faced) necessity? Did the Bengal Renaissance start here or . . . or were these just the early markers of a movement – an expanding, experimental social psychology – already well under way? Who can say?

One thing worth considering is how the Rani, Sri Ramakrishna, the Brahmo Samaj and the Bengal Renaissance all have in common a sense of moving forward while still looking keenly back. A kind of easy modernity which passionately celebrates its conservative – even (wince) 'primitive' – past. It is intrinsically Kali-esque in nature. It somehow magically transcends the pair of opposites. It is at once of now and of then. A synthesis. A counter/pro-imperialist,

counter/pro-capitalist farina pudding of yes and no. A milky
(distinctly non-transparent) anti/pro-nationalistic faith-fuelled
blancmange.

Let's get back to the dreams. Because there's still another
dream (a second/fourth!). But before we home in on that, let's
imagine the Rani hunting for her piece of land. Or the Rani's
agent (in all likelihood). He sails up the great Hooghly (well,
it's actually the Thames: some swampland down near Canvey
Island in which we've raised a couple of mock-palms. Although
his *grab – brig – katra* – I forget which – is a 100 per cent
faithful copy, etc. etc . . .) searching diligently for the perfect
spot. And he finds several.

It's a matter of common knowledge that the western bank of
the Ganga is considered more holy than the eastern side. So
that's where the Rani started her search (hence instantly putting
paid to the 'first night of the voyage' scenario). But nobody
would sell her land on the western side. We are told that the
reason is petty jealousy. Perhaps with an added, extra
sprinkling of good, old-fashioned caste-based (and let's not
forget sexist) *hauteur.*

So they turn their search to the eastern bank and discover
the ancient Muslim funeral ground near Dakshineswar with its
shrine to a holy saint (not to mention a large adjacent plot
which supports the bungalow of a nameless European.
Although that's not actually terribly romantic or interesting).
Some may think it unpropitious to build a temple over a
graveyard. But this is a Kali temple. And Ma Kali is a natural
habituée of the cremation ground, is she not?

The land was purchased and building commenced. The
designs were magnificent (of course) yet still traditional and
classically – *classically* – Bengali. The whole enterprise (buying
the land, shoring up the embankment, raw materials, labour
and another secondary investment in productive land elsewhere
to enable the temple to be self-sustaining after the Rani's death)

meant a total outlay of something approximating one and a quarter million rupees.

The Rani has persistently made a habit of favouring local craftsmen in many of her numerous commercial and creative commissions over the years. She understands the real ecology of business. She is at once a financial whizz and a respecter of niches. She sees the individual's face behind each fast-rupee. The Rani has commercial nous; more important yet — commercial *soul*.

The second dream involves (oh yes — that second dream . . .) the commissioning of the Kali image for her now (*quick!* Fast-forward the tape!) almost finished temple. Unlike its giant and spectacular carapace, the image that lies at its heart isn't huge. It's actually quite petite, standing at only thirty-three and a half inches tall. It should also be noted that just as soon as the sculptor commenced carving the image the Rani undertook a series of severe austerities (which are required by the scriptures). She spent much of her time in telling beads and prayer. She bathed three times every day. She ate basic vegetarian fare.

The image was soon completed and the Rani was utterly delighted with it. But before she could finally install it, the temple complex still needed a few extra tweaks and modifications. There were several irritating delays (remember the swift and that quick peek we had at that large pile of raw materials still waiting to be used near the plate-washing *ghat?*). In the meantime Ma Kali was stored in a box. But she wasn't happy there. She began to perspire. Eventually she contacted the Rani (finally! The second dream!) and told her that she wished to be removed from her box and put in the temple IMMEDIATELY.

Gulp!

Ma Kali, the great creatress, is no respecter of contractual deadlines, it seems. So the Rani — in a panic — searched her calendar for an auspicious day for the ceremony. But none suggested itself. So she installed the image anyway, with great aplomb, and under considerable personal duress, no doubt.

If the Rani's dreams are to be taken seriously, we must inevitably conclude that Ma Kali is not a goddess to be lightly trifled with. She is impatient, unpredictable and imperious. It should also probably be borne in mind that loyal devotion to such an irascible deity may well involve a certain number of personal privacy violations, funny turns, broken arrangements, cancelled holidays, prodigious financial outlays, etc. etc. Argh. But we kinda knew that already, didn't we?

Here follows a timeless and unifying spiritual message — via the 24-hour/7-days-a-week live broadcast channel of Sri Ramakrishna — to all religious zealots, humourless fundamentalists and wishy-washy-western New-Agers:

The Master wants GOD-
realisation *not* SELF-
realisation!

It's a subtle distinction, but the ego becomes God. God does not become the ego.

Ah,

'God is in all men,
But all men are not in God,'
The Master shrugs.

Mathur Nath Biswas is wandering around the Dakshineswar
Kali Temple grounds when a tearful, almost hysterical Sri
Ramakrishna comes running up to him, stark naked.

Sri Ramakrishna (*petrified*): 'Mathur! *Please!* Please help me!
Something dreadful has happened!'
Mathur Babu (*visibly alarmed*): 'Just calm down, Gadai. Catch
your breath.'
Ramakrishna (*shaking like a leaf, starting to hiccup*): 'It's awful,
so awful. I'm so *hic!* scared!'
(*He points to his genitals, mutely.*)
Mathur Babu (*staring down at Ramakrishna's genitals, somewhat
perturbed*): 'Gadai, what's the matter? Tell me!'
Sri Ramakrishna: 'I was . . . *hic!* I was urinating in the *hic!*
pine grove when I suddenly saw a . . . *hic!* a tiny worm
[*shudders, uncontrollably*] crawling out from the end of my
nunu!'
Mathur Babu continues to gaze at Sri Ramakrishna's penis
as he quietly digests this momentous piece of news, then he
gazes up into Ramakrishna's eyes (only just suppressing a
smile).
Mathur: 'Gadai, I can sincerely promise you that this is
honestly nothing to be too concerned about.'
Sri Ramakrishna (*with childlike credulity, still hiccuping*):
'Are you – *hic!* – sure, Mathur?'
Mathur: 'Yes. Absolutely . . . [*thinks for a moment*] . . . in fact
it's . . . well, it's actually very *good* news.'
Sri Ramakrishna (*brightening*): 'Really?'
Mathur: 'Oh yes. Because all human beings have a worm in
their body exactly like this one of yours.'
Sri Ramakrishna (*astonished*): 'They do?'

Mathur: 'Yes indeed. It is the worm of lust, and it is responsible for generating lustful ideas and feelings and urges within us. But the Mother has just seen fit to rid you of yours! Gadai, you are indeed truly blessed!'

Sri Ramakrishna clasps his hands together, delighted. His previously crestfallen face is now wreathed in beatific smiles.

Oh which of us can truly comprehend the divine play of Sri
Ramakrishna? Is he man or child? Leader or follower?
Masculine or feminine? Radical or conservative? Idiot or
genius? A god, a god-man or just too, too human?
Is this book a farce, a comedy, a tragedy or a melodrama?
What *is* this?
Who *was* he?
Who the heck *was* Sri Sri Ramakrishna?
Eh?

Eh?

?

!

Twenty or so years later, during a festival being attended by the immensely famous and popular philosophers and social reformers Keshab Chandra Sen and Pratap Majumdar, a craven admirer approaches them and starts to gush . . .

Craven admirer: 'I see seated here before me Gauranga and Nityananda!' (*Two legendary fifteenth-century incarnations of Krishna and Balarama.*)

As it transpires, Sri Ramakrishna also happens to be sitting nearby. Keshab turns to him and (possibly a little embarrassed, perhaps a tad vainglorious) murmurs:

Keshab: 'Gauranga and Nityananda, indeed?! What then are you?!'

Without so much as a moment's pause, a beaming Ramakrishna responds:

Sri Ramakrishna: 'I am the dust off your feet!'

Ah . . .

'Sri Ramakrishna –
He'll never be caught napping!'
Keshab Sen chuckles.

Uncle very often talks about how the image of Ma Kali was left inside a box while the temple was being completed and how the closely confined goddess started to sweat. This idea seems to preoccupy Uncle a great deal. I think this is because when he looks at the world – when he gazes all around him – Uncle often sees God being packed away in a box and ignored. Uncle thinks that the modern world and the big city of Calcutta want to wrap God up in soft muslin cloths and just place him aside. Uncle thinks that God is simply another distraction in this busy life of ours. Of course we can bring the box down from the attic during religious festivals. We can gently unwrap God then. But once the flower garlands have wilted, the candles are blown out and the incense has burned down, God is shoved back away again until the next time he is required. Perhaps for a wedding. Perhaps for a birth. Perhaps for a death.

And Uncle also sees many different kinds of god being worshipped today. There is the god of words (or the god of the many scriptures), there is the god of strict rules (of caste and of our different and conflicting worship traditions), there is god with form and god without form, of course. But none of these gods does Uncle worship exclusively. And we must never forget that there are also the gods of lust and the gods of money – the gods that Uncle most truly fears and despises.

Uncle thinks of nothing but God, and so he is constantly searching for other people – fellow travellers on the path of faith – who may worship the same kind of god that he does. This God who dwells like a flickering flame within his own wildly beating heart. Uncle longs for intelligent talk about God. He thirsts for it. He feels starved of it. He longs to meet people who might teach him something he doesn't yet know. If he hears of such a person on the temple grapevine he will track them down and present himself before them. He will take the dust off their feet. 'I have heard that you have seen God,' he will say, and his yellow, moon face will be alive with joy and hope.

But Uncle is often disappointed. And he is often humiliated. Indeed, we are both often humiliated, because I am always with Uncle, accompanying him to these different addresses and offering an introduction for Uncle. Such lofty individuals can be very cruel. They don't understand Uncle. They can't see that Uncle is unlike other people – that Uncle is special. And Uncle will not put on any airs and graces. Uncle is incapable of such things. Uncle is uncalculating. Uncle has an open heart. But these individuals expect more than this. They look at Uncle and see a poor and uneducated village boy who stammers when he talks and smiles and smiles and can barely keep his wearing-cloth on.

Sometimes I wish Uncle would try and be just a little bit less like, well, like himself. But Uncle never listens to me.

And Uncle takes his disappointments very hard. Although the humiliations do not bother him. Not one bit. Uncle has no ego. When people laugh at Uncle he just laughs along with them. Uncle shares in the joke. He laughs at himself the loudest of all. But I know that Uncle hates to feel alone. He wants others to love God as much as he does and to share in this love with him. But then who may love God as much as Uncle? How, I wonder, might that be humanly possible?

Uncle will not see that his approach to religion is slightly unbalanced. But who would dare tell Uncle this? Not me. Uncle understands God. Uncle *knows* God. But I understand everything that surrounds God – an understanding that in Uncle's mind is insignificant and amounts to nothing. Uncle has no interest in balance. Uncle cannot see past God. Beyond God is *maya* – simply lies and illusion – Uncle says.

But how would the world be if everyone in it was like Uncle? How might we all manage? I tell Uncle that as good *brahmins* we are taught that there are four main goals in our human life, and that for our ultimate happiness we require a small portion of them all. The first of these is *dharma*. *Dharma* refers to the maintenance of our moral codes and rules. We want to live a good and virtuous existence in a world where these values are understood and cherished. Then there is *artha* which is something I myself am very concerned with (but Uncle not one bit). *Artha* is our material prosperity and security. Next is *kama,* which refers to our emotional happiness and fulfilment; the pleasure of good friends and family, for example. Finally there is *moksha,* which is liberation, the realisation of the self and spiritual freedom. And this goal – *moksha* – is Uncle's main preoccupation. This is all that Uncle thinks of. So I, foolish Hridayam, must quietly fret over everything else.

There is plenty to worry about. Especially since Uncle has begun to increase his devotions to the god Rama by taking on the attributes of his most perfect and loyal servant and companion, Hanuman. Hanuman is a god in monkey form, so Uncle has lately transformed himself into a gibbering ape. This ape-Uncle is very difficult to engage with on any level. This ape-Uncle travels everywhere on all fours, at incredible speed, his hands often curled into fists as he moves.

Not long ago Uncle and I planted a *panchavati* – a circle of five holy trees – and this is Uncle's favourite spot now. The ape-Uncle feels at ease here. And also in the big old banyan, where the ape-Uncle likes to perch and scratch himself and squeal at the crows and at passers-by. The ape-Uncle makes no eye contact. In fact the ape-Uncle's eyes are small and dark red. They move restlessly about.

Uncle's hair has grown long and become very dirty and matted. The ape-Uncle picks at his scalp and then nibbles at the old skin and **salt** that he removes from it. This ape-Uncle cannot often be persuaded to wash himself or to dress. His wearing-cloth is tied around his waist and hangs down at the back like a tail.

This ape-Uncle will only eat fruits and roots. His nails and his teeth are a sickly yellow. People are afraid of and also amused by this ape-Uncle. I am exasperated with him. But I am afraid also. Because it is difficult to find Uncle inside this creature. Sometimes I worry that I will never see Uncle again.

Recently it has been observed (by one of the temple guards) that the ape-Uncle is starting to grow a tail of his own. There is a small, white, bony lump at the base of the ape-Uncle's spine. If one stares at it closely one can sometimes see it move around of its own accord. Like a tiny thumb.

I worry for Uncle. I hate this ape-Uncle. I want my dear, dear old Uncle back again. Now I think about it, I regret all that I have said previously about Uncle's childlike ways. At least a child has a pure heart. A child is innocent. But this creature? This ape-Uncle? It is furtive and mischievous. It throws soft fruit at passing pilgrims. It wrestles with the temple dogs. There's no end of mischief it might get itself into.

Can God be here? In this wretched place? Hello? *Hello?* Is God here? Here beside ape-Uncle? I swear I can see nothing but a filthy monkey covered in fleas and circled by swarms of buzzing flies. Gadai! My dear friend! Where are you? Where have you gone? Uncle! Beloved Uncle! Come back! Come back to me, please!

Oh, this latest crazy phase of Uncle's *sadhana* is truly a fearful blight on us all!

Eight haiku

Sri Ramakrishna says:

Please make some *effort* –
However small it may be
Or you shan't find God.

When searching for God,
Take one small step towards him
And God will walk ten.

There are two main paths:
There is the path of knowledge [1] –
Or of devotion [2].

The path of knowledge [1]
Means killing attachments through
Renunciation.

[1 = *Neti! Neti!* Not this! Not this!]

Constant devotion [2]
To worship God in your heart:
Is the path of love.

[2 = *Iti! Iti!* This! This!]

I have cooked the food –
Now just sit yourself down, please
And partake of it!

Be a cast-off leaf –
Just blown around by the wind,
And you will find God.

Ask me for nothing –
Your prayers will be answered
If Mother wills it.

The curious fable of the straightening of the crooked heart of Girish Chandra Ghosh

or

How sometimes doing nothing is the hardest path of all

Once upon a time there was a man called Girish Chandra Ghosh who was rather famous in the state of Bengal on account of his being one of India's most celebrated writers, poets, playwrights and novelists. In fact the handsome(ish), disarmingly funny and devastatingly witty Girish might credibly be ascribed the honour of being the Father of the Golden Age of Bengali Theatre. But alas, while undoubtedly brilliant and immensely talented, Girish was also a notorious drunk and a voracious libertine.

Poor Girish suffered a fair portion of personal tragedy in his lifetime. As a child aged eleven he lost his mother, then his father three years later. He responded to these awful traumas by growing up into a wild, dissolute and cynical young man. He was fearless, pugnacious, argumentative, cunning and irreverent – quite the cock o' the north, in fact! But Girish was also – at root – a bit of a soppy idealist. He was secretly quite kind and sweet, although of course he didn't tend to make a great big song and dance about it!

While an active member of a notorious gang which generated endless amounts of mischief in his local neighbourhood (this naughty lad thought nothing of desecrating the images of Hindu gods and goddesses), Girish also, somewhat paradoxically, liked to raise money to help the poor buy food or medicine or to cremate their dead.

When he was a little itty-bitty boy, Girish's wise old grandmother had liked to entertain him nightly with marvellous stories from the Indian epics – those astonishingly colourful tales of adventure, heroism and mythology – which the little itty-bitty Girish truly loved. One night she described, in great detail, a moving scene from the *Bhagavatam*. In this scene the adorable Krishna is compelled by his powerful uncle Akrura to leave behind his idyllic home of Vrindavan, thereby abandoning the happy troupe of innocent shepherd boys and girls who had, hitherto, been his constant, all-singing, all-dancing childhood companions. When his grandmother reached the point in the story of Krishna's actual leaving – during which packs of weeping *gopis* clung on to the reins of his horses, howling with despair – Girish suddenly interrupted her and demanded to know if the adorable Krishna was ever to return during his lifetime to his happy idyll of Vrindavan. On being gently told that he would not, Girish burst into violent tears, stormed off in a huff, and for quite some time thereafter refused, point-blank, to listen to any more of his ancient grandmother's cruel and destructive tales.

Dear Girish was in possession of a fine and sensitive soul (and an artist's eye, and a poet's sensibility) but this rather naughty man was definitely not a lover of authority or of rules. He had a questioning mind ('But why, Grandma? Why? Why? Why? *Why?*'), yet he was very easily disillusioned ('I hate you! I hate you! I hate you! I *hate* you!'). And while having experienced what would generally be considered a series of strange and miraculous signs and visions at various critical stages in his life – not least the appearance of a glowing, scarlet-clad female form by the side of his sickbed during a severe bout of cholera, who cured him with an imaginary offering of *prasad* [*insert fairy wand tinkle sound*] after doctors had abandoned *every last shred* of hope in his future recovery – he was still deeply resistant to the idea of sacrificing his many idle pleasures to dedicate himself to God.

The mysterious, magical and moon-faced *guru*, Sri Ramakrishna [*whose name must always be accompanied by the jaunty parp-parping of a clown's horn*], was, for quite some time, an intermittent presence in Girish's exotic Calcuttan-based social *milieu*. He met him (*yay!*) – and was singularly unimpressed by him (*boo!*) – on several occasions at the houses of various friends and acquaintances. But gradually the *guru* (*parp-parp!*) who would not be called a *guru* (*parp-parp!*) – who would not be called *anything*, in fact (*silence*) – seemed to insinuate himself into naughty Girish's consciousness (and then, rather more fatally, into the core of his fragile and tender soul).

'Will the crookedness ever leave my heart?' a winsome Girish once demanded (probably somewhat tipsily) of the mysterious and moon-faced Sri Ramakrishna (*parp-parp!*) after a certain period of polite acquaintance.
Sri Ramakrishna (*parp-parp!*) nodded. 'It will go,' he gently confirmed.
But Girish wouldn't be so easily convinced. He asked a second time, then a third. 'Will the crookedness ever leave my heart?' Each time Sri Ramakrishna (*parp-parp!*) calmly and smilingly responded in the affirmative.

Sri Ramakrishna(*parp-parp!*)'s relationship with Girish wasn't ever going to be plain sailing (of course not! Because where would be the fun in that?!). He (*parp-parp*) firmly believed that Girish was, by nature, of a 'heroic' disposition, and that people of this particular bent must always be allowed a certain measure of licence and only ever be *very carefully* handled (if at all).

Because of this belief, Sri Ramakrishna (*parp-parp!*) always refused, point-blank, to impose any kind of nasty or difficult rules or restrictions on Girish. So naughty Girish would often turn up at the temple or the theatre drunk and insult Sri Ramakrishna (*parp-parp!*) in front of everyone! But Sri Ramakrishna (*parp-parp!*) never reacted harshly or meanly

136

or stood in cruel judgement over poor, silly Girish. Good
heavens, no! In fact Sri Ramakrishna (*parp-parp!*), employing
what was manifestly a profound and impressively mature insight
into basic human psychology, eventually contrived to convert a
man who was considered completely unconvertible simply by
dint of refusing to change him *in any way at all*!

After a long, long period of sadness and carousing and
bust-ups in whore-houses, dear, darling Girish finally decided –
completely of his own volition – to surrender himself, heart and
soul, to Sri Ramakrishna (*parp-parp!*). He tearfully presented
himself before the *guru* (*parp-parp!*). He was willing to submit
to anything, he said. No. Seriously. This isn't just the drink
talking – anything, *anything* . . .
'What must I do?' he demanded (on bended knee).
'Do exactly what you are doing now,' the moon-faced Sri
Ramakrishna (*parp-parp!*) advised him. 'Keep holding on to
God with your one hand and on to the world with your other.'
After a moment's thoughtful consideration he (*parp-parp!*) then
added, 'And just think of God a little, if you can, in the
morning and the evening.'

Oh dear, oh dear, oh dear. Just as soon as these magical
words were spoken, poor, silly, foolish Girish immediately
began to doubt that it would be possible for him to observe
such a high level of commitment. I mean to think of God,
each day, with such fearful *regularity*? A man with *his* busy
lifestyle?!

Sri Ramakrishna (*parp-parp!*) noted the slight element of
reticence in Girish's demeanour and so suggested, 'Well, how
about if you remember God when you eat and when you go
to sleep?'

Again, poor, silly Girish was troubled by the thought
that this was just *way too much* to ask of himself. He lacked
self-discipline. He knew it. He was impetuous and bad and
ungovernable. He liked to sing bawdy songs and pee in the

street. He was a notorious potty-mouth! So to be expected to remember God? *God?* Before eating and sleeping? *Every single day?*

Sri Ramakrishna (*parp-parp!*) once more detected Girish's patent lack of enthusiasm. He (*parp-parp!*) prayed for a short while. Then he (*parp-parp!*) opened his eyes. 'Very well,' he smiled (*gasp!* The *guru*'s teeth are all yellow and full of blackberry pips!), 'if you can't even manage that, then why not give me your power of attorney? I will be responsible for you. And if I am responsible for you, you won't have to do anything at all!'

[*Please be aware of a deep and ominous percussive sound that is growling and rumbling away in the background. It is almost inaudible to begin with, but then grows louder and louder with every passing second. NB : This growling, rumbling percussive sound will henceforth replace the clown's horn whenever Sri Ramakrishna's name is mentioned.*]

Delightedly, even ecstatically, the foolish, foolish, *foolish* Girish immediately agreed to this kind offer. Sri Ramakrishna (*ominous rumbling sound*) had set him free! He now needed to do absolutely nothing – *zilch! Nada!* – to acquire spiritual fulfilment. *Yaaaaaaay!* A delighted Girish left the Master (*ominous rumbling sound*), feeling an extraordinary sense of lightness and relief.

Dum-de-dum-de-dum-de-dum! Tra-la-la-la-la! Oi!

A few days later, however, while in Sri Ramakrishna(*ominous rumbling sound*)'s presence, Girish perkily referred to some great scheme that he was undertaking (in the theatre, perhaps) with the phrase, 'I'm going to do this!'

Ta-dah!

Hardly were the words out of his mouth before Sri Ramakrishna (*ominous rumbling sound*) raised a hand and quietly interrupted him with, 'If God wills it. From now on, Girish, you must add 'if God wills it' whenever you make such statements.'

Eh?!

Girish gazed over at him, startled.

'Remember, the *guru* is God, God is the *guru*.' Sri Ramakrishna (*ominous rumbling sound*) smiled. 'SO GOD HAS YOUR POWER OF ATTORNEY NOW!!!!'

[*Dreadful cacophony! Cymbals being crashed, xylophone being bashed as a large drum-kit is kicked over.*]

Poor, stupid, lazy Girish suddenly realised – but way too late – that he was now Sri Ramakrishna(*ominous rumbling sound*)'s *slave*! The Master (*etc.*) had his power of attorney! And now he would permanently be compelled to think of God *ALL THE TIME! AT EVERY MOMENT! FOR-EVER-AND-EVER-AND-EVER-AND-EVER!*

Girish had – through an excess of laziness and complacency – unwittingly allowed himself to become nothing more than a blank-eyed zombie, a lifeless puppet, permanently compelled to bob up and down, up and down, up and down at the *guru*'s every idle wish and whim!

(*Curtain falls.*

Tumultuous applause!

Curtain rises.

All participants line up to take their bows.

The actor playing Girish performs a strangely stiff and unsettling curtsey as the actor who plays Sri Ramakrishna tugs away, menacingly, at his strings.

Curtain falls.

Applause fades. Everyone charges into the foyer and mills around aimlessly. Atmosphere of nervous confusion.)

The End.

1858. The Rani and her son-in-law, Mathur, kindly employ two of Calcutta's top female prostitutes to try and help cure Sri Ramakrishna of his deep psychological ills

Sri Ramakrishna returns to his room after a short stroll in the flower gardens to discover two of Calcutta's most legendarily beautiful, high-class prostitutes perched quietly upon his bed. They are happy – nay eager – to perform his each and every bidding. Sri Ramakrishna gazes from one exquisitely attired, bejewelled and fragranced beauty to the other, then falls to his knees, with a gasp of pure joy, and proceeds to worship them both, in tandem, as perfect embodiments of the Divine Mother. The prostitutes run from his room in a heady profusion of jangling anklets, utter confusion and tears.

Yogin Ma is one of Sri Ramakrishna's most faithful women devotees.
1886, Varanasi

When she meditates
Yogin Ma's trance is so deep
Flies nibble her eyes

1882. A bemused and benighted widow, who seems to be suffering from a strange kind of indigestion, bemoans her total inability to draw away from the Master while clutching at her chest, traumatised:

Sri Ramakrishna
Has tied a string to my heart
And keeps yanking it!

Aaaargh!

Winter 1859, at the Dakshineswar Kali Temple (six miles north of Calcutta)

I cannot say with any certainty whether it was Mathur Baba's physician – with all his special dietary rules and his expensive powders and unguents – who finally cured Uncle of that terrible, burning sensation in his chest. But I do know that I overheard Uncle telling someone that he had been concentrating during his most intense periods of meditation in the temple on his own sin – and also on its destruction – and that during one such meditation he suddenly had a vision in which a red-eyed, black-skinned creature came reeling out of his body and staggered around as if the worse for drink. Shortly after, a second person emerged – with clear eyes and a serene appearance – wearing the ochre cloth of a monk. This second person carried a trident and he attacked the red-eyed, drunken creature with it and killed him. From this moment onward, Uncle claimed, he was freed from all his former discomforts.

I was working hard at the Kali Temple and I was worrying greatly about ape-Uncle – so much so that it is difficult for me to recall in what order these events came about. But just as the pain in Uncle's chest disappeared, so too did ape-Uncle suddenly scamper off. When ape-Uncle left, Uncle was blessed with a great boon in the form of a vision of Sita, Rama's divine consort. Sita is truly the embodiment of all female virtues. Her name in Sanskrit means 'furrow', because to produce bounty a field must be carefully tended and ploughed. There are very many sources to her name and her story, but Sita is greatly loved because wherever she is worshipped she always brings benevolence and fecundity. When the beautiful goddess appeared to Uncle she told him that she was happy with his service to Rama and then entered his body, uttering the words, 'I bequeath you my smile.'

It strikes me as curious that Sita's name means furrow –
in the way a brow may be furrowed into a frown – and
yet what she gifted to Uncle was the very opposite of a
scowl.

In truth, I cannot recollect ever finding Uncle's smile
anything but charming (even as ape-Uncle, there was a certain
magnetism to it), but after Uncle's vision of Sita the smile on
his lips was a thing of such beauty that people would gasp when
they saw it. And Uncle smiled constantly. When he prayed or
he sang or he chanted or he slept (which was rarely) or he
danced or he talked, Uncle would always be smiling. He would
radiate joy and peace and great serenity. That's not to say Uncle
was always happy. Not at all. Uncle still struggled in his
spiritual journey. He was often upset and confused. But his
smile would light up his eyes and play around his lips even
then – even during our darkest hours.

One could light a room with Uncle's smile. One could melt
ice with it. Uncle's smile could warm any soul and bring
comfort to it. To be the recipient of one of Uncle's tender smiles
is to feel like the richest man on earth. It is at once feminine
and warm and comforting and holy. It is a most gracious and a
most loving smile.

Oh, how I hunger and thirst for that smile of Uncle's! But
presently I am most cruelly deprived of it, because Uncle has
returned to Kamarpukur to stay for some months with his
beloved mother.

Chandradevi, after many years of very little contact with her
youngest son, had lately been receiving mixed reports about
Uncle's progress at the temple, and had become, as a
consequence, sick with worry about him. Uncle's mother is
most adored by Uncle – as any good mother surely must be by
all but the most ungrateful and disloyal of her offspring. Uncle's
mother was Uncle's first great love, after all. And her example
has stood as the foundation stone of what has become his most

natural and most powerful spiritual mood of childlike love and devotion to the goddess Kali.

Uncle's great loves are his two mothers. Uncle venerates them both and seems perfectly oblivious to Chandradevi's faults: her simplicity and her naivety. Perhaps this is because Uncle has chosen to adopt some of those qualities for himself (Uncle can be very simple and naive on occasion), although in Uncle these faults find a strange kind of perfection.

Because Uncle cannot be expected to do anything on his own, I journeyed home with Uncle and helped him to find his bearings for a while. But then I returned with a heavy heart to my duties at Dakshineswar. I cannot pretend that I did not think it was good for Uncle to get away from the stressful atmosphere of the Kali Temple. Uncle had been in a state of heightened, spiritual emotion for far too long. He was very thin and exhausted and confused. Uncle was a small boat being tossed around in a great spiritual storm. It was most necessary for him to pull into a safe port for a while. And where better or safer a port than Kamarpukur?

Uncle has now been gone for almost a year and I miss him every moment. Life is flat without Uncle. There is no colour in the divine worship. Sometimes, I must shamefully confess, I have felt as if Uncle has stood in the way of my progress in life; how may I hope to find my own path if I am always helping Uncle to find his (especially when that path is fraught with chaos and danger – a briary thicket that I must be constantly hacking through with a blunted knife)?

But now that Uncle is gone I pine for him terribly. In the way that Uncle pines for Ma Kali, I pine for Uncle. There is something so special about Uncle, and a little part of whatever is so special about Uncle rubs itself off on me, too, just because I am always close to him. When Uncle is here, I become the precious setting in which the jewel of Uncle may be shown off to its very best advantage. I hold Uncle firmly so that the light may hit his many, sharp, fine-cut surfaces and sparkle. When Uncle is not here, all I seem to do is talk about Uncle. People do not forget him, and I will not let them forget him, either. How can I? So much of my conversation starts and finishes with 'Uncle says . . . Uncle thinks . . . Uncle . . . Uncle . . . Uncle . . .'

Uncle is my compass now. I cannot negotiate the world without him. He is my still centre. Without Uncle everything just spins pointlessly around.

I know I should feel happy and calm without the chaos of Uncle complicating my life, but instead I am like a drowning man being dragged into an endless whirlpool. Where is my anchor? Where is my help? Where is my hope, if not in Uncle?

I have returned to the village to visit Uncle on two occasions and am very comforted to see that he is much more at his ease now. Uncle lives a quiet life at Kamarpukur. His spiritual moods appear less extreme. Although Chandradevi informs me that she does not see as much of Uncle as she would like – he spends most of his time alone at the cremation ground, lost deep in contemplation.

Even so, Chandradevi is most happy and grateful to have Uncle back home with her once more, but still she fusses and worries over Uncle as a mother will. She even set upon a scheme to get Uncle a wife! When I first heard of this plan I must admit that I was rather disconcerted. A marriage? A wife? Are there not already a sufficiency of problems for us to worry over with Uncle? And Uncle has made it very plain that he has no interest in living a householder's life. Uncle cares only for spiritual matters. Uncle cares not a jot for women or for gold. Was not the worm of lust expelled from his penis?

I spoke to Uncle about Chandradevi's plans, but Uncle just smiled and shrugged. He would not oppose his beloved mother. So a search was begun to find Uncle a wife. But there was nobody suitable in the nearby villages – no girl who could reach Chandradevi's high standards for Uncle. And of course Uncle's reputation generally preceded him. People love Uncle dearly but he is hardly to be considered good husband material!

The search for a suitable match went on for many weeks, until Chandradevi was quite despairing, and then one morning Uncle announced that he had found his future bride all by himself. We were very confused because Uncle had done nothing but sit in the cremation ground and pray and meditate and appear completely indifferent to the ongoing search. Even so, Uncle provided his mother with the name of a girl in the village of Jayrambati. This name was Saradamani. We had no reason to think that Uncle had ever met or even heard of this girl before. But when we went to the address a girl was there, just five years old, and her father was very happy with the prospect of a betrothal. And so Uncle was married, and then the young girl – a sweet and obliging child – was sent back to live in the bosom of her family until she came of age. Uncle, for his part, after all these excitements, was now ready to turn his mind, once again, to Dakshineswar and the Kali Temple. What a relief it was to prepare for Uncle's return! And yet why did my heart sink a little at the mere thought of it?

I swear I do not know whether I am coming or going with Uncle. But I have certainly missed his lovely smile and his constant scolding. Uncle is funny. While he is completely detached from all worldly concerns, he can still be very particular and fussy and sarcastic about the finer details of things. He is certainly a most demanding master. My heart always sings and jumps like a cricket when he is around.

1868, approximately
Sri Ramakrishna offers three humble starting-points for meditation

Imagine the sky –
Vast – grey – covered in dense cloud:
Stand and gaze, in awe.

Imagine a lake –
This huge expanse of water,
But utterly still

Imagine a lamp
With an unflickering flame –
Everything quiet

Shhhhh back there! We're *meditating*, you dullards!

1863, approximately, and Mathur Nath Biswas offers Sri Ramakrishna something to eat

Mathur (*proffering a fruit*): 'Will you have some mango?'
Sri Ramakrishna (*shaking his head*): 'No, thank you. This . . . [*indicates self*] has eaten.'
Mathur (*frowning, suspicious*): 'What do you mean? Why are you talking that way?'
Sri Ramakrishna (*surprised*): 'Does not the stump of ego block the path to God's kingdom? To enter the kingdom one must first leapfrog over that stump.'
Mathur (*smirking*): 'So now you refuse to use the word "I" because it is an expression of ego?'
Sri Ramakrishna (*nodding*): 'The great pandit, Gaudi, speaks in this style. I have been told that this is how all true renunciants express themselves.'
Mathur (*with a dismissive swipe of his hand*): '*Argh*, let Gaudi speak however he chooses! It's simply an affectation – an *expression* of his egotism. But you have no ego. There is no need for you to talk as these people do.'

   Sri Ramakrishna thinks for a moment, frowning slightly, then his gentle but perplexed brown eyes turn and settle, thoughtfully, upon the lovely, ripe fruit. Ah, but how the sweet-toothed Master adores a mango!

For the main meal:

Eat a little rice,
Perhaps a little spinach —
Chant God's name all day.

And as a quick digestif:

Bite on a chilli —
By accident or design,
Your tongue will still burn.

16 April 1886, the Cossipore Garden House, Calcutta

or

The perplexing tale of Pagli*
(* in Bengali, Pagli means 'mad woman')

Please remember God,
But if you cannot do that –
Then just think of me.

        Sri Ramakrishna

Ravaged by the final stages of throat cancer, barely able to eat, walk or speak, Sri Ramakrishna is staying in a large, upstairs room at a beautiful garden house rented by devotee Surendra Nath Mittra in the leafy suburbs of Cossipore. The Master's small band of exhausted and heartbroken disciples are nursing him around the clock and are eager to ease his evident – but unspoken – discomfort in any way possible. It is mid-April and very hot. Surendra has purchased some blinds for the windows to keep out the worst of the scalding light. But now it is night-time (if still airless) and the full moon shines with an almost supernatural brightness.

In the garden, a woman suffering from acute mental illness (the disciples call her 'Pagli') is crying and entreating whomsoever may listen to be granted access to the bedside of the dying *guru*. Pagli has chosen to worship Sri Ramakrishna ('the *guru* is God, God is the *guru*') in the spiritual attitude of the lover, and so she torments him, at every opportunity, with her passionate, crazy and utterly inappropriate displays of affection.

The disciples are sick of Pagli. She is prone to breaking into the house and forcing her way into Sri Ramakrishna's room to demonstrate her deranged love for him. She tortures him from her post in the garden with her hysterical screaming and her perpetual commotion. Recently, over-tired and exasperated, a couple of the disciples went so far as to beat her up. But still she returns, battered and bruised. Still she chides and wheedles and yells.

The *guru* (who will not be called *guru*) is quiet and uncomplaining. He receives visitors, even though speaking often causes his throat to haemorrhage. He has been banned from talking – he talks only of God – but he hoarsely whispers, nonetheless. When he is no longer able to talk he signs with an emaciated arm and fingers.

The Master(who will not be called Master)'s doctor (a spiritual sceptic) has forbidden him from entering into spiritual trances. During Sri Ramakrishna's trances, blood and energy automatically mass at his throat (might this be the reason for his cancer? Or perhaps his lifelong attachment to the hubble-bubble, or to chewing betel nut, a known carcinogen?). Of course Sri Ramakrishna has no control over his spiritual moods. If he is inspired by thoughts of God, if he hears religious singing, if he talks of the Mother, if he smells a particular flower used in worship, or a whiff of incense or of camphor, he will enter a state of ecstasy. He cannot help it.

His faith is killing him.

The disciples know that the Master has great supernatural powers (although he rarely uses them – he *disapproves* of them. God should be sought through love and devotion, he holds, not magic; magic confuses and inflates the ego . . . Although remember the woman who was instantly cured – by just a brief touch – of her insurmountable grief over the death of her daughter? Remember how a mere word or a smile have inspired states of terrifying spiritual ecstasy in numerous individuals that can last hours, days, even weeks?) and so they entreat him to cure himself, *please*.

Sri Ramakrishna is plainly horrified by these requests. His illness is part of the Mother's *lila*, he says. It is her sport. It is her divine play. It is her will. He recently had a vision in which the Divine Mother showed him his own emaciated corpse, and his bare back was covered in weeping burns and blisters. Horrified, he asked her why it was so. She then showed him how spiritual seekers touched him for good luck, and how their sins singed and sapped his physical self.

Poor Pagli. She has fixated on the *guru* in much the same way that the *guru* fixated on the Divine Mother at the onset of his own strange spiritual journey. She too can find no rest or peace without palpable demonstrations of love from her chosen ideal. In the past she has angrily accused the bemused Master of 'pushing her away, mentally'. She is implacable. She is frustrated. She is demented. She is a pest. Sri Ramakrishna has patiently explained to her that he sees all women as manifestations of the Divine Mother, that he is incapable of engaging with any woman except in that attitude. But Pagli refuses – or is unable – to understand.

Sri Ramakrishna is slowly dying, in incredible pain and scalding heat, but he cannot find a moment's peace from this, his most ardent and passionate disciple.

On that long, hot night of 16 April 1886, Girish – with his artist's soul – pleads Pagli's case before her many detractors. Did he not pester and insult the *guru* himself, for years, he demands, before he finally relented and saw the light? And now that he *has* finally seen it, how is it possible for him to resent the warped, emotional whirlwind of Pagli for enthusiastically embracing that exact same impulse?

The other disciples aren't receptive to Girish's kindly analysis (they could happily kill her for the trouble she's caused), but Girish still persists. He walks over to the window and peers out. There Pagli stands, in the garden, bathed in silver moonlight, her dark hair awry, her arms covered in bruises. She is calling the *guru*'s name as if her heart would break. 'Pagli is truly blessed,' he murmurs, turning towards the emaciated *guru*, his soulful eyes filling with tears, 'to love you this much. If she calls on your name with such faith and devotion, surely no real harm may befall her?'

The tormented *guru* will not speak. He just closes his eyes and smiles.

And now — oh dear — it's the bill!

If you have money
Then give it in charity —
If not, simply chant.

Hiss at the wicked,
Frighten them just a little,
Lest they do you harm.

I don't accept gifts —
We take no collection here;
That's why people come!

Winter 1864, at the Dakshineswar Kali Temple (six miles north of Calcutta)

The very instant Uncle set his foot back inside the Kali Temple compound, the spiritual madness overwhelmed him once again. But this time, if possible, it was magnified by a thousand. The terrible burning sensation in his chest returned, the sleeplessness, the restlessness, the delirium, the sudden explosions of uncontrollable grief. And these were now joined by constant visions, and sweats and violent shaking.

That serene, ochre-robed *sannyasi* – the monk – that came from within Uncle and killed his sin with a trident suddenly returned, but now its great ire was directed towards Uncle himself. It threatened Uncle. I would hear him talking with it and pleading with it not to harm him. This *sannyasi* would give Uncle no peace. It taunted and reprimanded him. It felt that Uncle wasn't trying hard enough to find God. But who, *who* might try harder than poor Uncle did?

I would sit on the veranda at night, not able to sleep, listening to Uncle's side of their countless arguments. I wanted to protect Uncle, to defend him against this trident-bearing creature who so cruelly cajoled and humiliated him, yet how might I possibly go about it? It lived inside Uncle's head! It *was* Uncle!

'But I *am* concentrating!' Uncle would wheedle. 'Please, I *am* trying. Why won't you believe me? I *love* God, I promise, I *promise*, with the whole of my being . . .'

Sometimes the ochre-robed *sannyasi* would travel to distant places. He would walk on a golden path and Uncle would call after him, anxiously, 'Where are you going? Hello? Hello? What do you see down there?' Often the *sannyasi* would return and tell Uncle what he had found. But Uncle would not share the finer details of these conversations with me, because he said I would not be able to understand.

Uncle spent all his time in meditation. His hair was very long and matted. He would sit still for such lengthy durations that birds would perch on him and peck at his head. Mice would clamber around in his long locks hunting for food. I once saw a snake slither across his lap. But Uncle did not move. Uncle was a lifeless stone – a rock – oblivious to everything.

When Uncle wasn't meditating and sparring with the ochre-clad *sannyasi*, then he was engaging in austerities. Uncle wanted to destroy any final residue of his *brahmin*'s pride. At night he would creep out of his room and head for the temple latrines. He would use his long hair to clean them. There was no dank corner or stinking hole that Uncle would not investigate and scour. To defeat his sense of natural aversion still further, Uncle would even go so far as to touch the faeces of strangers with the tip of his tongue. There was no degradation that Uncle would not submit himself to.

I was in despair. Because while Uncle was suffering, I was suffering *for* Uncle. Who can understand the pain – the nagging torment – of bearing witness to the one you love above all others punishing himself daily (and not even for vice or worldly advancement, but for otherworldly love)?

I had begun to lose all hope for Uncle. Once again, as before, I was exhausted and full of a terrible foreboding, but then suddenly, without any warning, two things happened to transform our fortunes, one hard upon the next. The first was the sad death of the Rani in 1861, and the passing of her estate into Mathur Baba's hands. In the past when I had complained to Uncle about our lack of money he would always pooh-pooh me. He said I was not to worry and that we would never go hungry because the Mother had told him in a vision that he would have four 'Suppliers of Provisions' throughout his life. Uncle was very confident of this fact. He had complete faith in the Mother. And (much as I had doubted him at first) Uncle's faith was rewarded, because it transpired that Mathur Baba was to be the first of these four.

After the Rani's death, Mathur Baba's devotion to Uncle – which was always strong – increased still further. Uncle had only to mention an idle whim or a passing need and Mathur Baba would instantly satisfy it. Thank God for Mathur Baba! I thank our lucky stars for his patience and his forbearance! Of course Mathur Baba is not an especially spiritual man – he is rich and he lives high and he enjoys his luxuries – but he loves Uncle dearly. One could almost go so far as to say that Uncle is Mathur Baba's greatest indulgence! How fortunate Uncle is that Mathur Baba is so firmly on his side now! Uncle has utterly beguiled him and without any particular effort. Uncle is simply himself – a clever but guileless child of the universe.

All the temple officials and administrators – even Mathur Baba's own private priest – have nothing good to say about Uncle. Not a word! They are deeply jealous of his attraction for Mathur Baba. They whisper and accuse him of devilry, of casting spells to bewitch Mathur Baba. Of course Uncle doesn't care a jot about such things. Uncle's mind is fixed on a higher plane. But I must sit and listen, clenching my teeth, to their constant gossip and their endless jibes.

On one occasion when Uncle was visiting Mathur Baba's residence he was left temporarily alone and fell into a sudden trance – something Uncle has become increasingly prone to – and as he lay on the floor, lost in ecstasy, Mathur Baba's private priest, Haldar, happened across Uncle and, finding him alone and defenceless, this scoundrel set about kicking Uncle and beating Uncle with all his might. Uncle's mind was falling in and out of consciousness. He could tell what was happening but he could not move to defend himself. When I found Uncle a short while later he was balled-up in pain and panting like a wounded animal. His ribs were cracked. He was horribly bruised. But he made me swear on my mother's life not to tell a

159

soul. 'If Babu Mathur finds out what Haldar has done he will sack him!' Uncle said. 'And what will become of his wife and his family then?' Uncle forced me to hold my tongue. And angry as I am, I must quietly endure it. Uncle insists that he wants no fuss or retribution. Uncle is surely a great soul. He is possessed by the spirit of true resignation. 'Dear Hriday, this is simply the *lila* of the Divine Mother.' Uncle laughs (then he winces, then he clutches at his chest, then he laughs once again).

I have always been very protective of Uncle, but from that time forward I was even more determined never to leave Uncle unsupervised for so much as a moment. Uncle is far too precious. And who would look after Uncle if I did not? Uncle could not be expected to take care of himself – especially now that he has so many jealous enemies and rivals. Although, in truth, I have often thought that Uncle's greatest and most dangerous adversary will always and for ever be Uncle himself.

At around this time – just after the Rani's death, and during Mathur Baba's increasing devotion to Uncle – another very important person entered Uncle's life who, thank God, was to quietly take the place of Uncle's mean and sharp-tongued *sannyasi* as his spiritual guide. Uncle was standing in the flower garden one morning, gazing over towards the main bathing *ghat* when he saw a beautiful, orange-robed *brahmini* alight from a boat. It is already well established that Uncle has no interest in either women or gold, but just as soon as Uncle set his two eyes upon her he became very excitable. He called me over and demanded that I go and introduce myself to her and then tell her all about him. Well, I was naturally perplexed and uncomfortable to approach a strange *brahmini* in such a forthright manner, but this is just life with Uncle, I fear. Normal rules and conventions do not apply here.

The *brahmini* – although not in her first flush of youth – was a very handsome woman. I told her about Uncle as she sat, cross-legged, in the welcome shade of the *chandni*. She listened very patiently, and then, instead of coolly dismissing me – as I imagined she must – she asked me to take her to Uncle immediately. I guided her to Uncle's room where Uncle was now anxiously waiting, and I was very astonished – once the formal introductions were over – that the *brahmini* and Uncle behaved towards one another as if they had known each other their whole lives! Uncle told the *brahmini* – who, as a true *sannyasi*, owned nothing in the world but two wearing-cloths and a handful of spiritual books – his entire life story, about all his spiritual aspirations and experiences, of how people thought he was insane, and how even he himself doubted his own sanity at times.

The *brahmini* nodded calmly throughout Uncle's tales. And when he had finished talking she told him – with many clever spiritual references and the paging through of books – that the whole world is mad for something – money, pleasure, love – and that this was perfectly normal. It just so happened that Uncle was mad for God. She then showed Uncle segments of the *bhakti* scriptures where all the symptoms that Uncle had been experiencing were described in great detail. She explained that Uncle had reached a state referred to in the scriptures as *mahabhava*: a condition of exalted devotion rarely ever seen except in the greatest of saints.

Furthermore, the *brahmini* then told Uncle that she was on a mission from God. She had been instructed to wander the earth until she met three spiritual aspirants, with all of whom she was to share the bounty of her extensive Tantric and Vaishnava knowledge. Uncle, it seemed, was to be the third of these disciples. She said that she had been wandering and searching for Uncle for many years.

Ah, how do I explain the sheer relief that Uncle felt upon his meeting with the *brahmini*? A charming bond was immediately established. Uncle became the *brahmini*'s little Krishna, and she his most beloved mother. I will not deny that I was slightly put out by the *brahmini* suddenly becoming Uncle's all in all. But the pressure of caring for Uncle had become very heavy at this time, and to see Uncle so relieved and so encouraged by the *brahmini* was of course a great boon for me as well.

The *brahmini* is a strong and most intelligent woman. She is a powerful spiritual force in her own right. As with all good mothers and teachers, she is very stern and controlling. But who am I to voice such an opinion? Who is Hridayram Mukhopadhyay? He is nothing! Nothing! The *brahmini* knows this. The *brahmini* is never rude but she sees straight through Hridayram. He is transparent to the *brahmini*. He is insignificant. He has simply to adjust quietly and uncomplainingly to her special quirks and her curious requirements. Hridayram's life with Uncle is a long game. The best players must always show a willingness to adapt. And so must he. This is his destiny. He is accustomed to being invisible. He is accustomed to always shining the light upon Uncle. The person who shines the light but who stands in the darkness is still holding the light in their hands, after all.

A fistful of dirt on this mysterious brahmini:

She was born in East Bengal. In some accounts she is around forty years of age, in others, fifty. She is clever and handsome, powerful and charismatic. She is an itinerant monk and an avowed intellectual, who (to all intents and purposes) lives freely – *sans* ties or protection – in nineteenth-century Bengali society. She is definitely a force to be reckoned with: a fixer, an opportunist, a mover-and-a-shaker.

Her avowed aim (her dream) is to firmly and fearlessly guide Sri Ramakrishna (the man who would be God), through the sixty-four dangerous and exotic disciplines of the Tantras, then – once these have been practised and mastered – to teach him the main ideas, rules and tenets of Vaishnavism.

The *brahmini* finally establishes the – let's face it – somewhat free-form and *errant* Sri Ramakrishna in a strong, traditional, faith structure. Having spontaneously arrived, after six years of complete devotion and dedication to the spiritual growth and well-being of the saint, she just as suddenly disappears.

Simply 'brahmini' –
This spiritual midwife
Stays anonymous.

His story. Records. Little. Else.

November 1884 (or some time thereabouts) at the Dakshineswar Kali Temple

Sri Ramakrishna is sitting in his room with a group of shocked disciples discussing the terrible way in which the infamous libertine and playwright Girish Chandra Ghosh has drunkenly abused and humiliated the *guru* at the theatre, in front of a large crowd, the previous night:

Irate devotee: 'Girish has gone too far this time. What he did was unforgivable!'
Sri Ramakrishna sighs then shrugs, sadly. He turns to another devotee, Ram Chandra Datta and asks for his opinion.
Sri Ramakrishna: 'What do you make of it, Captain?'
Ram Chandra Datta (*after pondering for a while*): 'I think Girish is like the vicious serpent, Kaliya, who has nothing to offer Lord Krishna apart from her venom. And so that is what she offers.'
Sri Ramakrishna smiles, nods, orders a carriage, and promptly drives over to Girish's house to forgive him.

1882 (or some time thereabouts). Sri Ramakrishna talks to a new disciple about sadness:

Misery is good!
If the whole world was happy
Who would chant God's name?

A passing observation

First the Rani, and now the *brahmini*? Both negotiating paths of such extraordinary freedom and flexibility within the restricting manacles of nineteenth-century tradition, sex and caste? How on earth did they manage it?

First answer:
Feminine guile!

Second answer:
Native wit!

Real answer:

Ah, Hinduism:
This, the Pair of Opposites,
Binds *and* releases!

Two haiku about Tantra

'Consciousness' – 'Being' – 'Bliss' –
All three are identical,
And all hail from God

(or)

'Chit' – *'Sat'* – *'Ananda'* –
You are one with the Godhead;
God lives within you

Winter 1881, at the Dakshineswar Kali Temple. Sri Ramakrishna finally gets to meet the one person he has been waiting for HIS WHOLE, DAMN LIFE!!

(Suggested subheading: True Romance! Uh . . . Oh. Although . . . gulp! . . . not with his wife . . .)

Part 1

The undoubtedly brilliant but somewhat cynical and world-weary eighteen-year-old Narendra Nath Datta is encouraged to visit the well-known (nay, notorious?) and rather eccentric *guru* Sri Ramakrishna by a couple of his friends. His mood on approaching the Master's domain is a little haughty and somewhat less than enthusiastic. He enters Sri Ramakrishna's room, sits down, and after some prompting (he has a lovely voice) is persuaded to sing. When his song is finished, Sri Ramakrishna (now forty-five years of age) beckons him outside, on to his northern veranda (which is protected – as it is winter – from strong winds and bad weather by a matted screen). He closes the door behind them with great care and deliberation. They are now completely alone. A curious scene here unfolds:

Sri Ramakrishna (*grabbing the bemused eighteen-year-old boy's hand and bursting into noisy tears*): 'You've come so late! Why has it taken you so long? Didn't you *know* how I've been waiting for you? I've been driven almost *mad* by the worldly talk of all these fools around me. I thought I would *burst* without anyone to tell my true feelings to!'
Narendra Nath Datta (*eyes widening with alarm*): 'But I . . . I don't . . .'

Sri Ramakrishna (*dropping the boy's hand, stepping back and pressing his palms together prayerfully as if addressing a deity*): 'I know your true identity. You are Nara, incarnation of Narayana. You have returned here to earth to relieve the burdens and sufferings of mankind!'

Narendra Nath Datta (*frankly astonished, and not a little horrified*): 'I'm . . . I'm not sure if . . .'

Sri Ramakrishna (*excitedly*): 'Wait! *Wait!* One minute!'

The *guru* dashes back into his room and returns, moments later (carefully closing the door behind him again), with a plate of Indian sweets. He then proceeds to gently push them, piece by piece, between the shocked teenager's lips. After several mouthfuls a startled Narendra speaks:

Narendra (*embarrassed*): 'Perhaps if you gave me the plate I could carry it back inside and distribute these treats among my friends?'

Sri Ramakrishna (*indignant*): 'No! These sweets are for *you*. They're *yours*. The others [*waves dismissively*] can have theirs later.'

The *guru* (who will not be called a *guru*) continues to feed Narendra until all the sweets are gone and the plate is empty.

Narendra Nath Datta (*dabbing anxiously at his lips. Perplexed. Feeling a sudden, slightly sickening sugar-rush, glancing towards the door*): 'Maybe we should think about joining the . . . ?'

Sri Ramakrishna grabs the teenager's hand again.

Sri Ramakrishna (*desperate and earnest*): 'I won't move from this spot until you promise me that you will return here again, *very* soon, and that the next time you visit you'll come alone.'

Narendra Nath Datta (*clears his throat. Uncomfortable. Slightly cornered*): 'Yes. *Yes.* Of course.'

Narendra Nath Datta returns to the Master's room and there he sings a second song. Later, travelling home in a hired carriage, he licks his lips and is startled to discover that they are still sugary from the sweets the Master has fed him. He is both thrilled and appalled by his recent encounter. He is also utterly convinced – more than he has ever been convinced of anything *in his whole, short life* – that Sri Ramakrishna is a complete lunatic – a crazy madman – a cunning and dangerous monomaniac.

Ah . . .

To be wooed with sweets . . .
To be hand-fed the *prasad*
By a crazy man!

Psssst!

Please never go back!
Listen to your wise parents!
Don't fall for his tricks!

Are you listening, Narendra?
Hello? *Hello? Narendra?*
NARENDRA?!

Part 2

Oh dear. After a good deal of soul-searching . . . A few weeks later

Narendra Nath Datta returns to the Dakshineswar Kali Temple
alone and on foot. The last time he made the journey – when
he came with his friends – it was in a hired carriage. He'd
hardly noticed the distance. But this is actually – the teenager
quickly realises – a gruelling six-mile hike, and he is unsure of
the way. He keeps asking people for directions. He grows
increasingly stressed and exhausted. He is full of misgivings.
What draws him here?
What is this compulsion?

Eh?

Faith?
Boredom?
Naivety?
Spiritual hunger?
Vanity?
Stupidity?
    He has often heard mention of Sri Ramakrishna's 'incredible
attraction'. If the dark rumours are to be believed, this famous
guru is a still flame who draws fluttering moths to his light and
then singes their wings.
    Narendra finally arrives at the temple and makes his way to
Sri Ramakrishna's room. Sri Ramakrishna is – unusually
enough – alone. His room – with its red concrete floor spread
with straw mats – has few possessions in it. There is a
collection of pictures on the walls – of Hindu gods and
goddesses, one of Jesus . . .
On the right-hand side of the room are two beds, one larger,

one smaller, pushed up against each other (the larger benefits from the luxurious addition of a mosquito net). Sri Ramakrishna is perched on the smaller of these.

The *guru* (who will not be called a *guru*) greets Narendra joyfully. He beckons him to sit on the end of the smaller bed. Narendra tentatively does as he is instructed.

He observes that the Master is in a strange mood. He seems introspective, preoccupied. He is grumbling and muttering to himself under his breath. Narendra is somewhat alarmed by this, and is consequently on his guard.

There is something about the Master that confuses him (and it has confused many others). One might imagine that Sri Ramakrishna (with his childlike, almost feminine demeanour) would be small, even slight. And sometimes he is. But then at other times he seems perfectly . . . how to express it? *Huge*. He seems huge. Nobody quite understands how or why.

[When you inspect the few remaining photographs of the saint (a notable one in which he is in a trance-like state being watched by members of the Brahmo Samaj, and supported, from behind, by his nephew, Hridayram), he seems tiny – fragile.

After the *guru*'s death, when questions are asked about his size so that a marble sculpture can be commissioned, nobody can agree on how big he was. Eventually a coat is found (a green coat) and a photograph of the Master wearing it, and by dint of careful reckoning, it is decided that the Master was five feet eight inches.]

Narendra watches the Master with a combination of social unease, teenage *hauteur* and exhaustion.

The Master – after a little more muttering – turns, looks hard at the boy, then suddenly stands up and moves towards him. Narendra panics. Oh no! Is there about to be another of those exquisitely embarrassing scenes? Like the last time he visited?

He has barely begun to process this thought (and its concomitant dread) when the *guru* lifts his leg and places his bare foot firmly upon the teenager's body (where we do not know – the lower thigh? The hip? The chest?) and then everything goes completely haywire. The walls of the *guru*'s room collapse backwards, everything starts to spin at an extraordinary speed and the teenager has the powerful inkling that his consciousness – his essence – is about to be swallowed up into a massive, ravenous, rotating vortex; an all-engulfing void.

In terror he hears his own voice scream out (all signs of teenage hubris instantly evaporating), 'What's happening to me? Help! What would my parents think?'

The laughing *guru* lifts his foot and gently touches his hand to the terrified teenager's chest. 'All right,' he murmurs, half to himself, 'let it stop. This needn't happen all at once.'
And, just as suddenly as it emerged, the giant void disappears. The walls reform. Only a couple of seconds have passed, in real time, but entire continents have shifted within Narendra's consciousness.

He sits on the bed, slumped forward, struggling to catch his breath. The *guru* retreats. Once again everything about him appears small and harmless and childlike. He is now incredibly friendly and kind and warm to the visiting teenager. He offers him every sort of hospitality. And he is funny. He sings, he dances, he cracks jokes. He can be a bitch. He can be terse. He is an exceptionally droll impersonator. Before Narendra knows it a whole day has passed in his delightful company and it is time for him to return home again. The *guru* is dejected at the thought of him leaving. He visibly droops. He perches on the end of his small bed, shoulders slumping, chin on his chest, arms hanging, like a poignant little *pierrot* doll.
Only he himself – *Narendra Nath Datta* (it seems to the gilded youth) – has the almost divine power to activate him now.

Rational explanations for the previous incident . . .

How did this happen?
Hunger? The heat? Exhaustion?
It's incomprehen—

WAAAAAH!

Part 3

After several months . . .

Among Sri Ramakrishna's circle is a man called Pratap
Chandra Hazra. Sri Ramakrishna doesn't especially like him.
He finds him 'dry' or lacking in sincere spiritual inspiration.
Hazra is well-read and perfectly intelligent, but something of a
pedant (a quality Sri Ramakrishna especially loathes). And
even though he has a wife and a family in dire financial need
back in the place he calls home (somewhere near Hriday's
native village of Sihar), he still spends most of his time at the
Dakshineswar Kali Temple in the orbit of the famous saint,
loudly and piously practising *japam* on Ramakrishna's veranda
and doing his best to attract attention to himself.

Ramakrishna is often irritated by Hazra and what he
considers to be his unhelpful influence over some of his newer
(and most precious) devotees. The saint is not averse to making
the odd sarcastic aside at Hazra's expense. Although he has
finally come to realise (and how could he not?) that Hazra is
simply a part of the Mother's divine play. He accepts that Hazra
has been sent to plague him for a reason, as a lesson – in much
the same way that Krishna's most passionate devotee, Radha,
was persecuted by Jatila, her mother-in-law, so that her
constant meddling and interfering might make Radha love
Krishna still more – and that Hazra is therefore an essential
part of the Mother's divine scheme. And this knowledge – this
insight – makes him surprisingly tolerant of Hazra; even to
feel, at some level, a measure of gratitude towards him.

It is, nonetheless, a source of profound irritation to him that
Narendra, his most beloved devotee (the saviour of mankind,
the devotee Ramakrishna knows will bring his message to the
world), is great friends with this flawed individual and

consequently open to his malign influence. Often he will struggle to get the teenager's attention (the teenager – as he settles into his relationship with Sri Ramakrishna and becomes increasingly and delightfully aware of his own huge significance to him – will be cynical, argumentative, dismissive and cruel to the *guru*). He is arrogant by nature. He will sometimes make snide remarks about the *guru*'s lack of a formal education.

The *guru* has a very particular way of guiding people to spiritual fulfilment. You might call it 'the pick and mix' technique. He gets to know the person (inspecting their face, their hands, their tongue, their feet), asks them countless questions, then decides what spiritual approach most suits their needs. Ramakrishna is promiscuous by nature. There is no one route. No one-size-fits-all approach. And because Narendra Nath Datta is (in the *guru*'s mind, and in fact) destined to be his future mouthpiece to the world, he chooses to initiate this special disciple into Vedantic non-dualism, a highly difficult, obtuse and intellectual doctrine that teaches that the disciple and God are identical.

But it isn't all to be plain sailing. Hazra and the teenager certainly see to that. On one occasion Sri Ramakrishna comes outside on to his balcony to find the two of them engaged in a bitchy discussion about the credibility of the non-dualist approach. Narendra is pointing to a water pot that sits on the floor before them and is saying, 'Is this water pot *God*?! Is this cup, *God*?! Are you *God*?! Am I *God*?!'

They are laughing together, scornfully, at the very thought.

'What are you laughing at?' the childlike *guru* wonders, sweetly, and as he speaks he taps Narendra lightly on the shoulder, once again turning the teenager's entire universe on its head.

Narendra immediately becomes conscious of the fact that the whole world *is* God. The. Whole. World.
God!

He spends the entire day in this bizarre, heightened state. He tells nobody what is happening to him. He just hopes – desperately hopes – that it will wear off. But it doesn't. He travels home. Everything is God. He sits down to eat. The plate is God. The food is God. His mother who serves him is God. Her words are God.

And it continues. He attends college. He walks the streets. Everything is God. A carriage approaches him as he crosses the road – at high speed – but he can barely bring himself to move out of its path. It is God. And he is God. So he is the carriage. And they are all God.

Experts call this a state of 'divine intoxication'. It's how Sri Ramakrishna feels all the time. The *guru* lives in a perpetual state of divine intoxication (almost to the point of finding it a nuisance).

As a part of his intoxication Narendra has lost all sense of feeling in his hands and his feet. This makes him anxious. And as the ecstasy fades, over days, weeks, he continues to worry about it. Now he feels like he is trapped inside in a strange kind of living dream. He feels distanced. Numb. Weird. Woolly. As he walks down a street one day he falls to his knees and starts hitting his head against a set of railings to try and establish whether they are real or not.

His poor mother has lost all hope for him. That pesky *guru*! That pesky, pesky *guru*!

'My poor, darling Naren . . . He won't live long,' she murmurs.

Sadhana is reached
When you witness God's presence
In everything.

Part 4

1885, the Cossipore Garden House, not long before Sri Ramakrishna's death

Sri Ramakrishna is lying upstairs, desperately ill, when a certain amount of commotion erupts downstairs. The saint's faithful diarist and scribe, modestly known to the world simply as M (but known in day-to-day life as the much-loved and respected, if incredibly humble Calcuttan headmaster, Mahendra Nath Gupta) kindly informs the saint of what is unfolding . . .

Narendra Nath Datta, it transpires, has been sitting on the ground floor, meditating. And as he meditates he has the curious sensation of an intense, fiery warmth at the back of his head. He then loses all consciousness and experiences what is generally perceived to be the ultimate spiritual state, described by seasoned Vedantists as *nirvikalpa samadhi*. During this form of ecstasy the embodied soul is completely effaced and unified with God. It is known to be a rare, extraordinary, mind-blowing and ego-shattering phenomenon. Sometimes – indeed, often – people die when it happens to them. In fact – if we can fast-forward seventeen years – Narendra himself *will* die (at the horribly premature age of thirty-nine) the next time he enters this state. Although following his first experience Sri Ramakrishna calls him upstairs and tells him that he will not enter the state again until the Mother's work has been accomplished. And he is right. 'This revelation will stay under lock and key,' the *guru* says, holding aloft an imaginary key, kissing it, and then placing it into an imaginary pocket lying close to his heart.

But this is still Narendra's first experience of *nirvikalpa samadhi*. We have no idea how long his consciousness is lost to it in real time. All we do know is that when he begins to regain consciousness, he does so only partially. He can open his eyes and see his head (the tip of his own nose, his tongue), but the rest of his body is now invisible to him.

And this is the source of all the commotion. Narendra, in a panic, is crying out: 'Where is my body? Where is my body?' Another devotee comes running into the room (followed, no doubt, by a panting M) and tries to reassure the early-twenty-something-would-be-saviour-of-the-world. 'Your body is right here, Narendra! Don't panic. Your body is here!'
But Narendra isn't persuaded and he continues to wail.

At this point, M sensibly dashes upstairs to ask the *guru* what they can do to help. The *guru* receives the news of Narendra's perceived disembodiment with complete equanimity. Then he smiles. Then he swipes a limp hand through the air. 'Argh,' he whispers, with a hoarse chuckle, 'just leave him that way for a while. Let Naren have a little taste of his own medicine. He's certainly worried me for long enough.'

After the great guru's death, Narendra muses, somewhat astonished:

We were trained by him
Without even knowing it –
Just through fun and games!

:)

Mathur Baba is a great and a powerful man, and he truly loves Uncle almost as much as I do. But it took Mathur Baba quite some time before he could fully accept the sudden arrival of the *brahmini* and her great and immediate influence over Uncle's *sadhana*.

The *brahmini* has a very controlling manner and is of strong opinions, and after only a very short acquaintance with Uncle she became convinced that Uncle was an incarnation of God. Uncle received this shocking news with his typical, childlike innocence. He skipped off to see Mathur Baba and he gaily informed him of what the *brahmini* had said:

'Mathur! Mathur! The *brahmini* says that I am an incarnation of God!'

Mathur simply frowned and shook his head. He loved Uncle but he thought the *brahmini* had gone too far. He told the *brahmini* that there could only be ten *avatars* of Vishnu, as described in the *Garuda Purana*, and that this number had clearly already manifested. But the *brahmini* insisted that there were also twenty-four in the *Bhagavata Purana*, and that anyway it also states in this most holy and sacred of texts that Vishnu's incarnations are endless.

She showed the sceptical Mathur Baba the exact quotation. '*Whenever righteousness wanes and unrighteousness increases I send myself forth*,' she calmly read. '*For the protection of the good and for the destruction of evil, and the establishment of righteousness, I come into being age after age.*'

Mathur Baba merely sucked his tongue and scowled and gazed at Uncle suspiciously from under his lowering eyebrows. But was Uncle worried or disturbed by Mathur's doubting? Not at all! Uncle just clapped his hands joyfully and danced around and sang his sweet and charming songs in praise of his beloved goddess. He was completely unconcerned. For why should Uncle care about what people say? Uncle has no ego. Uncle only cares about God and nothing else.

But the *brahmini* would not be silenced. She stood up to Mathur Baba and told him that he should convene a conference of famous pandits to openly discuss the matter and come to a final decision upon it. Mathur Baba is a sensible and an educated man. He has a weakness for Uncle, a great weakness for Uncle – as I do – but he was not to be convinced so easily as all that. And it was only after considerable heart-searching – and with his deep misgivings – that the conference was eventually convened.

Yet what a great and learned occasion it was! The *brahmini* presented her case before the summoned pandits in grand style and with much detailed reference to the scriptures. The pandits were all very thoughtful and serious about what the *brahmini* had said.

Uncle sat among them, like a child, hardly paying any attention. To Uncle this was just the Mother's divine play, just her *lila*. Because for Uncle, fame and reputation are merely an illusion. They are *maya*. And yet even though Uncle made no effort whatsoever to convince or beguile the pandits, one by one they announced that yes, indeed, Uncle truly was an *avatar* (although when I questioned Uncle about this after, Uncle just threw up his hands impatiently and said, 'Pah! What do *I* know about such things?').

Mathur Baba is a freethinking man. Who can be sure whether the pandits convinced *him* of Uncle's being an incarnation or not? I love Uncle as much as it is possible to love another human being, but I must confess that I was yet to be fully won over by their many and clever arguments. Perhaps I simply do not possess the kind of mind that would be liable to understand the finer details of such lofty issues? When I dwelt deeply on the matter I would merely flip-flop like a landed

187

fish! Because one minute I would really and truly believe in their decision, then the next I would be terribly confused and perplexed. How could I be absolutely sure? How might I finally decide and feel secure?

It wasn't too long after that conference, however, before Mathur Baba fell neatly into line with the pandits' opinions. Late one afternoon, just before the start of the evening *arati*, Mathur Baba came running to see me as I was rinsing Uncle's *dhoti* in the plate-washing tank. 'Hriday,' he panted, 'something truly extraordinary has happened! I was standing by a window in the *kuthi* gazing over towards the temple, and I caught sight of your Uncle, deep in thought, pacing up and down on the temple's north-eastern veranda. But as I stood and I watched him he was suddenly transformed, and in place of your Uncle I saw the goddess – I saw Ma Kali herself – quietly pacing, deep in thought, upon that same veranda, and then, when she reached the furthest extent and slowly turned around, I saw Lord Shiva, walking back towards me again. I stood there for many minutes, Hriday. I closed my eyes several times and I blinked. But when I opened them, still, it was *them*, Hriday, the Great Goddess and her holy spouse, both apparently contained within the earthly form of your beloved Uncle. I swear my heart almost stopped beating there and then. I was so filled with awe and fear that I could scarcely breathe.'

Mathur Baba covered his chest with one hand and then reached out his other to touch my forearm. I could feel that his fingers were icy cold and still trembling violently. Yet before I could speak and offer any sort of consolation he quickly continued. 'I left the *kuthi* and I ran straight to your Uncle, Hriday, and I confronted him. I told him what I had seen . . .'

'How did Uncle react?' I wondered, almost to myself.
'Your Uncle was not at all happy!' Mathur exclaimed, astonished. 'In fact he reprimanded me quite severely. "Stop all this fuss and commotion!" he snapped. "And please leave me in

188

peace! Is it not bad enough already that everyone in this temple thinks I have cast a wicked spell on you? Take control of yourself! What will they think if you continue to behave in this way?" And then he sent me off with a flea in my ear. That is why I have come to you with this news, Hriday. For who else might I possibly confide in?'

Mathur burst into noisy tears and I – humble and lowly Hriday, Mathur Baba's newest spiritual confidant – was obliged to shake water from my calloused, working hands and embrace this great and soft and wealthy patriarch as if he were merely a sobbing village boy.

In that instant I was possessed of a most powerful feeling, not of fear, nor even of compassion, but of overwhelming triumph. Perhaps I had not been so foolish after all to dedicate my services so wholeheartedly to Uncle? Because of what real import was the mere 'truth' of the matter – whether Uncle was an incarnation of God or not was surely just a trifling issue – if we had the belief and the loyalty and the support of a wealthy, powerful and influential man like Mathur Baba?

Hmmm. Interesting . . . [*plucks at chin, thoughtfully*]

Sri Ramakrishna –
Why did you choose to marry
Then live as a monk?

If you are a god
So your wife – by extension –
Must be a goddess . . .

Mustn't she?

?

OK, so we're still coming to terms with the sudden shock of the Rani's passing (although she will doubtless pass again – and again, and again – in a variety of media), and we've also painstakingly created a little elbow-room for the elusive brahmini (seamlessly! Quite seamlessly!), and before too long, we'll probably need to engage with the self-effacing conundrum that is Sri Ramakrishna's wife, Sarada Devi, aka the Holy Mother – but before we do that:

Some minor wrangles: or, well, perhaps just the one:

Remember **labon**?

Salt?

Bangladeshi for nun?

And remember Hridayram? Or Hriday? Who *serves* his great master so dutifully (and through this service, the saint claims, will find God)? Well, the English translation of his name, Hriday, actually means 'pure heart'. And sixty-two years after the death of the great Bengali saint, Sri Ramakrishna – a prophet without a prophesy, a *guru* without a system, a bizarrely exclusivist egalitarian – will come another saint (*gasp!*), hot on his heels, to this lost and chaotic and sprawling metropolis, who will breathe sharply down his neck (Ramakrishna wears his unpretentious white *dhoti* with its bright red trim, this other 'impostor' saint wears an unpretentious white sari, fringed in blue) and even (dare we say it?) threaten to partially overshadow his startling Calcuttan legacy.

She will be unconventional, too. She will sidestep all traditional formalities. She will refuse to accept government funding for her charitable endeavours because she will not waste so much as a precious second on (argh – yawn – eye-roll) *pen*-pushing. She will not embrace modernity, *per se*, only the dignity of work, of rolling up one's sleeves and mucking in, of good, honest sweat and heartfelt sacrifice.

Like Sri Ramakrishna she will eschew aversion. She will actively embrace filth. Which is fortunate. Because she is here, right here, in the heart of the slums of this belching, rotting, teeming city. She will love the unloved, the unlovable. This is her *mantra*. And there will be *no official record of her work*. Neither saint will leave their own private paper trail. To them, books – articles – lectures are all silly and worldly and stupidly vainglorious.

Ah. They are close, so close, these two.

In 1952 this other saint – this new (let's just come out and say it) *foreign* saint – will establish a Home for the Dying a stone's throw from Kalighat, the most famous and ancient of all the Kali temples, and it will be a place of selfless service called Nirmal Hriday (Home of the Pure Heart). But here their parallel journeys take somewhat different routes. Mother Teresa (for it is she – who else?) will dedicate her life to an entirely practical kind of service. She will pitch in and get her sari filthy. Then she will trudge to her un-air-conditioned cell, utterly exhausted, and wash it, herself, in a bucketful of cold water. Sri Ramakrishna? Although his legacy – in the hands of Swami Vivekananda (his beloved Naren) – will be improving and altruistic, the saint himself (the source of this great movement which will inspire the likes of Mahatma Gandhi) will be surprisingly indifferent to human suffering. He will not focus on anything – *anything* – bar the pursuit of God. He is not remotely political. He is not remotely social. He is not remotely incensed or incendiary or indignant.

Sri Ramakrishna is constantly united with God through ecstasy. But the *devi* – the goddess – has told him (many times, in many visions) that he must remain in a state called *bhava samadhi*. The Hindu scriptures teach us that once God has been fully realised the human body will naturally just shrivel away. But Sri Ramakrishna has been given a mission to serve humanity by teaching us to *see* God. And to do this (on a

practical level) he develops various techniques to try and keep
the waves of ecstasy that naturally infiltrate his body and his
consciousness – hour by hour, minute by minute, second by
second – at bay. He smokes, he chews betel, he drinks iced
water. He tries to maintain a few tiny vices. It's as if he is a hot
air balloon, floating, inexorably, up and up to heaven, but every
so often he turns down the heady stream of helium, just to lose
a bit of height. And this is where we meet up with him – as he
draws a quick breath before taking off again – on this strange
planet we call earth.

And Mother Teresa's story? It couldn't be more different. But
it is still curiously intertwined. Because she is here – is she
not? – at Kalighat (a place that Sri Ramakrishna regularly
frequented) and she is extremely unwelcome to begin with. The
building she takes over to commence saving the dying in was a
former Kali temple, but by 1952 it has been abandoned, has
fallen into a state of chronic disrepair, and is inhabited by a
group of local thieves and pickpockets who make a living out of
preying on visiting pilgrims. The local council are persuaded to
hand over the building to her. But the local people are not
happy. And why would they be? Why *should* they be? Because
what kind of a message does it transmit (uncomfortable?
Embarrassing? Colonial?) that a tiny woman – a Catholic,
more to the point – should have come to this sacred Hindu spot
to perform her do-gooding services here?

The nuns are regularly menaced and threatened. But they
refuse to be intimidated. On one occasion the Chief of Police is
called to try and calm down an angry mob that is marching on
the place intent upon its destruction. He holds back the crowd
with an outstretched palm and calmly informs them that he will
rip the home down himself, with *his own bare hands*, if a single
man or woman among them is willing to step up and promise
to perform the miserable work that the nuns are undertaking.
Nobody volunteers. The crowd disperses.

Not long after, one of the priests of the Kalighat Kali Temple collapses in the street, dying of consumption. He is covered in blood and froth. No one will approach him. But the saint, on hearing of his predicament, rushes out and gathers him up in her tiny, powerful arms. And she gives him temporary respite: a wash, a bed, a sip of something, a meal if he can manage it. She offers this poor priest of the Kali Temple a place to die, with dignity. And he gratefully accepts her offer. And all the muttering and the rumbling soon ends, after that.

But before we get *too* carried away with this . . . let's just . . . let's just retrace our steps for a moment . . .

In the popular mythology of Rani Rashmoni we are regularly informed that she established (way, way earlier than Mother Teresa; in the first half of the nineteenth century) a Home for the Dying in a place called Nimtala, where a burning *ghat* was first built in 1828. Did the Rani herself build the *ghat*? We know that she built several *ghats* (Babu *ghat*, and another in Ahiritola). Nimtala *ghat* and its cremation ground would later be much frequented by Beat Poet Allen Ginsberg and others of his ilk. Whether the Rani funded the *ghat* itself isn't made clear. But the Home for the Dying is a dead cert. Such homes get their first mentions – historically speaking – in association with the early Christian Crusaders. And what is Mother Teresa, if not a Crusader, of sorts? Although at the saint's home in Kalighat, the residents are not preached to. They are not converted. They are offered only basic care, companionship, dignity in death (insofar as that is possible), and perhaps a small mouthful of sacred Ganges water as they draw their last breath.

Mother Teresa sees God (or Jesus) in all the hopeless. When she dresses a gangrenous limb, or cleans up a pile of vomit, she is serving God-in-man.

It's worth noting that in 2010 plans were afoot to upgrade the legendary but severely dilapidated burning *ghat* at Nimtala. The great Bengali Renaissance poet, Rabindranath Tagore, was cremated there. They built a small monument in his honour. It was thought that it might be nice to change the name as a mark of respect. Although when we look back to the original name – Nimtala – we discover that its origins are in the old Neem tree that stood in that very spot, for many centuries, and under whose holy and welcoming shade, it just so happens, Job Charnock first landed in Kolkata – which was not even yet Calcutta – on 24 August 1690.

Sometimes, when you read the assorted literature on the subject, it feels as if Mother Teresa (does she take her prefix from Ma Kali? we wonder) was the first person ever to invest any concerted energy in Calcutta's lost and her dying. But what of the Rani's home? Where was it, exactly? Who ran it? And what did it consist of? History is hoarse – it has no proper voice to tell us. But what we can be quite certain of, is that these are two women – two good, clever, inventive, powerful women – working, together, in Calcutta, under Ma Kali's forbidding glare. They are creating a legacy – shaded by the *Paramahamsa*'s great, white wings – of faith and unity and tolerance and service and care.

How curious, to have two great saints in such close proximity! What does this tell us about Calcutta? I wonder. Perhaps only that it is a place most in *need* of faith. In *need* of hope. A lost place. A hungry place. A desperate place. A city run under the brutal, clear-eyed and merciless auspices of the goddess Kali. The creatress, the destroyer. The mother, the murderess.

And this is enough (isn't it?). Enough of Mother Teresa? For this book? For the Cauliflower®? With its bad haiku and its sketchy budget? Simply to know that she was there? That sixty-two years after the main event this tiny, industrious, inventive, creative, ferocious, prune-faced saint came along and took a low bow? Isn't that enough?

195

Yes?

Yes?

Although there is a bizarre footnote . . . Because one thing we
now know, much to our consternation – to our astonishment –
of this blue-tinged saint (unlike her so-recent predecessor, after
whose servant she quite unwittingly named her Home for the
Dying), is that while *he* was overwhelmed by the presence of
God, *she* was signally *under*whelmed by it. This great, modern
heroine, this mysterious power, this taut nerve of a woman
who was driven almost to distraction by her urge to serve, to
save, was actually *without* God. But nobody – aside from her
spiritual confessor – knew it. Because such was her love of God
that she made an oath to live and serve *without* him. Without
solace. Without comfort. Without inner peace. She gave it up.
She sacrificed it. And more to the point, her God *took* it. He
snatched it away from her. He left her dry and alone. Empty.
Hollow. A spiritual husk. And so she became – in her own
words – a Saint of Darkness. A black hole. And she gave up
any hope, any comfort ('consolation' the religious call it) for a
period approximating – her secret oath promised – *infinity itself.*
To serve. To inspire. She gave up her very *soul* for all eternity,
to live without love, for love.

And why? Because she loved God so much. And in her
beautifully, *crazily* warped conception of it, a true saint – a
great saint – always humbly sacrifices the thing that they love
the most.

Ah, the pair of opposites!

I give you two saints:
One quite bloated with God's love –
And the other? *Starved.*

1864, the Dakshineswar Kali Temple (six miles north of Calcutta)

There is so much great potential in Uncle, and very often it saddens me that Uncle seems determined not to make full use of it. Late on in his Tantric *sadhana*, Uncle secretly confessed to me that he was now possessed of the eight Miraculous Powers. I became most excited at this news. Uncle could – if he wished – reduce his body to the size of an atom, or have ready access to any place on earth, or realise whatever his heart desired . . .

Of course armed with such valuable information I at once set about thinking of many interesting and lucrative ways in which Uncle might make good use of these new powers of his, and Uncle – with his habitual childlike spirit – was at first very enthusiastic about my many schemes. But then, after a little while, he became uneasy and restless and said that he would go to the temple and pray to the goddess to find out which acts *she* wished to see him perform with them. When he returned from praying Uncle was very grave and sober. 'The goddess has told me that I am to hold these new powers of mine in as much esteem as I would hold excreta,' he said. From that moment onwards Uncle refused to talk of such matters with me any further. And if I dared to raise them with him – and sometimes it was hard for me to resist – he would become quite incensed.

At another time Uncle caught me deep in conversation with Mathur Baba who had enquired about the best ways in which he might secretly leave his vast inheritance to Uncle. Mathur Baba and I were coming up with all manner of excellent plans when Uncle happened to enter the room and – even though our talk immediately stopped – he somehow caught a whiff of what was being discussed (Uncle has a great talent for the reading of minds – this is one of his eight powers, after all) and became instantly furious. He accused us both of trying to ruin him and then ran away almost in tears.

I wish Uncle knew what was best for him.
I wish Uncle knew what was best for us.

Mathur Baba loves to spend his money on Uncle in any way he can. He once bought Uncle an exquisite Vaishnava shawl and presented it to him. Uncle – with the spirit of a child – took the shawl and felt its quality and admired its decoration and arranged it across his shoulders and twirled around his room in it. He was quite delighted with the gift. And so he went out into the temple grounds and pranced around in his new shawl, showing it to anyone and everyone who would care to stop and take a look. His moon face was beaming with joy and excitement. It was truly lovely to see him taking such innocent pleasure in Mathur's generous gift.

But then Uncle's mood suddenly changed. He began to scowl. 'Tell me, Hriday,' he murmured, plucking at the shawl nervously. 'Will this beautiful shawl bring me any closer to God?'
Oh how was I to answer him? My heart sank. I glanced away. I said nothing. And then before I could stop him, Uncle had ripped the shawl from his shoulders and had thrown it on to the ground and was spitting on it, with hatred, then began jumping up and down on it. Next he ran off to find a match so that he might burn it – this hateful shawl, this beautiful shawl, this expensive shawl – because it could not bring him closer to God. No. Worse even than that. Because Uncle felt that to love earthly possessions – to feel such attachments – was to be drawn further away from God.

I am only thankful that Uncle was gone for some time trying to find a match so that I could take the shawl and hide it from him.

You might be forgiven for thinking that Mathur Baba would be cross with Uncle for treating his generous gift so shabbily, but Mathur Baba, on being told of what Uncle had done, just nodded his head, approvingly. 'It is perfectly right that your Uncle should have behaved as he did.' He smiled. Because Mathur Baba can find no fault in Uncle. Which I suppose is just as well – for us all.

I love Uncle dearly. And Mathur Baba's judgement in such matters is extremely sound. But it is sometimes difficult – even for one as close to Uncle as I am – to fully comprehend which things Uncle will embrace and which he will reject. I am not accusing Uncle of inconsistency. It's just that my worldly mind cannot entirely fathom the choices Uncle makes with regard to Mathur Baba's spending. Uncle is very specific about the gorgeous Varanasi saris, or the exquisite gold jewels that he wishes to dress the image of the *devi* in, for example. No expense will be spared over those. And he will encourage Mathur Baba to spend endless amounts of money on drawing visiting pandits and *sadhus* to Dakshineswar. Which other temple offers so many wonderful gifts and incentives for its holy visitors? In fact Uncle encourages Mathur Baba to hold many spectacular concerts and performances and festivals, and of course Uncle will always be found sitting, clapping joyously, at the centre of all these. If Uncle takes a shine to a particular actor or musician or dancer then Mathur Baba will – according to the level of ecstasy or spiritual fervour they transport Uncle into – shower them with lavish gifts. But Uncle is a spiritual child, he will not just try one sweet but many sweets, and having encouraged Mathur Baba to give to one performer, he will then promptly fall in love with another and then another until even Mathur Baba's endlessly deep coffers (and his great patience) seem in danger of running dry! But what does Uncle care about such matters? When Mathur Baba's store of gifts runs out Uncle will simply take off his own clothes and present these to the actor! Uncle is a child. Just a child.

This attitude of the child has always been Uncle's natural and habitual spiritual mood. Why else is Uncle so drawn to the

200

brahmini who treats him like a mother would and lets him sit on her lap and strokes his hair and sings him songs and feeds him with chunks of creamy butter as he perches there? Although following Uncle's undertaking of the sixty-four Tantric disciplines – and his great success in all of them – Uncle and the *brahmini* hadn't rested on their laurels. They then set about exploring more fully the many spiritual moods of *bhakti yoga*, which celebrates the different forms of devotional love for a personal God. The mood of child and parent Uncle had already explored, so too that of the devoted servant to his master (in the form of the monkey chief, Hanuman), and so next Uncle took it upon himself to worship God as a lover.

It was during this time that Mathur Baba hosted the grand Annameru with Uncle's happy encouragement. Never in my life had I seen such a colourful and extravagant religious event! Mathur Baba stinted on nothing. At the heart of this festival is the customary mountain of food. Mathur Baba gave to the pandits and visitors over a thousand *maunds* of rice and the same in sesame. He handed out gold and silver and silks and every other kind of luxurious object one could possibly imagine. He hired the best and most famous singers and performers. The event lasted for many days and caused much excitement. And as I watched Uncle sitting joyfully at the centre of it all, falling constantly in and out of ecstasy, I couldn't help thinking back to when the Dakshineswar Kali Temple first opened, and how the mounds of food prepared then were just left to rot or thrown into the holy Ganga.

My, how things had changed! And who might we say was at the very root of this transformation? Was it not Uncle? Perhaps by encouraging Mathur Baba to spend so selflessly and extravagantly on others, Uncle himself (who is given pride of place by Mathur Baba at every wonderful celebration) was unwittingly gaining the credit and the attention and the admiration of all those who attended? Was not Uncle the true host of this magnificent event? And all without having spent a single rupee himself?

Oh, Uncle is not nearly so foolish and innocent as he might at first appear! Uncle is truly a genius! And where is the harm in it? Because if the people learn to love Uncle and Uncle loves the goddess then surely only God himself is the ultimate victor?

Of course not everything connected to the Annameru was unstintingly positive. It was at this time that Uncle's mother, Chandradevi, decided to visit the temple in person to see her son, and then resolved to stay on. She was now determined to live out her last days close to the holy Ganga. And Uncle was most delighted to have her staying with him because he loves his mother dearly. I was not quite so happy because I am the person who cares for Uncle, and now, I suppose, I am also the person who must care for his ancient mother.

I think it only fair to say that Chandradevi and I have never been especially close. There has never been any serious animus between the two of us. It is simply what they like to call 'a clash of personalities'. For some reason Chandradevi has never trusted Hridayram. He can see it in her eyes. Or perhaps it is only that he serves her son so well that she is sometimes at pains to find ways to serve him herself, and thus her pride is wounded? Who knows?

Whatever the reason, Chandradevi quickly established herself in the tiny storeroom at the foot of the *nahabat* close to the Bakultala *ghat*. It is an inhospitable space but she seems perfectly content with it. And Mathur Baba is very happy to have her there because they can talk endlessly about Uncle together. Chandradevi loves to reminisce about Uncle's childhood. But she is a simple soul and much given to curious flights of fancy. I once heard her telling Mathur Baba about the circumstances of Uncle's conception: of how her husband, Kshudiram, was on pilgrimage in Gaya, to absolve the sins of his ancestors, and on his final day made an offering in the

202

temple of Vishnu. He was filled with a great sense of lightness and joy on this occasion, and that night, while he slept, he had a strange dream in which he entered the temple again and saw all his ancestors lined up before him. He was so happy to see them! He fell down in tears and took the dust off their feet in gratitude. And as he lay there a glorious light filled the entire temple, emanating from a Divine Being (was it not Vishnu himself?), who spoke to him, saying that he was so delighted with Kshudiram's service that he would be born to him as a child so that Kshudiram might continue to serve him. Kshudiram appealed to the Being not to follow this plan because his circumstances were so humble, but the Divine Being would not be dissuaded.

When Kshudiram returned home from his pilgrimage (Chandradevi continued), he made no mention of his dream to his wife, but she, without any prompting, asked if it were possible for a Divine Being to sleep in a human bed, because one night, while her husband was absent, such a Being had appeared in the bed beside her. A few days later, on entering a temple of our Lord Shiva, she had noticed waves of divine light emanating from the image and moving towards her, and before she could tell her friends about it, the waves had engulfed her and her surprise was so great that she had promptly swooned.

A short while later – greatly advanced in years as she was – she discovered that she was pregnant.

Such are the stories that Chandradevi tells to Mathur. In truth, I cannot remember if I have heard these stories before. I must confess that they seem somehow familiar. And – like Uncle – Chandradevi is incapable of calculation. She is very innocent. She is naive and silly. Although I would never go so far as to call her an imbecile. She is my aunt, after all.

I know that Chandradevi is happy to be here, and her needs are few. In this regard she is just like Uncle. She does not miss her village home because the rumours about Uncle had been a kind of torture to her simple soul. The villagers had accused Uncle of all kinds of craziness in his pursuit of God – many of which were of course perfectly true. And now Chandradevi is to be here in Dakshineswar, close to her beloved son, to witness some of these crazy behaviours for herself! Perhaps, in time, she will even start to feel that remaining close to Uncle is not such an undiluted blessing after all?

Because the meandering river of Uncle's *sadhana* has taken another strange turn of late. In his desire to perfect his worship in the divine mood of the lover (*madhura bhava*), Uncle has decided to focus all his attention on his beloved Krishna. And the best way to love Krishna, Uncle says, is by imitating the behaviour of his most ardent admirer, Radha. And so this is what Uncle does.

Uncle has lately transformed himself into a woman to offer his love to his most dearly beloved. And Mathur Baba is there to indulge Uncle in all his desires in this regard. Having thrown away the shawl in complete disgust, Uncle has now permitted Mathur Baba to buy him the most glorious saris and bodices and jewels and the most expensive, handmade wig, and Uncle dresses up in them at every opportunity and behaves exactly as a woman would. This has caused great consternation at the temple where people mutter that such behaviour – such *luxury* – is inappropriate to a man who has renounced all connections to the material world. But Uncle and Mathur don't care a jot. Everything about Uncle has now become feminine: his voice, his walk, his laugh, his interests, his conversation. I – Hridayram – am now serving a woman. This makes me feel very uncomfortable. I have lately taken a wife and it is hard to explain all this to her. She is frightened of Uncle, and she is frustrated that I am spending so much time in his service, and in the service of his mother, too. When will I ever get around to serving *her?* she wonders.

Uncle now spends much of his average day in the company of women. Recently he moved into the women's apartments in Mathur Baba's Janbazar home and has become one of the family. The other women accept him completely as one of their own. At times even I have trouble recognising Uncle as he moves among them.

Uncle still loves to make ornate flower arrangements and to decorate the Radha-Govinda image at the temple with them. He also prays to the goddess that she will permit him to have Krishna as his 'spiritual husband'. Perhaps the goddess is jealous of losing her favourite child's exclusive attention (in the way a mother can sometimes be jealous of sharing her favourite son with a new daughter-in-law?), because for some reason this part of Uncle's *sadhana* is unbearably slow, and Uncle is becoming perfectly disconsolate. He is lovelorn. It is so strong, this loneliness of Uncle's, that it has started to remind me of many years ago when Uncle first pined for the love of the Divine Mother. He is refusing his food. He cannot sleep. That burning sensation is back once more. He moans and wails and claws at his clothes. But he does so in a most beguiling and feminine manner. Uncle cries like a girl. He says that the bones in his body seem all disconnected with unrequited love. He finds it difficult to move. He is disjointed. He can hardly walk, just totter around and then swoon.

I have a new wife at home and suddenly it feels as though I have a new wife here at the Dakshineswar Kali Temple. But she is a bad wife. The worst wife. She is a mad wife. She is perfectly demented.

Oh, how am I possibly to make sense of Uncle's *sadhana*? How many different courses can this unpredictable river run? How many ways can one man hope to see God? Why is Uncle not simply contented with all the great bounty he has earned so far? How can Uncle choose to put us through such torture, just when it finally seems like things are starting to go so well for us all? I wish I could understand it! I just wish I could make some sense – however small – of the great and most perplexing mystery of Uncle!

Why practise so hard?　　　[*you may ask?*]
I must live an austere life
As an example!

[*duh!*]
. . .

If you undertake
A *fraction* of what I do
Then you will see God!

NB

Keep focused on God.
And public opinion?
Ha! Just spit on it!

A Chapter of Accidents

(Oh, all right. Let's just call it A Page or Two of Accidents)

In 1865 (approximately)

Sri Ramakrishna enters a sudden and unexpected state of
ecstasy and inadvertently topples into a smouldering pan of
charcoal. He has to be pulled out, still unconscious. His hand is
badly burned and it takes several months to heal.

Some time later . . .

In the middle of the night Sri Ramakrishna is suddenly
possessed by the idea that he is Radha and goes to the Rani's
beautiful flower gardens to pick roses for her beloved Krishna.
While so doing he unexpectedly enters *samadhi* (ecstasy). He is
eventually found by a watchman, still unconscious, tangled up
in the bushes, bruised and covered in scratches.

Some time later . . .

While walking to the Kali Temple, Sri Ramakrishna enters a
sudden and unexpected state of ecstasy and collapses to the
ground, his arm badly twisted under the dead weight of his
torso. The arm is broken. The *guru* is very confused when
he eventually regains consciousness. His wrist is carefully
bandaged, but the saint persists in pulling the bandages off and
wailing like a toddler. He can't understand this injury. Why
would the goddess allow something so dreadful to happen to
her faithful servant? He walks around, showing his broken

wrist to anyone who will take an interest, and – much to his long-suffering devotees' consternation – plaintively asks if they know how to cure it. He remains for what seems like an inordinately long duration in the mood of an utterly forlorn and betrayed infant.

Some time later . . .

One morning everyone suddenly realises that Sri Ramakrishna is missing in action. A search party is sent out but the *guru* is not found. Ramakrishna's wife, Sarada Devi, flies into a terrible panic. She is convinced that Sri Ramakrishna has entered an unexpected state of ecstasy while standing by one of the temple *ghats* and has fallen into the Ganga and drowned.

People are growing increasingly convinced of this and are, quite naturally, deeply traumatised, when the saint is finally discovered in the dense thicket beyond the *panchavati,* cheerfully meditating under a spiky bush, the bottom of his tender feet cut to ribbons by thorns.

And all too often . . .

Visits to the museum, the circus, the theatre, the park etc. are destroyed when the excited *Paramahamsa* inadvertently enters a state of ecstasy and has to be carried – limp and insensible – back to his hired carriage and promptly driven home. Everything reminds the *Paramahamsa* of God. God sends the *Paramahamsa* into ecstasy.

Sometimes the *guru* feels the odd moment of pique that the goddess is always so determined to cut short his measure of earthly enjoyment. It's so irritating that he never makes it as far as the giraffe enclosure at the zoo because the lion always calls

to his mind an image of the goddess Durga (often depicted in Hindu art riding a lion as her steed), and then . . .
Ooops! There he goes! Quickly! Catch him, Hriday!

Aw. Just when everyone was starting to have themselves a little bit of fun, horrid, old God felt the need to elbow his way in and spoil it all.

:(

Samadhi:

We call it a gift . . .
But when you think about it,
Isn't it a curse?

1864. Several pages of lost and quite badly water-damaged jottings by an amateur anthropologist:

... of two Bengali Hindoos and their curious activities at the Dakshineswar 'Kali' Temple during the course of several weeks in the Summer of 1864. While my Hindi is excellent, I'm afraid that my Bengali is — at best — rudimentary, and both subjects are fluent in

. . . moon-faced and rather charming young man who is often addressed as 'Sri' Ramakrishna and is a permanent resident at the Temple where he lives in a large corner room of the owner's private house (or 'kuthi'). 'Sri' Ramakrishna – henceforth SR – is very highly regarded by the wealthy Temple owner (a broad, amiable, giant-mustachioed gentleman), to the extent of having his own personal servant.

&

(2) An older monk from . . . (not yet certain), who is much less social and gregarious than SR and is known by the name of Jatadhari. Jatadhari is an itinerant 'Sannyasi' who recently visited the temple to attend a lavish festival being held there (see notes re. 'Annameru'). He has stayed on, although plainly a very quiet and anti-social character by nature, presumably due to his having recently established a relationship with the aforementioned SR.

It should probably be noted that SR is often to be seen worshipping the statue of the Temple Goddess Kali while dressed in women's clothing. He sings and fans the statue with a special 'Chamara' (or blonde-coloured, yak-tail whisk). When SR dresses as a woman – in sari and bodice, wig and veil – he does so quite convincingly. Jatadhari wears the traditional ochre cloth of a monk. Jatadhari seems to find nothing strange in SR's dressing as a woman (although I have noticed that several of the Temple officials and some of the other Temple priests find the presence of SR somewhat grating . . . It is entirely possible that the Temple owner has hired the servant as a kind of bodyguard for his unconventional protégé). SR likes to

... *Jatadhari* which appears to be predicated on *Jatadhari's* obsessive regard for a pendant (or amulet) he wears of the Hindoo God Rama as a child (they call him, in the child state, '*Ramalala*'). *Jatadhari* spends much of his day worshipping this pendant. From experience I know that the God Rama is generally worshipped with flowers, fruits and buttermilk. Mondays and Saturdays are auspicious days of worship for this particular Hindoo God.

Nobody at the Temple appears especially concerned by *Jatadhari's* activities aside from SR who seems to have taken a special interest in him.

At first this interest consisted in SR sitting a short distance away from *Jatadhari* and witnessing his worship in a respectful manner.
It soon became clear during the course of several days, however, that SR had observed something special about *Jatadhari's* worship (I am uncertain of what this may be – possibly just his great application and quiet yet intense focus on his Chosen Deity).

. . . respectful observation, SR acquired a number of essential provisions (he seems to have unlimited access to the Temple stores) to aid Jatadhari in his worship. The monk was evidently very pleased by SR's interest in his activities,

. . . prone to entering what the Hindoos like to call 'a state of ecstasy' (Samadhi). When this happens his mouth smiles, his eyes roll back in his skull and he will suddenly lose all

. . . approached Jatadhari and asked if he might be initiated by the monk into his very particular form of worship (initiation in this instance would be by dint of the acquisition of a special 'mantra', i.e. a Sanskrit sound, word or syllable which is held by the Hindoo to contain its own intrinsic, spiritual power). Jatadhari seemed perfectly happy to oblige him (I did not actually observe the initiation ceremony). Following his initiation SR would sit, utterly still, for hour after hour, just gazing at the amulet. His bodyguard would call him for meals but SR just ignored his increasingly frustrated appeals

. . . unkempt. The wig sitting rather lopsidedly on his head. It soon became evident that SR had lost all ability to close his eyes. I approached him at one point and asked, in Hindi, if he would close his eyes for me. He seemed to understand what I was saying but his eyes were unblinking. I blinked my own eyes at him, repeatedly, but he just shook his head and laughed. He tried to force his eyes shut with his fingers but he could not. He offered me a chance to try for myself and I did. The eyes were

. . . closer inspection that they were actually caring for an imaginary child, which both men are able to see running around them.

It should be noted that Jatadhari is very patient with the child, very quiet around it (is eager not to draw attention to himself in this regard), but SR – the more exuberant personality – seems to find the child quite exasperating. Yesterday afternoon I witnessed SR trying to take his leave of the child (the child is typically to be found in and/or around the general location of Jatadhari's special amulet). The child refused to allow SR to take his leave of it. From SR's behaviour it appeared to be repeatedly calling him back to spend time with it. On one occasion the child pulled at his hair and SR yelled furiously. On another occasion the imaginary child went running towards the Hooghly River and both men were to be seen bounding after it, presumably to stop it from

Sri Ramakrishna says:

It's good to question!
Scepticism is a path
To realise God.

Five strange incidents involving the Master's first 'Supplier of Provisions', Mathur Nath Biswas

1) 1866 approximately

Mathur Nath Biswas is aware of the fact that Sri Ramakrishna is fully capable of transmitting the state of ecstasy (which the saint experiences regularly) merely by dint of the lightest of touches. He is not an especially spiritual man – and cheerfully admits as much – but is very eager to experience this seemingly magical state, so he asks Sri Ramakrishna to touch him and let him feel it. Sri Ramakrishna tries to persuade Mathur that this is not a wise idea. The Master instinctively knows which types of devotion are most beneficial to his individual devotees (in Mathur's case his easiest path to God is through loyal service to his *guru*, i.e. Sri Ramakrishna himself . . .

I have cooked the food
I have laid it on a plate
Just eat and enjoy!).

But Mathur (a man who greatly appreciates his earthly pleasures – so why not now heavenly ones to boot?) doggedly persists. The Master diligently tries to fob Mathur off with his stock response, i.e. that he has no personal power to transform anyone at will, that only the Divine Mother has this power, and he acts solely through her. Still, Mathur nags away at Sri Ramakrishna until eventually the saint promises to ask the Mother and see what she decides. Mathur goes home, mollified.

A couple of days later, Mathur suddenly experiences the state of *bhhava samadhi* (a lower state of ecstasy in which the individual still retains some measure of normal consciousness). He finds the experience devastating. He is unable to get anything done, make any decisions. He bursts into tears, constantly. His heart pounds. After three days trapped in this joyful hell he sends for Sri Ramakrishna, collapses to the ground in front of him and clasps both of his feet. He wants the Master to take away this state of ecstasy. He cannot endure it. His life has become completely unmanageable.

'But you begged me for this, Mathur!' Sri Ramakrishna exclaims.

'I know, I *know*, but my life is in ruins!' Mathur bleats. 'Ecstasy suits *you*, Father. But it's not *right* for the rest of us. Just take it away, take it away, *please*!'

Sri Ramakrishna – after a few seconds of delicious procrastination – lightly touches Mathur's chest with his hand and Mathur instantly returns to his normal, ebullient, generous and unapologetically worldly self once more.

Phew!

2) Around two years earlier

Mathur's wife, the Rani's daughter Jagadamba, is struck
down with a severe case of dysentery. After several weeks of
intensive treatment her doctors declare that there is nothing
more they can do for her. Utterly desperate, Mathur comes to
see Sri Ramakrishna and asks him if he can help. Of course
Sri Ramakrishna will never countenance the idea of using his
so-called 'occult powers' unless the Mother wills it. But the
case of Jagadamba is slightly different, as Mathur cogently
explains . . . His vast inheritance, it transpires, is *entirely
dependent* on the survival of his wife (who is the actual heir to
the Rani's immense estate). If Jagadamba dies, Mathur makes
clear, not only will he – Mathur – lose all his money, but he
will also lose his controlling interest in the Kali Temple.

Ah, what is a poor *guru* to do under such circumstances?
Suddenly (quite miraculously) the saint's tender heart is filled
with compassion. 'Don't worry,' he assures Mathur, 'your wife
will be cured.'
By the time Mathur Nath Biswas reaches home that night,
Jagadamba is already commencing her miraculous recovery.

And the Master? The very moment Jagadamba's health starts
to improve, Sri Ramakrishna is struck down with a chronic
case of dysentery himself. It torments him for six months. He
suffers quite dreadfully.

The Mother does have a rather dark sense of humour.

3) 1865, or thereabouts

During Sri Ramakrishna's practice of *madhura bhava* (or the sweet/conjugal mood) Mathur holds a spectacular five-day festival at his magnificent home in Janbazar for the Durga *Puja*. Such is Mathur's enjoyment of this festival that, as it draws to its natural climax – and the magnificent image of Durga is to be taken and immersed in the Ganga – Mathur becomes overwhelmed by a spirit of childish petulance and suddenly refuses – point-blank – to say the final prayer.

He has a monumental public meltdown and (certainly not for the first time in his life) behaves like a toddler who has devoured rather more red sweets than are entirely good for him. He is completely over-stimulated. He will not stand for the festival to be done with and for the prevailing mood of celebration and communion and extravagance and blissfulness to be brought to an end. He becomes utterly hysterical and threatens bloodshed – or worse – if anyone tries to take the image away from him. He begins to guard it, ferociously. Mathur's wife, Jagadamba, and several other people try their best to talk some sense into him, but Mathur refuses to be altered from his course. This festival will go on FOR EVER (d'you hear?) or he will not be held responsible for the consequences!

Eventually Jagadamba – in total desperation – calls on Sri Ramakrishna.

Sri Ramakrishna goes to see Mathur and asks him why he will not let the priest immerse the image. Mathur says that he loves the Mother too much and that he cannot bear to be separated from her, so the worship must simply continue on indefinitely. Like an overwrought and (let's face it) over-indulged teenage girl, Mathur – at this precise moment in time – simply CANNOT LIVE without the Mother.

Sri Ramakrishna listens attentively to Mathur and then smiles (who better than he to understand such spiritual and emotional excesses?).

'What does it matter if the image is taken to the river?' he murmurs, lightly rubbing Mathur's chest as he speaks. 'Surely this . . .' – his hand rests over Mathur's frantically beating heart – 'is where the Mother truly dwells?'

Mathur is immediately calmed by the *guru*'s touch and promptly allows (much to everyone's abundant relief) the image to be taken away and immersed.

4) 14 July 1871

On this day, at 5 p.m., Mathur Nath Biswas, Sri Ramakrishna's
most loving and generous benefactor (aside from the Divine
Mother herself, of course) breathes his last following a vicious
attack of typhoid fever. During his brief illness, Mathur's
beloved *guru*, Sri Ramakrishna, never pays him a visit (perhaps
because typhoid is contagious). The *guru* sends Hriday, his
nephew, to Mathur's home each day (or perhaps Hriday goes
of his own volition) for regular updates on Mathur's progress.
The day that Mathur dies, Sri Ramakrishna enters a long period
of *samadhi* in the late afternoon. When he emerges from it he
tells his nephew that Mathur has passed away at five o'clock.
This fact is duly confirmed a short while later. When people –
years after – ask the *guru* if Mathur (in exchange for his
extraordinary fifteen years of service to the *avatar*) escaped the
dreaded burden of rebirth, the *guru* merely mutters that when
he died Mathur 'still had a taste for enjoyment'.
Earthly attachments, it seems, are a serious long-term
stumbling block to eternal bliss (no matter how great and
generous and heartfelt your service).

Uh . . .
So that's a resounding 'no', in other words.

5) *1869 or thereabouts*

Mathur develops a giant abscess (its location is undisclosed; but
creative licence dictates that we imagine it pulsating, ominously,
on the cheek of one buttock) and is forced to stay in bed for
many weeks. During this time he constantly begs for Sri
Ramakrishna to pay him a visit, but the hard-hearted *guru*
simply ignores his requests. Messenger after messenger is
haughtily informed by the *guru* that he has no power to cure
the abscess so there is simply no point in him visiting Mathur.
The plaintive requests continue to roll in until eventually
(probably under pressure from Hriday) a grumpy Sri
Ramakrishna goes to visit his richest and most generous
devotee. Mathur, in evident agony, delighted to see the Master,
reaches out a hand from his sickbed and whispers, 'You
have come! Please, will you give me a little of the dust off
your feet?'
Sri Ramakrishna gazes down at him suspiciously. 'Why?' he
snarks. 'Will it cure your abscess?'
Mathur is mortified. 'I have a doctor to cure my abscess,
Father,' he insists. 'I want the dust off your feet simply to guide
me through the ocean of *maya*.'
At this, the reluctant *guru* enters a state of ecstasy and Mathur
is finally able to place his head on to the *guru*'s feet and receive
his blessing.
He recovers shortly after.

Sri Ramakrishna has many visions of God in many different forms, but ultimately . . .

If given the choice,
I love to see God's *lila*
As a human being.

There have been so many dreadful arguments over recent days
that poor Uncle has become quite exhausted with it all. This
tense atmosphere is not good for Uncle. He has returned to his
home village to recuperate after an especially exhausting phase of
his *sadhana* combined with the after-effects of the severe case
of dysentery which Uncle says he took upon himself voluntarily
in exchange for the life of Mathur Baba's wife, Jagadamba.

Some of the tension has been between Uncle's wife Sarada
and the *brahmini*. Uncle's wife – still a young girl, but with a
most obliging and modest nature – has come from her father's
village to visit us and Uncle is delighting in teaching her many
valuable spiritual and domestic lessons. Uncle is, of course,
most particular about how a home should be run, and how a
person should deal with their neighbour, and what is the best
kind of cloth or bowl. I know to my cost that Uncle is just as
fastidious concerning his domestic affairs as he is with regard to
his spiritual life. And Sarada is very happy to learn from her
husband. She is a most serious and receptive pupil.

But the *brahmini* seems to feel that Uncle is wasting his time
with such piddling preoccupations, that Uncle should be turning
his mind to higher issues.

Sarada would never be so forward as to direct a word of
criticism towards someone so lofty and wise and clever as the
brahmini, but it is plain for all eyes to see that a war of sorts
is being fought between the women of the house over the
ownership of Uncle. And everyone must take their side – apart
from Uncle himself, of course, whose mind is far too elevated
to dwell upon such petty matters.

The *brahmini* is strong meat – especially in the eyes of the
local women, who are honest but simple creatures by and
large. They follow caste and other rules and traditions most

ferociously. The *brahmini* is an independent spirit, however, and she is accustomed to living freely and unselfconsciously with only her heart as her guide.

Well, everything came to a head when a villager of lower caste came to visit Uncle and was provided with a meal. Caste rules dictate that this man should clear away his own dish after eating, but the *brahmini* – who was perhaps a little too eager to show off her powerful position in Uncle's household – simply took the dish away herself. Of course at the temple such behaviour may be tolerated, but not here in Uncle's village. Immense distress was caused by the *brahmini*'s behaviour and all the women were in a terrible flap about it. Did the *brahmini* care about this? Not at all! She thought the women were being small-minded and ridiculous. The women were profoundly injured by the *brahmini*'s attitude. Eventually I was obliged to step in on behalf of the women and I'm sad to confess that a great store of ill-feeling that had been festering for many years between myself and the *brahmini* was now brought out into the light. The *brahmini* accused Hridayram of being ignorant and controlling – of exploiting Uncle for his own selfish gain. Hridayram accused the *brahmini* of identical crimes. A dreadful atmosphere was thereby created. And these arguments continued to bubble and to fester until, thoroughly tired and exasperated, Hridayram was eventually forced to draw Uncle's attention to them so that he might use his wisdom and his authority to calm things down a little. Uncle was most upset that such a bad atmosphere had been generated by something so small and insignificant as the casual removal of a dish, but instead of rounding on Hridayram – or the women of his house – he turned and told the *brahmini* that her behaviour had been inappropriate. The *brahmini* did not take this criticism seriously at first. She thought Uncle was just joking. But more fool the *brahmini*, because anyone who is truly close to Uncle knows that while he himself has thrown off the burden of caste as a part of his *sadhana*, he by no means advocates such behaviours in others less far advanced in their spiritual journeys than himself. Quite the opposite in fact. Uncle holds that in order to move past the constricting burdens of social and caste rules, we must first obey them with great diligence and understand their significance. He could see why these rules served an important purpose in the spiritual lives of the village women. For all his many eccentricities, Uncle has never been a believer in throwing the baby out with the bath water.

The *brahmini* is of course accustomed to playing the role of mother with Uncle (indeed, with us all), but in this instance Uncle would not play his accustomed role of child. He did not back down with her and so she soon became very angry with him. It was sad to see. She felt betrayed by Uncle, and confused. But then she went off on her own and considered the situation very deeply for a while. She realised – much to her horror – that she had broken her own golden rule and had become much too attached to Uncle. In her desire to teach and nurture him she had forgotten her own path, her real calling: that of a true renunciate – a *sannyasin*.

So it was with many tears and some embarrassment and regret that she decided to leave Uncle and move on. In a matter of hours she was gone. All the tension instantly left the household.

Uncle loves the *brahmini*, but in truth I think he had already outgrown her. After completing his *sadhana* of the *madhura bhava* and having been granted extraordinary visions of first Radha and then his beloved Krishna, Uncle's mind had now finally begun to turn towards the ultimate *sadhana*: the non-dual discipline of the Vedanta. The goal of *sayujya*, of bodylessness, of *nirvana*.

For anyone familiar with Uncle's immense attachment to the Divine Mother this might seem to be a controversial decision by Uncle. How might he possibly hope to step beyond the goddess who is the beginning and the end of all his spiritual aspirations? Ah, who may hope to answer this question? Not a worm such as me! Although Uncle's tastes are notoriously catholic. Like a child, he is naturally most curious and promiscuous. Yet did the Mother not dwell at the very core of his heart and soul? Was the Mother not the very roots of the green and sprouting tree of Uncle?

At around this time two important people arrived at the Kali Temple. The first was Uncle's beloved nephew Akshay – the son of Uncle's brother Ramkumar – who came to the temple to take the place of Haladhari. Akshay is most beloved by us all, and, like Uncle, a great spiritual aspirant. The second person to come was an itinerant *Paramahamsa* who Uncle simply called Tota Puri or the Naked One. Tota Puri was a tall, gaunt and severe-faced mendicant with long and matted hair. He had been wandering for who may guess how long from his home in central India through to Bengal, travelling from temple to temple to teach and to share his great spiritual wisdom. He remained in no place for more than three days before he moved on. Tota Puri – as a serious practitioner of the non-dual discipline – had no time at all for idol worship which (like others of this disposition) he held in great contempt. On one occasion when watching Uncle clapping his hands and chanting the Mother's name, as was his wont, Tota Puri sharply demanded, 'Ha! Are you fashioning *chapattis* that you clap your hands like this?!' To a refined mind such as Tota Puri's one may only hope to see *Isvara* (the indivisible *brahman* united with its power) through the path of the intellect – by a calculated act of the will.

But after arriving by boat at the *ghat* his eyes were for some reason irresistibly drawn to Uncle who was sitting in the pleasing shade of the *chandni*, wearing only his simple cloth, radiating sweetness and holiness as Uncle inevitably must. Immediately Tota Puri approached Uncle and asked if he had learned, or might be interested in learning, the Vedantic discipline. Uncle considered this question and then answered in a manner typical of himself: 'I have no idea of what I should or shouldn't do. Only Mother knows. I do as Mother commands.'

Perhaps thinking that Uncle referred to his own birth mother, Chandradevi (who had always harboured a deep horror of Uncle becoming a mendicant monk), Tota Puri thought hard for a moment and then said to Uncle, 'Well, go and ask your mother. I shall not be here for very long.'

Without another word Uncle went to ask the Divine Mother at the temple and she told him that Tota Puri had been sent to teach him. Uncle returned to the Naked One, quite beaming with joy, and agreed to become his pupil, but only on the understanding that the main part of the initiation (where Uncle would shave his head and remove his sacred thread) might take place in private for fear of distressing poor Chandradevi.

And so it was. After a period of intense discipline and learning, late one night, in the *panchavati*, the *Homa* fire was lit and Uncle made offerings for the satisfaction of his ancestors, and to his own soul. Many sacred *mantra*s were uttered and oblations made, including Uncle's sacred thread and his tuft of hair. Next Uncle sat with Tota Puri inside the wooden meditation hut, dressed in an ochre cloth and *taupinas* and the Naked One guided Uncle in the familiar instruction of *not-this, not-this*, whereby Uncle would imagine everything in the world – everything of name and form – and then turn himself away from it, mentally, while identifying himself, all along, only with God – with consciousness-knowledge-bliss – with the indivisible *Brahman*.

Well, it did not take Uncle long to enter into a semi-trance-like state, but just as soon as he did he was confronted by his beloved Kali, the Divine Mother, his companion and inspiration throughout his many years of *sadhana*. How might he possibly hope to escape her holy form? Time and time again Uncle listened to the instructions of Tota Puri and time and time again Uncle closed his eyes and saw the Mother. Finally he exclaimed, in despair, 'It cannot be done! I cannot dive into the self! I cannot resist form!'

Of course Tota Puri was profoundly exasperated. He looked around him, scowling furiously, until his eye alighted upon a sharp shard of glass which he took up and stabbed between Uncle's eyebrows, exclaiming, 'Concentrate on *this*!'

Uncle did not flinch or falter. He closed his eyes tightly, concentrated with all his will, and when the form of the Divine Mother appeared before him – as he knew that she must – he took in his hand the sword of knowledge and savagely chopped his great beloved in half with it.

Ahhhh! At once – without hesitation – like a small stone falling through warm, clear water, Uncle descended from the world of name and form and into *nirvikalpa samadhi*. Tota Puri left the meditation hut and sat outside it for three days and nights, waiting for Uncle to re-emerge. But Uncle did not re-emerge. Finally, the Naked One entered the hut and discovered Uncle sitting exactly as when he had left him, the shard of glass still rammed between his eyebrows. Uncle was perfectly still. There were no signs of life in him. No emergence of breath. No movement of the chest. Tota Puri was astonished. He could not believe that Uncle had attained the ultimate Vedantic state within only three days of practice – a state that it had taken him forty long years to achieve. And so – after a brief period spent in considerable awe and wonderment – the Naked One began the laborious process of drawing back Uncle's consciousness to his stiffened, lifeless body by various subtle means and devices, not to mention the loud and cacophonous reciting of the appropriate holy *mantras*.

Tota Puri remained at the Kali Temple for nine months with Uncle, establishing him very firmly in the *nirvikalpa* plain of consciousness, and when he finally departed, Uncle – who will never do anything by half measures – determined to remain in that plain of non-duality – completely merged with God – for an uninterrupted period of six months.

You cannot imagine what torment this decision unleashed upon us! For who else might be expected to take care of Uncle's mother during this most dangerous and secretive phase of Uncle's *sadhana*? Hridayram, of course! Chandradevi was already very over-protective towards Uncle and frightened of losing yet another of her beloved sons, so to protect her from Uncle's activities Akshay and Hridayram between them undertook a careful balancing act – forever struggling to keep Chandradevi preoccupied and distracted.

Uncle's mother – who we already know had never been especially fond of Hridayram, nor he, indeed, of her – now began to develop the idea that Hridayram was in fact an evil and conniving devil, only intent upon exploiting and manipulating her poor, innocent son. And as if this was not hardship enough, anyone with a small measure of scriptural knowledge must surely know that to remain in the non-dual plane of consciousness for any lengthy period of time is immensely dangerous to a person's physical health. So with Tota Puri now gone, how was Hridayram to make Uncle – who sat immersed in *samadhi* like an unresponsive rock – perform all his necessary bodily functions? How might Hridayram hope to make Uncle eat or drink or wash or defecate?

Two things alone helped us to survive this considerable trial – by far the most trying and dangerous period of Uncle's *sadhana*. The first was the welcome assistance of a monk who arrived at the temple around this time, and – being an expert in this field – helped Hridayram to feed and maintain Uncle (sometimes, I confess, only through acts of minor violence). The second was a vision that Uncle had been granted from the Divine Mother – a vision he had been granted on three occasions, in fact — which calmly informed him that for the benefit of mankind he would soon be obliged to descend from the *nirvikalpa* plain and instead remain in *bhavamukha*, a lower plain of dual consciousness. What would we have done without this holy instruction? Where might we have ended up without the Divine Mother's timely help and guidance? Truly, truly, *truly*, it does not even bear thinking about.

The great Indian saint Ramprasad (a passionate adherent of the 'sweet' mood, and worshipper of Ma Kali) once said — rather cynically — of nirvikalpa samadhi/the non-dual worship:

We adore sugar,
But we just want to *taste* it,
Not to become it!

A brief diversion to the Camargue:

24 May. In perpetuity. Saintes-Maries-de-la-Mer, France

Just over a thousand years ago, the dark-skinned Romany
peoples from northern India first arrived in Europe. This original
group quickly fractured. Some – the Gitanos – ended up in
Spain where they are justly celebrated for their flamenco music.
The Roms – with their ancient language – inhabit central
Europe. The Manouches – also musical – travelled up to the
north. The Romany culture was – and remains – a culture of
displacement, of persecution, of marginalisation, of movement.

A thousand years earlier (the year 42), we are told that the
three Marys (Mary Magdalene, Mary Salome, Mary Jacobe:
all of whom – the Gospels tell us – bore witness to Christ's
crucifixion) have arrived in a seaside town in Gaul after being
sent out of Palestine during the Christian persecutions in a boat
without sails and without oars.

This town will later be called Saintes-Maries-de-la-Mer, and
the supposed relics of the Marys will be held and venerated in
a Catholic church there.

These Marys will prove contentious – if only because there
are so many of them. Aside from these three there are several
others, too. There is the Mother of God, Mary. There is Mary
of Bethany. There is the prostitute Mary who rubs perfumed oil
on Jesus's feet.

So many of them! So many Marys. And the fractured
narrative of Christianity sometimes mixes them up and confuses
them. In the complex figure of the Magdalene they become pre-
eminent one moment (she is the first person to speak to the

risen Christ) and then marginalised the next (roundly condemned as a woman of ill virtue). So many women sharing just one name! Marys, Marys everywhere . . .

In 1521 another saint will join this mess of Marys at Saintes-Maries-de-la-Mer: St Sara, described as 'a charitable woman that helped people by collecting alms, which led to the popular belief that she was a gypsy.'

But this newer saint, this *arriviste*, this impostor saint, Sara, also has many faces. In some accounts she is Mary Jacobe's black Egyptian maid. In others she is a Rom, living on the banks of the Rhône, following a polytheistic faith (the statue of Ishtari – goddess of fertility, sexuality and war – is carried into the water and immersed, every year, so that benediction may be received by the Rom peoples). This polytheistic Sara is blessed with a vision that the three Marys who witnessed the death of Jesus are coming to France in a boat. St Sara the Kali goes to the beach and sees them, and through her prayers and her assistance they are brought safely into shore. She is a kind of pre-post idol-worshipping Christian midwife. A saint of welcome.

Of course because this story takes place over a thousand years prior to the Romany people's first arrival in France we must view it as a kind of wishful thinking; a rewriting of history, a helpful (nay, even opportunistic) Romany-style piggy-backing on to the early – first-generation – Christian story. It's a poignantly juxtaposed symbolic re-enactment of the economic, social and spiritual welcome the Romanies themselves most desperately hoped for (and still hope for) in Europe.

In the nineteenth century a tradition begins of the relics of the three Marys being taken from the church down to the Mediterranean to commemorate their journey.

In 1935 the Marquis de Baroncelli (a French writer, cattle farmer, friend of the Romanies and fierce proponent of the culture and traditions of the Camargue) persuades the Catholic Church to allow the Romany peoples to take their own St Sara (a black-faced, doll-like creature with a red ribbon at her neck) down to the sea.

She is Black Sara, saint of the Romanies. She is a saint with many roots, of many origins. Like Kali she plays with time. Like Durga she is taken to the water. She is accepted by the Catholic Church – tolerated – but formally unrecognised. She aims to include but often alienates (the little town she lives in finds the massive, annual influx of Romanies – often intent on arranging marriages, making money and settling scores – both terrifying and overwhelming). She is the saint who is no saint. She is the un-saint of the pretence of belonging. She is welcomed through gritted teeth. She is the curious contradiction, the gaudily dressed and the raucously celebrated. She is the incoherent, the sincere, the love, the confusion. She is everything and nothing.
Who is Black Sara?
The impostor? The mother? The creatress? The ancient? The merging? The last word? The first word?
She is so dark, so mysterious, so magical, that if you draw too close doesn't she almost threaten to disappear?
Who is Sara la Kali?
Who is she?
Ah.
Don't you already know the answer to that question?
Sara la Kali is the Pair of Opposites.

1874, approximately

Sri Ramakrishna is irritated when a disciple – Sambhucharan
Mallick, his second Supplier of Provisions – calls him *guruji:*

'Who is the *guru?*
And who is the disciple?
You are my *guru!*'

Of course Sambhu blithely continues to address the prickly but
charming *guru* as *guruji* just the same.

1876, approximately

Since Sri Ramakrishna rarely sleeps for more than a couple of hours a night, he may often be found – several hours before sunrise – wandering restlessly around his room, or climbing up on to the roof above and gazing out at the Ganga, or strolling up and down his verandas, or mooching around in the temple gardens. Whenever he draws close to the *nahabat* during his regular perambulations (the tiny storeroom at its base now home to his wife Sarada Devi, his beloved niece, Lakshmi, and often several other visiting women, all somehow crammed in with their cooking utensils, groceries, water jars and – because of his weak stomach – Sri Ramakrishna's own special dietary provisions) the *guru* will clap his hands and cry out, 'Lakshmi! Lakshmi! Get up! Get up! Chant the name of the Divine Mother! Get up! Get up! Waken your aunt! The crows and the cuckoos are about to sing!'

The women – exhausted after a long day of mundane chores and cooking – will refuse to rise at this ungodly hour. Sarada Devi will mutter to her niece, 'Ssssh! The birds aren't singing! Don't respond!'

But more often than not, if the sleepy women unite to stage a mutiny, the mischievous saint will cheerfully generate unspeakable levels of wakefulness and consternation by playfully pouring a jugful of water under the doorsill (and drenching their thin, straw mattresses with it).
Argh!
Time to get up, ladies!
Chant the name of the Divine Mother!
Come on! Come on!
Rise and shine!

In the final years of her life, Ramakrishna's ancient mother, Chandradevi (now in permanent residence with him at the Dakshineswar Kali Temple), starts to develop paranoid fantasies about his servant and nephew, Hriday. After the tragic death of Sri Ramakrishna's other nephew, Akshay (from a mysterious fever in 1869), she starts to believe that Hriday has murdered him and constantly tells Sri Ramakrishna that Hriday is secretly conspiring to kill him and his wife, Sarada, too.

Another of her bizarre fantasies centres around food. She will never permit herself to consume her lunch before she hears the blowing of the conches in Vaikuntha. Vaikuntha is the god Vishnu's heavenly abode, a realm (not unlike Sri Ramakrishna's Kali Temple) of fun and love and feasting.

Of course Chandradevi is not yet a full-time resident of Vaikuntha, and the sound that she thinks is the blowing of conches is in fact the loud whistle informing the workers at the local Alambazar Jute Mill of their half-hour lunch break.

By and large it's perfectly fine that Chandradevi should wait to eat until the 'conches' have been blown. The only problem with this charming scenario arises during Sundays and holidays when the mill is closed and the whistle is not sounded. Chandradevi will then go hungry. If pestered to eat she will indignantly demand how she might possibly be expected to take food herself before it has been offered to Lakshmi and Narayana (Narayan is a form of Vishnu and Lakshmi is his consort)? Hriday is phlegmatic about this and tells Sri Ramakrishna that if the old woman is hungry she will simply disregard this eccentric and utterly self-imposed sacred injunction of hers. But Ramakrishna can't bear the idea of his mother's health weakening due to a lack of food, so will spend hours trying to tempt her with succulent portions of Krishna's *prasad* from the temple.

On one occasion Hriday comes up with a scheme to deceive the old woman by hiding outside her room and whistling on a pipe at the appropriate time. But Chandradevi – innocent as she is, simple as she is – will not be taken in by Hriday's cunning ruse. In fact it probably only intensifies her paranoid fantasy that Hriday is a dangerous and manipulative charlatan.

But it can't be all bad, can it? At weekends and during holidays Sri Ramakrishna's time is generally taken up by scores of visitors to the Kali Temple, so his doting mother may be expected to see considerably less of her son on these occasions. Unless she suddenly refuses to eat, that is.

Ah the conches! The conches! Whither the heavenly conches of Vaikuntha?!

Whither, indeed.

1875. The guru's sadhana is now complete. He has been told by Ma Kali that he has been placed here on earth for the benefit of mankind. But while local notoriety and the loyalty of a clutch of passionate devotees is all well and good, a serious guru (even one who will not call himself a guru) needs proper disciples. So Ramakrishna waits and he waits. And he waits.
OH WHEN, OH WHEN WILL THEY COME?!

He stands on the roof
Wailing into the darkness
For his disciples!

Perhaps something – or . . . or some*one* – might be putting them off?

1869, the Dakshineswar Kali Temple (six miles north of Calcutta)

I could never be angry with Uncle. No. Not ever. But my heart
has been broken twice over and I am not sure who will be able
to mend it aside from God. Last year, after our return from
Kamarpukur, Mathur Baba and his wife Jagadamba invited
Uncle and myself on a grand pilgrimage to all the holiest places
in north-western India: to Deoghar and Allahabad and Kasi
and Varanasi and Vrindavan. There were 125 people in our
party. Oh, the adventures that we had! Mathur Baba booked
four entire railway carriages for our private use which could be
unhooked from the main engine if we decided to tarry. We
travelled in such elegance and style (although Uncle and I
climbed off the train a few stops before Varanasi and
accidentally got left behind – but were then promptly rescued
by a kind official of the railway company!).

Over 100,000 rupees were spent on the trip. Mathur Baba
was shaded, at all times, by a servant holding a silver umbrella
and accompanied – to the fore and to the rear – by liveried
servants with silver maces. He was like a great prince.
Everywhere he went people stared after him in amazement.
He hosted special feasts for local *brahmins*. He rented two
magnificent houses and we lived there for several months in the
lap of luxury. He even hired Uncle a palanquin so that if he fell
into ecstasy on his way to visit the many temples he would not
harm himself unduly. And of course wherever Uncle travelled
in his palanquin, loyal Hridayram was always in attendance,
like a shadow, walking several paces behind him.

Uncle's body has become very soft and tender and womanly
since he completed the discipline of the *madhura bhava*. Uncle
is so sensitive now, so open. He sees God in everything.
Sometimes if Uncle is staring at an expanse of grass and
someone strolls across it Uncle will shudder, as if they are

carelessly walking across his own tender torso, and his body will exhibit severe bruising after. Or if a driver whips a horse Uncle will cry out, in misery, 'Why are they hitting me?!' I once found Uncle writhing with pain by the main *ghat* at the temple and believed that he had been soundly beaten, but then Uncle explained to me that he had merely witnessed an argument between two fishermen, and when it came to blows he felt the sudden exchange of punches raining down – one after the other – upon him. Uncle is so very sensitive. The lightest touch of a sinful person will leave marks and bruises on his skin.

Ah, there was so much grandeur and yet so much terrible poverty on our pilgrimage! Uncle's heart was greatly moved with compassion on many occasions. At a village near Deoghar he obliged Mathur Baba to give a piece of wearing-cloth and a good meal to an entire village. When Mathur Baba resisted Uncle's desperate request he threatened to stay with these humble people for ever and to live among them as one of their wretched number. Mathur Baba loves Uncle very dearly and cannot bear the idea of being without him. So he had no option but to grudgingly comply. The good-quality cloth was ordered in huge quantities from a warehouse in Calcutta.

At Kasi Uncle discovered the *brahmini* and went to visit her several times. Then at Vrindavan Uncle made the acquaintance of yet another holy woman whose name was Ganga Mata. As soon as this old woman set her eyes upon Uncle she became convinced that he was the incarnation of Radha. She called him her *dulali* (her darling) and immediately invited Uncle to stay with her and set up a permanent bed in her small room for him. Of course Uncle promptly complied with her request. Uncle is like a child! He is so unconstrained! He acts suddenly and impetuously as a child might. He felt an instant attraction to Ganga Mata – was perfectly besotted by her, forgot to eat or to sleep, just followed the old lady around like a lost puppy – and resolved to stay and live with her in Vrindavan from that moment onwards.

I cannot begin to describe the distress Uncle's crazy decision generated among our party. Had I not spent many long years nursing Uncle through his *sadhana*, six of these enduring the constant interference of the headstrong *brahmini*, only for Uncle to now abandon all that we had worked for to live with an old holy woman who would sing with him and dance with him and seemed to take a vindictive sort of pleasure in clambering up on to Hridayram's shoulders like an ancient monkey whenever she entered one of her many maddening trances?

Mathur Baba was in a dreadful state, unable to leave without securing the return of Uncle. My patience was greatly tried by Uncle. I tried to impress on Uncle's mind that he had responsibilities back at the temple, and that he had a weak stomach and needed to be constantly tended, but Uncle just laughed and paid me no heed. Only following days of endless negotiations was Uncle finally persuaded to come back with us after he suddenly remembered his ailing mother and how her heart might easily break if we returned to Dakshineswar without him.

When I arrived back at the temple, tired from my lengthy trip and perhaps even a little exasperated with Uncle, I discovered that my wife was very ill. She died shortly after. I was inconsolable. I had loved her so dearly, but sometimes she would accuse me of not loving her nearly so dearly as I loved my Uncle. Is that why she died and left me? Out of jealousy?

My wife is now gone, and what have I in return? I have Uncle. But had my beloved Uncle not been perfectly happy to abandon us all in Vrindavan for some insignificant holy woman he had known for a mere day or two?

During this time of my great suffering, Uncle continued on with his *sadhana*. He met a Muslim man by the name of Govinda Ray and was persuaded by him to practise the worship of Islam. He learned all the many rules of this faith, uttered the name Allah with great devotion, prayed three times daily and Mathur Baba even went to the trouble of hiring a special chef to cook Uncle Muslim food.

Uncle embraced his new Islamic faith wholeheartedly. He lost all interest in the deities at the temple. Then following three days of intensive trances – and the complete abandonment of all his previous behaviours and prejudices – Uncle was finally blessed with a vision of the Prophet Muhammad who walked slowly towards him and entered his body.

Uncle now believes that there is only one God, and that this God is formless but also with form. This God is beyond our humble understanding. To illustrate his theory, Uncle often tells a story about a group of blind men being led towards an elephant. The person who leads the blind men to the elephant tells them its name and asks them to describe what they find there. Each of the blind men approaches the elephant and places his hands upon it and carefully touches it. One man feels the tusk and reports back that the elephant is smooth and sharp, another feels the ear and reports back that the elephant is like a winnowing fan, another feels the leg, another the tail, another the vast flank. All the blind men have felt the elephant, and all of them have described it with perfect sincerity and accuracy, and none of the men is wrong about what they have encountered. But none will have experienced the entire elephant, their minds can only engage with just a small part of it, and their ideas will soon become fixed and unbending about what an elephant is. And so it is with faith. Each of us feels only one part of the elephant and refuses to understand that there are many parts and many ways to feel it, and that whatever our own experience, it should never be considered complete because God is, after all, like the elephant, a great and an incomprehensible beast.

Uncle recounts this story all the time; and another about

maya being like the green layer of pondweed on a lake which you can push aside with your hand, and another about the worldly man being like a snake swallowing a mole, and yet another about the world being like a hog plum (only stone and skin) . . .

In fact Uncle is very patient when people ask him about God. He tells them that there is only one Truth and that we are all seeking this same Truth, but that because of differences in languages and climate and temperament we like to call the Truth by a variety of names. But Uncle insists that everyone may find God if they are sincere and they long for him.

Uncle does not mind repeating all his best stories time and time again. Sometimes I think Uncle should save his best tales and not exhaust himself with constantly talking. He should book a lecture hall and send out invitations and tell them only to a special few, then take a collection afterwards, the way a proper pandit does. What is to be gained by Uncle telling them to anyone and everyone who turns up at his room and has the inclination to listen? But Uncle is a child. He is open. He has his own special way of seeing things and of doing things. Uncle will never be told how to think or to feel.

When Uncle's beloved nephew, Akshay, became ill after being forced into a marriage against his natural inclinations, Uncle hardly seemed to feel anything at all. He simply blamed it on the inauspicious timing of his journey (in the month of Chaitra). And when Akshay's condition worsened, Uncle calmly warned that the signs were not good for his recovery. We brought Akshay back to the temple and I arranged the best possible treatment for him, but his mysterious fever grew still more intense. Sick with worry, I turned to Uncle and asked for his help, but Uncle simply shrugged and said that the goddess had already told him the poor boy would die. Uncle is a child who will always speak his mind, but I soundly reprimanded him for these cruel words just the same. Uncle was indignant at this stern treatment and threw up his hands, exasperatedly. 'Do I want Akshay to die?' he demanded. 'I speak only under Divine Influence. It is the Mother who decrees this, not me!'

And the Mother is never wrong. Akshay died in his twenty-first year. He had been most kind to me after the recent passing of my wife, and now he, too, was gone. I wept many bitter tears for Akshay, but for as many tears as I wept, Uncle equalled my great quantity – and indeed he surpassed them – with many tears of his own: tears of laughing ecstasy.

I wonder if Uncle would laugh so heartily if his loyal Hridayram passed away? Who can tell? I try my hardest to push these dark thoughts from my mind, because who have I left now but Uncle? And it should be remembered that Uncle is a model of detachment. It was ever thus. Uncle cares only for God and nothing else. Perhaps I should try and follow Uncle's good example and seek God instead of earthly pleasures? Perhaps Uncle has cleverly trodden the wisest and the safest path all along? Worldly attachments are fleeting and painful! Who better than Uncle to teach me – by his words and his example – how best I may protect myself?

Uncle sees God in everything: in the pretty smile of a young girl and in the wide grin of a rotting corpse. They are all the same to Uncle.

Although after poor Akshay died in the *kuthi*, Uncle wasted no time in moving out of his room there and into another on the edge of the main courtyard with two verandas and a view of the Ganga. He insists that this new room of his is much better than his former one. It is a good room, there is no doubt. And perhaps it is only wishful thinking on my part, but I can't help suspecting that the *kuthi* reminds Uncle of his beloved Akshay, and the thought of still being there without him pains him more than he cares to admit.

Ah. Perhaps Uncle's enviable sense of detachment isn't quite so perfect as he thinks it is after all?

In summary

Sri Ramakrishna, he say:

If you feel *longing (i)*,
And a sense of *devotion (ii)*,
Then you will see God.

He also say:

The different faiths
Are nothing more than mere paths –
They are not the goal.

1886, deep winter, the Cossipore Garden House

Swami Ramakrishnananda, a leading monk of the Ramakrishna Order, is given the *guru*'s name when the order is formed after the *guru*'s death in tribute to how loyally he served him during his final year of life. On one occasion the future swami had rushed outside in the middle of the night in the freezing cold wearing only a thin cloth to perform some necessary (and probably rather sordid and degrading) service for the terminally ill *guru*. Sri Ramakrishna is skeletally thin and weak. He can do nothing for himself.

When the future swami returns to the room he finds that the emaciated *guru* has somehow climbed out of bed, crawled on his belly across the dusty floor and is reaching up a wasted arm to grab something off a hook. The future swami is naturally both horrified and incensed. 'What on earth are you doing?' he demands, finding it impossible to disguise the exasperation in his voice. 'It's much too cold to be out of bed!'

The panting *guru* slowly turns, and, with an immense effort, holds out his own dressing gown (a thick shawl) which he has somehow managed to pull from the hook. 'I couldn't bear the thought of you being cold,' he croaks. 'Please. *Please.* Take this.'

The future swami tearfully receives the cloth, but later gives it away, feeling himself utterly unworthy of such an extraordinary gift.

He brought me to the
    banqueting house,
And his banner over me was
    love.
Sustain me with cakes of
    raisins,
Refresh me with apples,
For I am lovesick . . .

Song of Solomon, 2:4

Secular topics
Will sometimes be introduced,   [*the guru shamefacedly
                                  confesses*]

To make people smile.

:)

Ten slightly irrelevant answers to nine slightly irrelevant questions you didn't even know you'd asked about the Divine Mother, Sri Sarada Devi

1) Sri Sarada Devi is not a terribly good cook. Because of his sensitive stomach, Sri Ramakrishna (for the vast majority of his adult life) can only ever eat very plain, bland foods (oh and sweets; lovely, sticky, creamy sweets – plenty of those). Nothing too spicy, nothing too oily, in other words. The saint's niece Lakshmi's mother is an excellent cook and sometimes prepares dishes for him when he's visiting Kamarpukur. Sri Ramakrishna is known to eat Lakshmi's mother's food and to announce delightedly, 'Whoever cooked this is a specialist!' But then, when he samples something Sarada Devi has prepared for him, to snort drolly and mutter, 'And whoever cooked this? *Hah!* A quack!'

2) Sri Sarada Devi is painfully shy and modest. She will usually only ever converse with the *guru*'s disciples by whispering her responses to a close, female companion. She will rarely appear in public, and if she does, she is often veiled.

3) When Sri Ramakrishna loses his voice towards the end of his life he usually indicates that he is talking about his wife Sarada by dint of making a small, circular gesture close to his nose (a visual reference to her nose ring).

4) Sri Ramakrishna's gruelling twelve-year period of *sadhana* is generally accepted as having come to its conclusion (or at least to the end of its most difficult and challenging phase – the *guru* never really stops his spiritual journeying; in 1873 he will embrace Christianity) with the worship of Shodasi in 1872. A few months earlier the Holy Mother (Sri Sarada Devi), then

only eighteen years of age, arrives at Kamarpukur with her father and some women of her village, on the pretext of attending a festival in Calcutta and bathing in the Ganga. In reality, though, her aim is to see her husband after a long, four-year gap.

The Holy Mother's life in her native village has not been easy over the past few years. She is known as 'the madman's wife' and is universally held as a figure of pity and ridicule. During the course of her lengthy journey to Calcutta, Sri Sarada Devi falls ill and when she arrives at the Kali Temple a concerned Sri Ramakrishna sets up a bed (a separate bed) in his own room for her. But after a short interval Sri Ramakrishna (now officially a monk, although he never wears the ochre cloth) decides to challenge himself – as a part of his *sadhana* – by sharing his own bed with his young and attractive wife without submitting to lust or to temptation (during the course of their 27-year-long marriage their relationship remains happy and unconsummated).

In June 1872, during a special festival at the Kali Temple, Sri Ramakrishna makes all the necessary preparations in his room for an important 'mystery' worship. This worship (it soon transpires) is the worship of Shodasi, an aspect of the goddess Durga, the Queen of Queens, a sixteen-year-old girl who represents the sixteen different types of desire. The teenage Sarada is led into Ramakrishna's room and is placed on a chair and worshipped there (sixteen objects are offered, water is liberally splashed, *mantra*s are chanted) in a lengthy and ornate ritual. After several hours the worshipper and the worshipped become completely identified with the *devi* in a mutual state of *samadhi*, and from this time forth Sri Ramakrishna believes – or professes – Sri Sarada Devi to be a living incarnation of the goddess.

5) Sri Sarada Devi's needs are few. For the vast portion of her married life she dwells (separate from her husband) in a tiny

storeroom at the base of the *nahabat,* a tower built by the Rani for musical performances. Because of her immense modesty she surrounds the base of the tower in grass screens. Whenever anything interesting is happening in Sri Ramakrishna's room (which lies a stone's throw away) he flings open his door so that she might hear, and she secretly observes unfolding events through a small spy-hole which she has painstakingly cut into the straw matting.

6) After several months of sharing Sri Ramakrishna's room with him it transpires that Sri Sarada Devi is getting very little sleep because of her husband's frightening and erratic night-time activities. Sometimes the saint will descend into *nirvkalpa samadhi* as he lies next to her in bed and she becomes fearful that he is actually dead. She tries to revive him but is often unable to do so and is forced to call on Hriday for assistance. On discovering how anxious this is making her, Sri Ramakrishna suggests that his wife goes and stays with his aged mother in the tiny *nahabat* where at least she can be expected to garner herself a few hours of undisturbed sleep. But not too many, obviously, or he'll fill a jug in the river and soak her mattress with the contents.

7) The *guru*'s niece, Lakshmi (who is ten years Sarada's junior), is the Holy Mother's constant companion. Lakshmi has learned the basics of reading in her home village, and Sri Ramakrishna (although virtually illiterate himself and a despiser of 'knowledge') encourages her to teach these to the Holy Mother. Once they have been mastered, he hires a student in Calcutta to raise them both to an even higher standard of literacy.

8) Sri Ramakrishna has a devotee called Golap Sundari, generally known as Golap-ma. She is a widow who has also lost her two children (her son as a boy and her daughter as a

young woman). When the *guru* hears Golap-ma's sad story he cheerfully informs her that she is actually very lucky, because God always helps those who have no one else to turn to. He then instantly cures her of her overwhelming burden of grief with a quick, light touch.

Later on he tells the Holy Mother that in the future, when he's gone, Golap-ma will be her permanent companion. And so – aside from a difficult year in 1887/8 when the Holy Mother returns to a life of loneliness and penury in Kamarpukur – it eventually transpires. Golap-ma does in fact become the Holy Mother's ferocious, self-appointed guard dog. The Holy Mother depends on her completely. She nervously holds Golap-ma's hand climbing in and out of carriages, and when appearing in public makes a habit of always humbly walking several paces behind her.

Golap-ma is tall and stern and very traditional with a high-pitched voice and a slightly tactless manner. She regularly offends people without really meaning to, and the furious disciples often ask the *guru* to reprimand her, but he never will – at least, not in person. He finds Golap-ma much easier and more receptive to his discipline in her dreams.

Golap-ma dedicates her entire life to the service of others. The Holy Mother tells a story about a trip they take together to Vrindavan. In Krishna's temple a stir is caused during the *arati* when a baby defecates on the tiles. Everyone is horrified, and shakes their heads and tuts disapprovingly, but it is only Golap-ma who – without a word – tears a strip off her own sari and quietly and uncomplainingly cleans it up.

Of course there are several women devotees who, over the years, serve Sri Sarada Devi with incredible kindness and humour and devotion, but Golap-ma is her rock. She indignantly protects the Holy Mother from insensitive devotees who sometimes pester her. She runs the Holy Mother's household with an extraordinary meticulousness and efficiency.

Like the *guru* she loves (although it's questionable whether she actually loves the Holy Mother still more), she abhors any kind of pointless waste. Every household scrap is carefully disposed of or recycled: food leftovers to the cows; bits of orange peel are dried in the sun and then used as fuel. Even the stalks of the betel leaves are neatly put aside and fed to the guinea pigs (who adore them).

9) Sri Sarada Devi is a difficult individual to pin down – so quiet, so unconfident, so obliging, so self-effacing. It's often easiest to get a sense of her through her relationships with others. Towards the end of her life, on a visit to Varanasi, the Holy Mother is sitting with Golap-ma and a small group of friends when a woman approaches (having heard that the Holy Mother is *in situ*) hoping for an introduction. She apprehends the group and is initially unable to tell which of them is Sri Sarada Devi. Because Golap-ma is tall and stern-looking with an authoritative air, she initially holds out a hand to her. Golap-ma says nothing, merely points, stony-faced, to Sri Sarada Devi. The woman turns, slightly embarrassed, and offers her hand to Sri Sarada Devi. Sri Sarada Devi, not missing a beat, silently points back to Golap-ma. The woman turns, perplexed, to Golap-ma. Golap-ma points, scowling ferociously, to Sri Sarada Devi. Quick as you like, Sarada points, eyes twinkling, to Golap-ma. And so it continues, until Golap-ma eventually snaps, bellowing at the terrified woman, 'What's wrong with you?! Are you *completely* incapable of telling the difference between a human face and a divine one?!'

10) On their final trip to Varanasi together, talk between Golap-ma and Sri Sarada Devi turns to liberation in death (to die in this ancient city is a promise of liberation) and Golap-ma, after some thought, looks Sri Sarada Devi square in

the eye and passionately declares, 'Liberation? What's the point in that? I don't *want* liberation. I want *you*!'

Aw.

Although . . .

But what foolishness!   [*Sri Sarada Devi retorts,*
                            scandalised — quite ruining
                                the lovely, sisterly atmosphere]
Don't you know that the Master
is liberation?

Remember this? From earlier?

If given the choice,
I love to see God's *lila*
As a human being.

I sleep, but my heart
    is awake;
It is the voice of my beloved!
He knocks, saying,
'Open for me, my sister, my
    love,
My dove, my perfect one;
For my head is covered with dew,
My locks with the drops of the night.'

Song of Solomon, 5:2

1881, approximately. The Dakshineswar Kali Temple. The Master's room. The Slacker approaches the Master

Lazy truth seeker (*exasperated*): 'My life is so busy. Finding God is so difficult. And prayer and *japa* take up so much valuable time. Perhaps you might like to give me some experience of God directly?'
Sri Ramakrishna (*closing his eyes with a sigh and entering into samadhi*): 'Oh, Mother! This person won't do anything for himself! What now? Am I to be expected to make curd from milk, then butter from curd, then to plop the butter directly into his mouth?!'

15 August 1886
Bring out your hankies. No. Put them away again. No. Bring out
your hankies. No. Put them . . .

Aaaargh!

The 'is he?'/'isn't he?' death of Sri Ramakrishna

My, oh my, what an extraordinary scene . . .
It is late at night. Let us imagine a beautiful but waning moon
hanging loosely upon – almost in danger of falling from – its
inky peg of sky. This moon reflects a thin, silver path into the
mysterious and still-inkier holy river below. The Ganga seems
restive. She sighs. The stooping willows try their best to
comfort her by lightly dragging the feathery tips of their
branches across her sacred, puckering brow. But the river will
not be mollified.

It's a melancholy world! Yet Sri Ramakrishna – mere hours
from death – is in a cheerful mood. Earlier that same afternoon
he has consulted the almanac to find out if 16 August 1886 is an
auspicious day.
Ah, yes! Look at that! It is! Good.

He has no voice left, but somehow, miraculously, he has
contrived to spend two entire hours in the afternoon talking to
a well-to-do visitor about *yoga*. He even manages to consume
half a cup of liquid farina pudding prepared by the anxious,
loving hands of the Holy Mother. But he is warm. *Very* warm.
He is hot – feverish.

The devotees prop him up against five pillows and ten of them
are fanning him in unison while Narendra (the *guru*'s most
beloved) gently massages his feet. Every so often the *guru* whispers
to Naren, and also signs when his voice gives out, 'Take care
of them. Take care of my boys. Please – please take care of them.'

Eventually he asks to be laid down on his side. He doesn't seem unduly bothered about the pain which must, in all candour, be perfectly excruciating.

Over recent days he keeps murmuring that the vessel which is floating on the surface of the ocean is now two-thirds full of water. Soon, very soon – and suddenly – it will fill up completely and plummet to the ocean bed. When he is dead, the *guru* seems to think that he will spend some considerable period of time under the surface of the sea.

He often points to his – 'this' – body and whispers, 'There are two people here: one is the Divine Mother, and the other is her loyal devotee. The devotee is sick.'

He no longer appears able to see the edges of things. Everything – including himself, his devotees – is now just God. Simply God. It is all God. A joyous mess of rapidly vibrating, dividing and coalescing, multicoloured particles of light. How on earth might he be expected to delineate between . . . ?
Life and death?

But there are still some hard facts remaining – some constants, some certainties: he expects to be reborn in a north-westerly direction (Canada? San Marino? *Belarus?*) in approximately 100 years' time (an *avatar*, Sri Ramakrishna avows, must always submit – nay, embrace – rebirth for the universal benefit of mankind). The *guru*'s niece Lakshmi and Sri Sarada Devi are not remotely happy at this prospect. They don't want to be reborn! Life is too long and dreary and tough! But if the *guru* is reborn, will they not then also be reborn along with him? Are they not, after all, an essential constituent of his divine play here on earth? The *guru* is amused by their palpable sense of disquiet. Don't they love him so dearly, he argues, that any kind of future existence – even a heavenly one – lived without him would be rendered unendurable?

At one o'clock in the morning the *guru* suddenly falls to one side. He emits a strange groaning sound and all the hairs on his body stand on end. Narendra releases the *guru*'s feet with a traumatised cry and sprints from the room. There is a doctor present (who is also a devotee). He takes the *guru*'s pulse, shakes his head and then begins to sob.

The young man who will one day become Swami Ramakrishnananda starts to roundly chastise everybody. How can they react in this way? Isn't the *guru*'s pulse constantly slowing down when he enters a deep state of *samadhi*? How can they be sure that this is any different?

The *guru*'s beloved nephew and servant, Ramlal, is not present. He has spent the night in the *guru*'s room at the Dakshineswar Kali Temple. He is immediately sent for. Who better understands the Master's curious physical and mental proclivities than his nephew, after all?

(*And Hriday? What of Hriday? His other nephew? Shouldn't Hriday be here?*)

Ramlal arrives in the Master's room at around 3 a.m., his cheeks already streaked with tears. He inspects his Uncle's body. Like the future Swami Ramakrishnananda he isn't certain that the *guru* has passed. He asks for Vishwanath Upadhyay to be called for.

In the meantime, about twenty devotees – including Narendra – have returned to the room and are seated on the floor and loudly – sonorously – chanting: '*Hari Om! Hari Om! Hari Om! Hari Om!*' in the desperate hope of calling the Master out of his deep *samadhi*. This chanting continues, uninterrupted, for the next twelve, long hours.

Vishwanath has arrived.

(*Quick! Make way for Vishwanath! What does Vishwanath say?*)

Vishwanath feels the *guru*'s body and detects some tiny signs of life.

'*Hari Om! Hari Om! Hari Om! Hari Om!*'

He comes up with the idea of rubbing clarified butter along the *guru*'s backbone (the channel of his *kundalini* – the source of

268

his prodigious, spiritual energy). This is gently and lovingly done.

'*Hari Om! Hari Om! Hari Om! Hari Om!*'

Initially there are signs of life, but then, ah then, slowly but surely, the *guru*'s body starts to turn cold.

'*Hari Om! Hari Om! Hari Om! Hari Om!*'

By one – two o'clock in the afternoon (but what meaning has mere time now?), the *guru*'s once bright eyes begin to close. His golden skin starts to dry and crack.

The chanting stops. Does it stop very suddenly, we wonder, or does it just gradually, imperceptibly, peter out? The tears – ah, the tears – begin to flow. He has left them. The Master is gone. Their beloved *Paramahamsa* is no more. The man who was Rama. The man who was Krishna. Their everything. Their all. The *guru* who would not be called . . . who would not . . . who could not be . . . The *guru* is dead. He is dead. He is *dead*.

How? But how? *How?* How is this possible?

Shhhh!

'The key to this room,'
He whispers, 'has to be turned
The opposite way.'

*In one swift move, Sri Ramakrishna cheerfully puts to bed that
eternal, Hindu bugbear of whether God is with or without form:*

If God was water . . .
With form he'd resemble ice.
Without? Clear liquid.

Such dreadful news: Mathur Baba – our great patron, our loving benefactor, our strong shoulder to lean upon – has been cruelly snatched away from us! He has been killed by a vicious strain of typhoid fever. Each day for several weeks I have travelled to Mathur Baba's home and sought reports on his worsening condition. My heart is so heavy. I am feeling so numb. When I think of how poor Mathur Baba has suffered my stomach twists and throbs inside my belly.

Uncle has been very calm. I keep telling Uncle that Mathur Baba pays for everything – for all our minutest needs – but Uncle simply shrugs. The Mother has promised him, Uncle says, that he will have four main Suppliers of Provisions in his lifetime. Mathur Baba is just the first of these. Uncle is extremely confident that there will be several others.

Uncle thinks himself immune to earthly attachments. He did not trouble himself to visit Mathur Baba in his final weeks. Perhaps Uncle felt that Mathur Baba might try and make him use his supernatural powers to heal him of his vicious disease? Mathur Baba has not been afraid of making such requests in the past, and Uncle has paid a high price for indulging him.

Mathur Baba is a fine man – a great man – and wealthy beyond our wildest dreams. He loves Uncle almost as much as I do. Uncle is his great joy, his delight, his passion. But Mathur Baba can often be hot-headed, too, and dangerously impetuous in his dealings with others. On one occasion he came running to Uncle after he had ordered his guards to kill a man during the course of a violent dispute with some other landlords. They promptly carried out his instructions – the man was murdered! Mathur Baba feared that he would now be imprisoned for his part in the crime. Uncle was the only person he could think of to turn to. And Uncle was furious with Mathur Baba! He was disgusted by his behaviour. Mathur Baba begged Uncle on his knees to save him from his awful fate and Uncle growled – as he always does – that he would place the matter in the hands of the Divine Mother. He stamped off to the temple and he prayed. And Mathur Baba was kept safe. He was preserved. Who can tell if Uncle was the sole reason for this fortuitous turn of events? But since this occurrence Uncle has been quite irritable with Mathur Baba, and although he loves him dearly he worries himself about Mathur's *karma*.

Mathur Baba has been a rock to us. He has always treated Hridayram with courtesy and respect, and where Mathur Baba leads others will surely follow. If Hridayram asks Mathur Baba for any little thing that Uncle needs Mathur Baba will always gratify his request.

Where will we be without Mathur Baba?

I asked Uncle whether Mathur Baba's faithful service to him will exempt Mathur Baba from the cruel cycle of rebirth, but Uncle has been strangely vague in his response. This has made me very anxious and doubtful. After the death of my beloved first wife – and then Akshay so soon afterwards – I have been turning my mind to spiritual matters. I have increased my devotions to Ma Kali in the temple. I have practised some austerities and am now saying *japam* quite regularly. Uncle is my example. Like Uncle I have sometimes taken off my sacred thread and put aside my wearing-cloth. Why should I not achieve all that Uncle has achieved if I focus my mind diligently just as he has done?

Uncle often says that if anyone cries out to the Divine Mother with a sincere and a longing heart then she will always respond. And Uncle is perfectly correct. It did not take long before my efforts were repaid by a series of brief visions and delightful, spiritual sensations.

Ah, these heavenly joys are truly intoxicating! No earthly bliss may hope to compare with them. But my achievements have been small and intermittent. I am very hungry for many more. I want to be just like Uncle and enjoy all the heavenly pleasures that he enjoys.

I have asked Uncle for spiritual guidance, but Uncle simply keeps on telling me that all blessings will be mine if I continue to serve him with my whole being. 'How will it be,' he asked, 'if we are both in a constant state of ecstasy? Who will take care of us then?'

Even Mathur Baba was highly critical of my new spiritual direction. When he found me late one morning (after my many chores were done) seated in the *panchavati*, surrounded by a small crowd of onlookers as I gasped and cried in ecstasy there (exactly as dear Uncle does), he scolded me soundly and asked where Uncle was and why I was not attending to him. He said that he and I had been placed on this earth to serve Uncle and not for any other purpose. He said that it was mere foolishness to try and impersonate Uncle. There is only one Sri Ramakrishna, he said.

Later I overheard him in conversation with Uncle, demanding to know why Hridayram was troubling himself with pointless austerities and *japam*. Uncle just shrugged and said that he had nothing to do with it. 'If Hridayram turns his heart to the Divine Mother then the Divine Mother will respond exactly as she sees fit,' he muttered. 'Do not worry,' he then added. 'She will give him a taste of bliss and then return him to his normal self again.'
Mathur Baba just laughed and said, 'Ah Father, I'm no fool. This is not the work of the Mother. This is all *your* doing.' But Uncle said nothing.

A few nights later I happened to see Uncle heading out of his room and making his way, alone, towards the *panchavati*. I went to fetch his towel and his water pot (thinking he might be in need of them), and as I ran along the path to catch up with him again I was overwhelmed by an exquisite vision.

Uncle – walking directly ahead of me – was suddenly transformed, on the inhalation of a breath, into a luminous, radiant being. His whole body glowed. He was no longer simply a man, but a million blinding particles of light. And as he walked his feet did not touch the ground. He floated just above it. I blinked and dashed at my eyes with my fists. But everything remained exactly as before: the water pot, the path, the trees. All except for Uncle, that is, except for luminous Uncle; glorious Uncle. And as I watched him I knew in my soul – or I was told – that Uncle is an incarnation of God. My heart was filled with inconceivable amounts of emotion. I could hardly breathe. I stopped in my tracks, my eyes streaming with tears. And it was in this brief moment that I so happened to look down upon myself and saw, to my great astonishment, that I, too, was luminous. Just like Uncle. I was luminous! Because I was Uncle's servant. And I was created to serve Uncle, from the same substance as Uncle. I was a little part of Uncle. I was reflected in his radiance.

I cannot be sure what happened next, only that the blissful waves engulfed me completely and I collapsed to my knees and began to shout. 'Uncle! Uncle! Sri Ramakrishna! We are not mortal beings! We are not mortal beings! I have seen it! I have seen what we are! We are luminous! We are made from God! Oh why, oh why is this happening to me? What shall we do now? Sri Ramakrishna! Sri Ramakrishna! What is our mission? Surely we must travel the world and liberate souls together!'

'Hush! Hush!' Uncle was suddenly standing by my side and his face was creased with rage. 'What on earth are you doing, Hridayram?' he demanded. 'Stop making a scene like this! People will think some dreadful accident has befallen us!' But I could not stop. I was overwhelmed by emotion. I was sobbing and calling and beating at my chest. Until finally Uncle lost his temper. 'This is impossible!' he exclaimed. 'Mother, please make Hriday his old, boring self again.'

Uncle lightly touched my shoulder with his hand, and as soon as I felt the light pressure of his fingers all the light and the joy abandoned me completely. I was back to my former self once more. But the contrast between these two states was so extreme. The joy had been so violent. And now the dullness that replaced it was unendurable.

'Why have you made me dull, Uncle?' I wept. 'Why have you taken my joy away from me?'
Uncle looked apologetic and almost sad. 'I haven't taken it away for ever, Hriday,' he said. 'You will get it back when you are better prepared for it.' And then he shook his head and added, 'To make so much fuss about a little bit of ecstasy! I experience such moods all day, every day. How would it be if I behaved as you just have?'

I will not call Uncle a hypocrite, but have I not stood by and watched Uncle behave like a madman throughout the long years of his own *sadhana*? Have I not watched him fall to the ground screaming and rub his face in the dirt crying, 'Mother! Mother!' Have I not scowled but said nothing as he crouched naked in a tree, urinating freely, producing the ear-splitting cries of a monkey? Have I not indulged and supported a million such extremities from Uncle? And now? To have my joy taken away after a single incident? Is this not too harsh?

Of course I heard what Uncle told me, but in truth I did not listen to him. In the weeks that followed I secretly continued on with my austerities. Then late one night, feeling myself possessed by a powerful spiritual urge, I walked to the *panchavati*, sat myself down on Uncle's special meditation seat and began to pray there. Yet within only a few, brief seconds of closing my eyes they sprang wide open again. What horror was this? I felt as if I had been covered in flaming charcoal – as if a pan of hot fat had been poured over my whole, miserable body.

I screamed in shock and in fear and in agony. The pain was unendurable! Mere seconds later I saw Uncle running towards me. 'What are you doing, Hriday?' he demanded.

'I am burning, Uncle!' I cried, almost insensible with the pain. 'I am burning! I am scorching – from my head to my feet! Help me! Help me!'

Uncle reached out his hand and he lightly touched my chest and instantly the pain was gone. I fell from the seat. I was shivering with shock. Uncle stood before me, shaking his head. 'Why are you persisting with this, Hridayram?' he asked, quite forlornly. 'Did I not tell you that serving me would be enough?'

Oh yes. Uncle did tell me. But was serving Uncle enough for poor Mathur Baba? Did serving Uncle so faithfully release Mathur Baba from the wretched cycle of death and rebirth?

I have learned my lesson. What other choice is there? My hands are now tied. I am bound to Uncle. I have accepted my place. I am resigned to it. So I continue to serve Uncle faithfully. But there is a shadow fallen across my heart. And there are voices that whisper to me, that taunt me – resentful voices, ambitious voices.

Sometimes I quietly ponder that conversation between Uncle and Mathur Baba, and how Mathur Baba thought Uncle was simply toying with Hridayram. How Uncle said that I would experience bliss and then return to my former self again. Uncle has many powers. I have witnessed his use of them. But why would Uncle, who loves Hridayram so dearly, use these powers to end Hridayram's bliss? Is Uncle only being self-serving? Does Uncle not think there is room enough in the Dakshineswar Kali Temple for two *Paramahamsas*?

These are dark imaginings. And I must be careful of them. Because Uncle has the power to read the thoughts of others. Uncle looks into people's minds and sees everything hidden there, as if he is idly peering at the contents of a glass case.

So I serve Uncle as dutifully as I can, although all my former habits and simple pleasures seem dry and tiresome to me now. What is the point in anything? Mathur Baba has gone, and with him all assurance of worldly comfort and happiness.

Ah, but my life winds on. I have taken a new wife. I have earned enough money over recent years to build a new worship hall in my home village. I am still a priest at the Dakshineswar Kali Temple. I have purchased a cow. And of course there is Uncle. There is always Uncle. Oh, surely that must be enough?

Approximately twelve years later. The struggling guru asks Ma Kali why he shouldn't be cured of his throat cancer:

'Ma, I cannot eat!'   [*the poor guru cries*]
'But you eat through all these mouths . . .   [*Ma Kali roundly
                                                  chastises him*]

Through your disciples!'

A momentous development: 6 November 1885, at Syampukur (Sri Ramakrishna's temporary residence in Calcutta), on the day of the Kali Puja

The Master has asked his devotees to make the necessary arrangements for the Divine Mother to be celebrated. That evening, the devotees bring numerous delightful offerings to the Master's second-floor room. What a spread! A plethora of ripened fruits and colourful, creamy sweets and bowls of fragrant rice pudding (baked with coconut milk and cardamom and rose-water and vanilla); plates bearing sandal-paste and vilwa leaves and burning cones of aromatic incense; there are mounds of flowers, especially generous quantities of Kali's favourite giant, trumpet-shaped hibiscus with its sumptuously long and arching yellow stamen poking – quite indecently – from the midst of its gaping, scarlet maw. All these are brought and respectfully presented before the beaming *guru*, who is smartly attired in a new wearing-cloth, and has been experiencing (quite involuntarily) a heightened state of almost perpetual ecstasy throughout the entire day so far. There are about thirty people present. The mood is joyful and harmonious.

The *arati* commences. But something is not quite right. There is no image of the goddess in the room. Sri Ramakrishna sits amid the offerings and tells the devotees to sit quietly with him and to meditate for a while. Time passes. (*Aaaauuuuummmm!*) And more time passes. (*Aaaauuuummmmm!*) And still more time passes. (*Hmmm?*) How much time? We cannot say. Then the *guru* quietly turns to Girish Chandra Ghosh and murmurs, 'It is the Divine Mother's day.'

Girish – who is an artist, and emotional by nature – is suddenly overwhelmed by an inexplicable feeling (hysteria? Mindless compulsion? Love?) and finds himself frantically grabbing garlands of flowers and tossing them at the *guru's* feet ('I do not know what took hold of me,' he says afterwards). All the while Girish is crying (accompanied by an equally fervent Ram Chandra Datta), *'Jai* Sri Ramakrishna! *Jai* Sri Ramakrishna! *Jai* Sri Ramakrishna!'

The remaining devotees, inspired by their example, then promptly follow suit, proffering a rich abundance of other objects to their beloved *guru*. One devotee prostrates himself before the Master, pushing his head against his feet.

'Jai Ma!' the devotees chant. *'Jai* Ma!' (Victory to the Mother!) Sri Ramakrishna instantly falls into a state of deep *samadhi*. He is facing north. He is holding his arms out as Ma Kali does in her sacred images: the fingers of one hand indicating fearlessness, the other granting boons. He seems to have no body consciousness and his skin . . . ah, his legendary, golden skin . . . it *glows*.

The devotees are mesmerised by the *guru*. They are in awe. They are transfixed. They are speechless. After a lengthy duration, furtive glances are exchanged, throats are nervously cleared, and then they quietly commence – with hushed and reverential voices – the singing of hymns. It's as if the Divine Mother herself is now inhabiting the *guru*. God is here, in this very room. She is he. He is she. They are one.

Extraordinary, eh? But let's shift our focus, just for a moment, from these curious activities joyfully unfolding in a slightly threadbare Calcuttan sitting room, to some other places in the world (Really? There are *other* places?), where, that same month, the Serbian army will occupy Bulgaria, Gottlieb Daimler will present the world with its first motorcycle, Pope Leo XIII will publish an important but slightly drab encyclical entitled *Immortale Dei* (about the delicate balance of relations between Church and state), and a meteor shower will be caught on camera for the first time.

Click!

Ten days earlier, Johannes Brahms, a composer, who, like Sri Ramakrishna, is both a traditionalist and an innovator ('Such a man, such a fine soul,' gasps Antonin Dvorak, 'and he believes in nothing! He believes in nothing!'), will premiere his final symphony: No. 4 in E Minor. He will conduct it himself, in Meiningen, central Germany, probably in a cheap suit, with no socks, and his giant beard shockingly unkempt. Brahms's dear friend, Hans von Bülow, on hearing the first movement of this new symphony on piano will exclaim, 'For the whole movement I had the feeling that I was being given a beating by two incredibly intelligent people.'

And so it must be this – this orchestrated beating; but what else? – that serves as the emotional soundtrack to the curiously smooth and strangely inevitable but still oddly faltering and clumsy transition of Sri Ramakrishna from man into God. We see the scene before us, once removed, through a series of tiny, glass slides with added colour (blotches of yellow and red and green applied with a possibly over-generous brush). Ah, here is the *guru* entering the room . . . Here is a close-up of his beaming face. Here are a group of passionate devotees . . . Here – goodness gracious – the next slide . . . a devotee collapsed in a clumsy heap, insensible with devotion, against a wall . . .

The ardent opening notes of Brahms's passionate 4th Symphony – the sweep of violins and the violas, the cellos – these notes newly hatched, just born, are spinning across the stratosphere: in the next slide the devotees are pelting the Incarnation with handfuls of giant hibiscus. What rhythmic instability the Brahms is conjuring up . . . ! How fragmented

282

the melody . . . ! How devastating the descending
sequence . . . ! Look at that! It's the *guru*'s feet . . . Oh!
And that! The curious arrangement of his golden fingers . . .

How ludicrously sincere and focused this music is – how
utterly romantic, how ridiculously over-wrought. Our hearts
are beating so violently. The fragrance of the flowers – the
warmth of the incense – the glow of the full moon. The
flutes . . . the clarinets . . .

And in the midst of all our sudden excitement (our perspiring
hands, our trembling breathlessness) the little wooden box of
precious slides goes cascading down on to the floor, disgorging
its contents. We drop to our knees. Our hands pat around
blindly to retrieve the slides. The floor is so dusty – the edge
of an old Turkish rug, frayed and curling, an old drawing pin,
a moth ball, a spider's web, the badly sanded floorboards
splintering into the pads of our tender, exploring fingers . . .
Oh but what joy! Eh? What drama! What mystery! What
seriousness! What obviousness! What silliness! What . . .
what *fun*!

Five minutes later . . .

Sorry . . . but I . . . did something . . . something quite
significant actually just happen there?

Like an apple tree among the
    trees of the woods,
So is my beloved among the
    sons.
I sat down in his shade with
    great delight,
And his fruit was sweet to my taste . . .

Song of Solomon, 2:3

Remember how Sri Ramakrishna once said:

The use of these words:
'*Guru*', 'Father' or 'Master'
Pricks my flesh like thorns!

Hmmm. So if those words simply won't do, then . . . then how
about . . . uh . . . how about: 'Incarnation'?

Might that possibly suffice?

When the lamp is lit
No invitation is sent,
But moths come in swarms.

Aw. Lighten up a little, will you?

You're in the orchard!
Why waste your time counting leaves?
Eat fruit! Be happy!

My Dear Dr Wainwright,

I trust that this letter finds you in excellent health. I am very well.
Papa – as I'm sure you can imagine – is positively blooming. He
spends every waking minute at the Indian Museum cataloguing and
displaying his precious and beloved artefacts. I wish I could give you
a more complete description of Mr Walter Granville's new building,
but suffice to say that it is handsome, well-aired and generously
proportioned. Papa never stops singing its praises (although it would
be difficult to imagine worse or more cramped environs than those
dreadful rented rooms in South Kensington!). He says that he feels
'the pure and adventurous spirit of Warren Hastings' constantly
guiding him. In fact after a late supper on Thursday evening
he even went so far as to lecture poor, darling Celeste (who is
currently indisposed and surviving only by gnawing listlessly
upon thin strips of sugar cane and drinking copious quantities of
double-boiled water) on 'the ancient primacy of the Brahmanical
writings . . .'!

Of course I immediately thought of you and raised a wry smile.
Indeed, this small exchange was – in all probability – the spur that
turned my thoughts to your many hilarious stories about the several
weeks you spent observing the curious antics of your eccentric,
golden-skinned Brahmin 'Truth-seeker' at the Dakshineswar Kali
Temple, and – still further – resolved me to visit these now-legendary
premises to try and meet with the infamous 'guru' for myself.

As luck would have it I had recently shared lunch with a Mr and
Mrs Peter Lamb who are staying at our lodgings and are eager for
diversions. Mr Peter Lamb is fascinated by anything water-borne
(aside, of course, from the dreaded cholera), and Mrs Peter Lamb
has a passion for all things horticultural. So it was that we ended up

288

adrift on a barge on the sparkling Hooghly – with Saaras, our trusty Hindoo guide (a renaissance man who speaks several languages, although it would be difficult to count English among the foremost of his many tongues), excitedly heading for an encounter with your dear 'Sri' Ramakrishna.

Saaras knew Mr Ramakrishna by reputation alone and seemed rather perplexed and alarmed by my desire to meet up with him, but then Saaras is a very modern-minded Bengalee. His dream is one day to become an engineer. Or a mechanic. Or even possibly a train driver. It was rather difficult (from his profusion of excitable hand signals) to decipher which of all of the above he truly aspired to.

I shall not bother you with my horribly laboured and ill-wrought descriptions of the grandeur of the temple, our magnificent approach from the river, the tumult at the ghat as we disembarked, the beggars, the bathers, the profusion of oiled bodies, the flies, the unspeakable heat, the blithely flowering oleanders, the overpowering scent of the roses in the gardens. I shall only trouble you with a description of my meeting with your beloved 'guru' himself.

After several, lengthy conversations in Bengalee we were directed to Sri Ramakrishna's room which is not – as you previously described it – in the grand Owner's House, but at the north-west corner of the courtyard and adjacent to the river with a semi-circular balcony, two verandas and perfectly enviable views on all sides.

Sri Ramakrishna was to be found sitting (cross-legged and perfectly alone) on one of these verandas loudly telling his rosary. The legendary charm – the childlike innocence and beaming smile – were not, I must confess, initially to the fore. Fifteen long years have passed since your delightful sojourn here, Dr Wainwright, and – by my half-baked calculation – the 'guru' is approaching his fortieth or so year, and now looks – it would be fair to say – somewhat less than golden; rather a little jaundiced and world-weary. He has gained some weight. He is no longer 'just skin and bone', as you once described him. First impressions were not propitious. The 'guru' was somewhat curt and abrupt to our guide during our initial introductions, but then, on espying my two mangoes (did you not say the 'guru' had a well-developed sweet tooth?), was suddenly the very acme of cordiality: palms were firmly pressed together, low bows were executed, etc. etc. The mangoes were then hurriedly snatched from my hands and carefully hidden away; Saaras claimed that they would be offered to the temple goddess during the evening worship and happily distributed among the devotees afterwards. Sri Ramakrishna then took us on a swift tour of the temple and the gardens. He seemed – to all intents and purposes – perfectly focused and sharp-witted, yet, every once in a while – and quite without warning – he would lean against a pillar or a tree or a wall, as if subject to a fit of uncontrollable swooning, then laugh, then talk to himself in what Saaras assured me was pure gibberish.

At one point he formally presented me with a fallen lotus flower (slightly crushed), then prostrated himself at my feet, then stood up again and chanted and danced (again, his dancing was not nearly so perfect or so effortless as you had previously described it), before sitting himself down under the shade of the large portico and proceeding to enthusiastically pray, encouraging myself and the Peter Lambs to follow suit. The Peter Lambs were nonplussed and we quickly beat our hasty retreat.

Sri Ramakrishna waved us off – most cheerily – after asking our guide for some kind of monetary remuneration for his time and his services (which was politely proffered by a tight-lipped Mr Lamb). And that – or so I thought – was an end to it . . . Oh, but it wasn't quite, Dr Wainwright, because as the barge pulled away from the ghat and I called out, 'Goodbye, Mr Ramakrishna!' a respectable-seeming Bengalee gentleman who was seated nearby shook his head, leaned over and quietly murmured behind his hand, 'That sorry article is not our esteemed Paramahamsa, madam!'

To cut a long story short, Mr Wainwright, we had been duped! The Bengalee gentleman, it quickly transpired, was an ardent devotee of the 'guru', and the individual we had recently spent our time with was merely his nephew, a man by the name of Harryday. I struggle to recall any mention of him in your many stories – but wasn't he perhaps the handsome but somewhat hapless character who followed the 'guru' around, preserving him from harm and dutifully cleaning up his various messes?

Our new friend, a Mr Ghatak (a matchmaker by trade, which, under the circumstances, seemed extremely appropriate, nay propitious), then proceeded to tell us all about his 'guru's' countless virtues. He told several funny stories. He said that while the 'guru' had the spirit of a child he was in fact a genius, that every sentence he uttered in conversation would be weighted with great gems of spiritual enlightenment. He also claimed that he was a brilliant mimic and a joker and that his singing voice, once heard, could never be forgotten. He said that there was never a man on earth in whose presence you could feel more loved, or seen or cherished.

Well, the Peter Lambs were perfectly entranced by Mr Ghatak's descriptions, and resolved, on the spot, to visit this adorable 'guru' with Mr Ghatak, by hired carriage, the following afternoon. I had already promised my services as typist to Papa and so was regretfully – most regretfully, I must confess – unable to accompany them. Of course you can well imagine how intrigued I was (after several hours of pummelling the keys) to find out all the gory details of the Peter Lambs' second visit.

And goodness me – it transpired that the second visit was still more perplexing than the first! When the Peter Lambs climbed into their hired carriage Mr Ghatak was already comfortably seated within, and on his capacious lap he proudly held a magnificent cauliflower as a gift for his precious 'guru'. Ah, Mr Wainwright, this innocent vegetable was shortly to be the unwitting subject of the most horrendous and embarrassing of scenes.

But first, the 'guru' himself . . .
The Peter Lambs were utterly charmed by him. When they arrived at his room (yes, the same room as the day before) the door was

open and the 'guru' was sitting in his bed – or cot – (he'd been suffering, I'm told, from a slight fever) deep in conversation with a small group of pilgrims who were lounging on grass mats liberally spread across the floor. Of course he doesn't speak a word of English (and even his Bengalee, I am told, is of the roughest hue) but the Peter Lambs found him captivating. At any given moment, they said, he would chuckle and break into song. And he was so graceful in all his movements. Mrs Peter Lamb found him delightfully gentle and feminine. Mr Peter Lamb found him to be a pinnacle of uncompromised machismo. The 'guru' is, it seems, all things to all people.

I shall not waste your precious time by extemporising about his golden skin and his heavenly trances (all of which you are familiar with to the point of tedium), but I must tell you about the reception of that most fateful of vegetables, the cauliflower. On arriving at the 'guru's' room the cauliflower was presented to him, much to his very evident delight. He took the cauliflower from Mr Ghatak and held it in his hands, simply marvelling at it, then he passed his palm over the top of it and murmured something, looking up, his eyes all aglow. Mr Ghatak happily interpreted (and I dare say he may have got his translations slightly confused), 'God is everywhere. God is in all of us. God is here – even here – in this humble cauliflower.' His eyes momentarily filled with tears. He pressed his cheek against the cauliflower's yellow crown. Then an intense anxiety suddenly gripped him and, glancing worriedly over his shoulder, he exclaimed, 'We must hide it! Quickly! Quickly! Before my nephew, Harryday, comes.'

Yet no sooner had he uttered these words than the aforementioned nephew strode into the room. His eyes scanned the scene and settled, almost immediately, upon the cauliflower. The 'guru' gasped, as if in terror, and tried to hide the cauliflower behind his back. The nephew pointed, his face darkening with fury. 'What is that?' he demanded. (These are mere approximations of the exchanges, obviously.)

'Please don't be angry!' the 'guru' whispered, cradling the contested vegetable to his chest. 'It was a gift!'

But the nephew was not remotely satisfied with this explanation. He leapt forward and tried to snatch the offending cauliflower from the 'guru's' terrified embrace. All the time he was harshly remonstrating with him, 'You know that you cannot digest it, Uncle! How many times do I have to tell you? Your stomach will not tolerate such foods!'

It did not take him long to wrestle the cauliflower from his desperate Uncle's arms. In that moment, Mrs Peter Lamb explained, almost tearfully, the 'guru' looked so tiny and defenceless that it quite literally broke her heart in two (Mr Peter Lamb, of course, wholly disagreed: the 'guru' was, he opined, the perfect example of masculine restraint and affronted dignity). Either way, Mr Wainwright, the startled Peter Lambs – and the assembled devotees – were not best placed to know how to react. Perhaps sensing his embarrassment at his extraordinary treatment at his own, dear relative's hands, one of the pilgrims asked the 'guru' a lengthy question of a spiritual nature. The 'guru', after a brief pause, began to answer him. The nephew, meanwhile, stood in the doorway, holding his trophy, taking every opportunity to roll his eyes, boredly, at each of his Uncle's intelligent pronouncements. Finally he left. The 'guru' smiled mournfully upon his departure, and – his cheeks streaking with childlike tears – confessed that he didn't understand why, if God had released him from all earthly ties, he still allowed his nephew to humiliate him so monstrously. Then, in the very next instant, he was cheerfully singing the nephew's praises again. Extraordinary!

When the Peter Lambs finally took their leave of the 'guru' (both now utterly besotted; Mr Peter Lamb is even considering learning a 'few choice phrases of the old Bengaleese' which he felt, on the 'guru's' tongue, sounded like a 'damnably fine language') the nephew approached the Lambs and asked them for money. He explained that his Uncle could not ask for himself (the 'guru' despises money, it

293

seems) but that he (the nephew) was solely in charge of his upkeep (although Mr Ghatak insists that there are others responsible for his day-to-day expenses, and that he also receives the minor privileges of a temple priest). The 'guru' was a child, his nephew maintained, and could do absolutely nothing for himself. And he had a poor wife to support. He also explained (and quite cordially) that his Uncle had destroyed his stomach during years of spiritual training so now could hardly eat a thing other than boiled rice and boiled milk and barely seasoned bitter squash soup. Cauliflower, it seems, made him subject to the most horrendous trapped wind. Mr Peter Lamb failed to specify whether money had finally exchanged hands. But it certainly may have been. Mr Ghatak was very upset about the trouble his cauliflower had generated. He claimed that the nephew guarded the 'guru' like a jailer and was constantly impersonating and undermining him. But he also admitted, in almost the same breath (just as the 'guru' himself had), that the 'guru' needed constant support and attention which the nephew offered unstintingly.

So that is where you currently find us, Dr Wainwright. Of course I am terribly eager to return to Dakshineswar to meet this captivating 'guru' for myself (although what's an uncontentious gift to take . . . A kilo of rice, perhaps?).

Oh, I am late for tea! Please offer my copious love to Beatrice and Henry and do forgive this unforgivably abrupt finishing off.

With all good wishes,

or

'Namaste!'

Miss Laura Bartholomew

PS: Papa, ever the natural scientist, wants me to be sure to assure you – for reasons of authenticity – that all the most important details of this curious little anecdote are absolutely true – the argument, the cauliflower etc. – but for some perverse reason (known only to herself) the author of

The Cauliflower ®

(can we even truly call her 'the author'? The collagist . . . ? The vampire . . . ? The coloniser . . . ? The architect . . . ? The plagiariser . . . ? The skid-mark . . . ?) has chosen to fictionalise this account.

x

LB

Girish Chandra Ghosh puts his beloved guru on the spot:

Girish, laughing, asked:
'Sir, are you man or woman?'
But he could not say.

Early autumn 1882, Jadu Mallick's Garden House

The *guru* (who will not be called a *guru*) is in the sitting room, weeping copiously, having become perfectly demented with love for Narendra Nath Datta.

Late December 1883, the Dakshinewar Kali Temple

The Master (who will not be called Master) is in his room, collapsed on his bed, weeping copiously, still perfectly demented with love for Narendra Nath Datta. A bemused devotee, Bholanath, is holding his hand and trying to calm him:
Bholanath (*concerned*): 'But is this appropriate behaviour, Master? To become so distressed because of a simple *kayastha* boy?'
Sri Ramakrishna (*briefly staunches his tears for a moment, thinks intently, hiccups, and then, at full volume*):
'WAAAAAAAAAAAAAAAAAHHHH!!!'

Six months later

One of the devotees, Prankrishna, fondly known as the Fat
Brahmin, tries to reason with Sri Ramakrishna (who is
currently in the rather unfortunate habit of endlessly holding
forth on the infinite virtues of Narendra Nath Datta):

The Fat Brahmin (*nervously but respectfully*): 'Father, if I might
just . . . If I could possibly interrupt you for a moment . . .
[*clears throat anxiously as Sri Ramakrishna – not much accustomed
to being interrupted – gazes at him, hawkishly*] . . . Narendra is
of course a lovely boy, but he has very scant education. Do
you think it might be a little rash to be so . . . so infatuated
with him?'
Silence
Sri Ramakrishna continues to inspect Prankrishna, blankly.

The Master gazes at Narendra, and sighs:

When I hear you sing,
A snake hisses, spreads its hood,
Holds still, and listens.

Several months earlier. The Master's Room. The Dakshinewar Kali Temple (six miles north of Calcutta)

Sri Ramakrishna is surrounded by visitors and devotees, but he refuses to acknowledge any of them, only Narendra:

Narendra (*embarrassed*): 'There are many people here to see you, sir. Do you think you might take the trouble to talk to some of them?'
Sri Ramakrishna (*glancing around him, perfectly astonished, as if they had all previously been quite invisible to him*): 'Oh . . . [*dazedly scratches head*] . . .'

Two months later. The Master's Room. The Dakshineswar Kali Temple (six miles north of Calcutta)

An exasperated Narendra Nath Datta sharply chastises the mooning and love-struck *guru*, warning him that if he doesn't gain some control over his adolescent ardour he will be in serious danger of damaging his reputation.
The startled and deeply hurt *guru* goes scuttling to the temple and prays to the Mother, then returns, a short while later, in high dudgeon:

Sri Ramakrishna (*hotly*): 'You rascal! For a moment you almost had me doubting myself, but then the Mother told me that what I truly love is only the God in you. Without the God in you I could not love you *at all*!'

Narendra Nath Datta laughs, bemused.

Shame, hatred and fear
Must be removed from your heart —
Before you'll see God.

. . . I have taken off my robe;
How can I put it on again?
I have washed my feet;
How can I defile them?
My beloved put his hand
By the latch of the door,
And my heart yearned for him.
I arose to open for my beloved,
And my hands dripped with
    myrrh,
My fingers with liquid myrrh,
On the handles of the lock . . .

Song of Solomon, 5:3

The guru openly and happily confesses:

Really and truly
I have no pride – not any –
Not the slightest bit!

When I consider it, I cannot fully comprehend it. I cannot
comprehend that Uncle is no longer here by my side, that Uncle
is no longer with me. Because Uncle is my every word. Uncle is
my every breath. Where is Hridayram without Ramakrishna?
Where is Hridayram without Uncle? I am torn apart. I am
empty. I am a pair of hands with nobody to serve.

And what was my crime? I had offered sandalwood paste
and flowers at the feet of Trailokya's daughter. Trailokya is the
temple owner. His daughter was a sweet child, only eight years
of age. I had seen her in the temple during *arati* and was
suddenly inspired. I took her and I worshipped her following
the ancient Tantric rights. No harm was done. But later the
owner's wife saw signs of sandalwood paste upon her daughter's
pretty feet and became enraged. She is a small-minded woman.
She is wealthy but ignorant. She thinks that for a *brahmin* priest
to worship a girl child of a lower caste in this manner is an ill
omen – that the child's future husband will now die after her
marriage.

But I meant no harm by it. Uncle is my example. Uncle is
always my example. Did not Uncle say that social and caste
rules were only to be maintained until we are able – with God's
help – to move beyond them?

It was the act of a mere moment, but the punishment
was swift and harsh. Hridayram was told to leave the temple
grounds and never to return. He quickly ran to his Uncle.
He told his Uncle what had happened. His Uncle said nothing.
His Uncle did nothing. His Uncle was a stone, a clod of
earth. What could his Uncle do? What could his Uncle say?
Hridayram turned and left. A short while later a temple
administrator asked Uncle to leave as well. Uncle did not
object. He just quietly picked up his towel, placed it over his

shoulder, and commenced slowly walking towards the temple gate. Uncle did not argue. Uncle did not fuss. Uncle did not look back. And that was all Uncle took – only his towel. Surely Uncle is the pinnacle of detachment and renunciation? But Hridayram is not like Uncle. Hridayram had grabbed what he could. No. I am not like Uncle. But surely this is because I care for Uncle? I must worry and think and plan ahead? I must plan ahead for Uncle?

Oh, when my fugitive eyes saw Uncle walking towards the gate, my heart was lifted. Suddenly there was hope! Yet before Uncle had reached the gate, Trailokya – apprehending Uncle's stately movements – hurriedly came to remonstrate with him. 'Sri Ramakrishna!' he exclaimed. 'This is a terrible misunderstanding.'

'Have you not ordered me to leave?' Uncle asked. There was no anger in Uncle's voice, only calm, only flatness.

'No, sir, no. It is only your nephew I have asked to leave,' Trailokya insisted. 'I have not asked you to leave, Father. You can stay, you must stay. Please, Father, please, promptly return to your room.'

At this, Uncle smiled, then he turned, still smiling, his towel still over his shoulder – the very image of detachment – and began walking, slowly walking, back to his room again.

So it was only Hridayram. It was only Hridayram who was obliged to leave. And Uncle would not go with him. But Hridayram tried. Hridayram tried to persuade Uncle to go with him. Had not the goddess shown him that they were created from the same luminous material, after all? If Uncle was God, was Hriday not God also? Had the goddess not clearly demonstrated to him that it was so?

Hridayram stayed at Jadu Mallik's Garden House for some days, trying to persuade Uncle that they should leave Dakshineswar together. Uncle sent Hridayram meals. Uncle visited. But Uncle would not leave the Dakshineswar Kali

Temple. Hridayram told Uncle of his hopes to set up a new Kali temple somewhere else. But Uncle was not ambitious to run his own temple. Uncle is not ambitious. Uncle is happy to stay exactly as he is, and Uncle has his other nephew – his other, younger, fresher, more handsome and helpful nephew, Ramlal – to wait upon him now. So when Hridayram persisted, when he nagged at Uncle, and wheedled and cajoled him, Uncle became incensed and finally, his eyes burning, he exclaimed, 'What am I, Hridayram? Will you treat me like some cheap trinket to be hawked from door to door?!'

It was finished. It was done. Twenty-five years of loyal service had all come to this – to nothing. And so Hridayram left with a heavy heart, a broken heart. He returned to his home village, to Sihar, and his family farm. But as he stood there and he quietly looked around him, he plainly saw that there was something wrong. There was something missing. Uncle. Uncle was not there. There was sky but no sun. There were stars but no moon. There were clouds, but no rain.

With Uncle gone, who is Hridayram, after all? Without Uncle how might Hridayram find his true path to God? Or even his path to worldly wealth? Because Uncle is surely the feast. Uncle is the heavenly carcass that the maggot of Hridayram must feed himself upon. Where has that carcass gone? How will Hridayram feed? How will Hridayram breathe? How can Hridayram even bear to look at himself, knowing that his hopeful face is no longer reflected in the heavenly eyes of Uncle?

Hridayram's health has broken down. Hridayram is a collapsing roof. He tries to save himself by remembering Uncle and doing just as Uncle does. Hridayram is no longer Uncle's shadow – he may not be permitted to stand close enough for that – but he is still his echo. He is practising the left-handed Tantric disciplines. These are dangerous disciplines. Uncle practised them under the *brahmini*, but he sternly warns others against them. Perhaps this is because Uncle fears that they will make Hridayram as powerful as he is? Did the goddess not reveal in her sacred vision that Hridayram is also made of light? Why did Uncle stop Hridayram's bliss on that fateful day? Was it love or jealousy that guided his hand?

Uncle has asked his Supplier of Provisions to send his sick nephew money. But this money has no life to it. It cannot grow. Uncle was the Wish-Fulfilling Tree, the *kalpataru*. All Uncle's leaves and branches tinkled like rupees. Uncle was the orchard and Hridayram the bird who pecked upon his fruit. Now Hridayram is just a beggar, crouching by the roadside. The fence of Uncle's orchard is too high for him to scale. Now Hridayram's only hope is for Uncle to persuade mere strangers, out of pity, to toss his estranged nephew rotting windfalls.

Uncle is free at last, is he not? Uncle is free of Hridayram. And now that Hridayram is banished, the bees are arriving in large numbers to pollinate Uncle's flowers. Uncle is blooming. But Hridayram watered Uncle and tended him before there were ever flowers. Hridayram waded through manure. Hridayram shielded Uncle from the violent blasts of his *sadhana*. But who will shield Hridayram?

Hridayram has become a hawker, selling clothes from door to door. He has been told that his Uncle is unwell, that his Uncle is dying, but he has not troubled to visit him. He keeps himself away. He is an abandoned dog. He wanders the streets searching everywhere for something, but finding nothing. He is hungry. His soul is aching. His heart is hollow. He is tossed between the storms of rage and the droughts of remorse. He knocks on doors and offers his wares. He is old and tired and worn.

Uncle sees God in everything. Is there God in Hridayram? He desperately yearns to find him. He is hungry for God. He is parched for God. He is panting. But when he thinks of God a strange thing happens: he can see only Uncle. His Uncle's back is turned. He tries to serve him but his service is rejected. Uncle kicks out his foot and the dog screams and cowers. The dog sits in dark corners, crying and gnawing at its own tail. Hridayram tries to serve Uncle but Uncle rejects his service. So he snaps at Uncle's hems. He nips furiously at his ankles. He smashes his loving fists against the wall of Uncle, but Uncle is a stronghold he can no longer assail.

They say Uncle is an *avatar*. They say Uncle will be reborn and reborn, and that the members of Uncle's divine play – his *lila* – will be reborn along with him. So there is to be no rest for poor Hridayram. No peace. And no path, except a jagged one. There is no truth, only confusion. There is no help. Who may he call upon? And who may call upon him? There is no hope. Because there is no Uncle. He was my master, my love, my *guru*, my ape, my wife, my corpse, my pain, my child, my disappointment, my every joy, my world.
But there is no Uncle.
I am a rent cloth. I am a spoiled meal. I am a shallow breath. I am a broken drum that can no longer be beaten.
Because there is no Uncle.

. . . I opened for my beloved,
But my beloved had turned
  away and was gone.
My heart leaped up when he
  spoke.
I sought him but I could not
  find him:
I called him, but he gave me no
  answer
The watchmen who went about
  the city found me.
They struck me, they wounded
  me;
The keepers of the walls
Took my veil away from me . . .

     Song of Solomon, 5:6

A dastardly plot

16 August 1886, the Cossipore Garden House. In dark corners, there's a whispering . . .

Outside in the hazy sunlight, a series of photographs is taken of the *guru*'s frail body as it lies in its coffin swamped in garlands of fragrant flowers and surrounded by a legion of devotees. A crowd has been gathering all morning. As one force, one voice, one colossal energy, they lift the *guru* on to their shoulders and march, singing rousingly, to the Cossipore Cremation Ground. A special banner has been made, covered in symbols of all the world religions. Firewood had been collected by those attending. The devotee who would become Swami Ramakrishnananda sits some way off from the giant pyre, clutching a fan, sobbing inconsolably.

The *guru*'s frail body is washed in Ganga water, dressed in a new cloth, covered in fresh garlands and placed on the pyre which is doused in sandalwood and rich, yellow *ghee*. The pyre is then lit. The flames lick and grow. The cremation ground shakes with cacophonous chanting, the violent beating of drums and the sounding of cymbals. Devotees pelt the burning body with flowers.

When the fire has burned itself out, three of the devotees collect the *guru*'s remains and tip them into a copper urn. On the march back to the Garden House (the urn carefully balanced on a devotee's head – Sri Ramakrishna has specifically asked that his earthly remains always be transported in this manner), one of the party is violently bitten by a snake (Ah . . . Perhaps it is the Master's legendary *kundalini*, out on the rampage, having fled from his burning body?). All hell breaks loose. An atmosphere of farce – of panic and chaos – is engendered.

The bite – potentially lethal – must be quickly and painfully cauterised by a hot iron.

Might the mischievous *guru* have been amused by this scene? Back at the Garden House the urn is propped on the Master's bed and the disciples sit around it meditating and chanting and exchanging fond reminiscences about the Master (Narendra does an excellent line in droll but intensely fond impressions of the Master emerging – startled and perplexed – from *samadhi*).

After only a few days, however, Ram Chandra Datta, who is renting the house, tells them that they will have to vacate the property by the end of the month and return back to their own homes. He also informs them that he will take the ashes and inter them at his Garden House in Kankurgachi Yogodyana. The disciples are upset and disappointed, and after intense discussions (did the Master not specifically ask to be interred by the Ganga?) resolve only to give Ram Chandra Datta a small amount of the ashes and keep the remainder for themselves. They ask Ram Chandra Datta to provide them with an urn, then, without him knowing, they place a tiny amount of the Master's ash into his urn and seal the lid. The vast remainder are taken, for safe-keeping, to Balaram Basu's house, but not before, at Narendra's instigation, the disciples all devour a small portion of the Master's remains so that they might become, in Narendra's words, 'living shrines' to Sri Ramakrishna.

The *guru*'s body – his human shell – has now, on two separate occasions, quite literally been consumed.

He died, virtually destitute, in 1899, but without his
encyclopedic wealth of biographical knowledge, the *Gospel
of Sri Ramakrishna* could never have been written. Hridayram
was the only living person to have stayed with the Master
throughout his epic, twelve-year-long *sadhana*, and as a
consequence, after Ramakrishna's death, he had every
opportunity to become a significant – even a respected –
figure within the nascent Ramakrishna Order. But he continued
to be a difficult and a perplexing character – a maddening
combination of helpful, self-pitying, resentful and unpredictable.

Shortly after Ramakrishna's death, the *guru*'s ashes (or at
least some of them) were installed, ready for worship, at Ram
Chandra Datta's Garden House in Kankurgachi Yogodyana (it
was a poignant interment. The disciple who would eventually
become Swami Ramakrishnananda became hysterical as the
spade patted the ground flat over the *guru*, crying, 'You are
hurting him! You are hurting him!').

Ram very kindly took pity on Hridayram and offered him
the job of priest there. It was an excellent position – full rent
and board and a generous salary. But after a few days,
Hridayram began behaving unpredictably, devouring the butter
and the sweets provided for the Master himself, and offering
only the remaining scraps (his own *prasad*, in effect) to his
Uncle. A shocked and exasperated Ram Chandra Datta
promptly – but regretfully – sacked him and sent him on
his way.

In those difficult final months, an unexpected discovery . . .

A devotee enters the *guru*'s room, but noticing that he has his eyes closed and seems to be resting (a rare thing for the *guru*), he prepares to tiptoe back out again. For some reason, however – a bedpan or spittoon that desperately needs emptying, a precariously balanced bowl of farina pudding, a buzzing fly, a fallen cloth, a dragging bed-sheet – he suddenly reconsiders and makes his way quietly over towards the dozing *guru*. He reaches out a gentle hand and touches him, very lightly, then starts, with a gasp, barely managing to contain a violent yell. He staggers backwards, blindly, his eyes rolling, his mouth slackening, as if slapped, as if tasered by a jolt of pure, undiluted . . .

Wooah! What the heck was *that*?!

The *guru* opens one eye, and peeks over at the devotee with a mischievous grin:

'Ah,' he hoarsely whispers, 'so you have found out my secret!'

Ecstasy. A protective shield of ecstasy. Powerful, constant, coursing waves of ecstasy are pervading the *guru*'s entire body. Sri Ramakrishna is cannily, naughtily, mercilessly, employing the handy device of spiritual bliss as pain relief.

Roll up! Roll up! Roll up!
For one day only! For this day only (1 January 1886 – the first
day of the New Year), your favourite guru, and mine, Sri
Ramakrishna, will be appearing, exclusively, in the guise of the
kalpataru – the wish-fulfilling tree!
Roll up! Roll up! Roll up!
Don't be late!
Don't miss out!
Come and see!

Well, by some miracle the *guru* has actually crawled out of his bed. For the first time during his stay at the Cossipore Garden House he is up, he is about, he is warmly dressed and he is planning to take a small constitutional around the gardens.

It is a public holiday. There are devotees everywhere: lying under trees digesting their lunches, sitting by the water, laughing, praying, saying *japa*, gossiping about the *guru* and about each other, telling jokes, having fun, picking flowers. It's a halcyon scene.

It should probably be observed – as we scan the local environs – that there are a few really rather important people missing. Some of the Master's closest and most trusted disciples have gone off – led by his favourite, Narendra – on a jaunt to Bodh Gaya. These core disciples – especially Narendra – are, at this stage in their *sadhana*s, very influenced by the Buddhist teachings. Several of them have avowed that they do not even think they actually believe in God. Sri Ramakrishna appears to take all this in his stride (what else can the poor *guru* do?). He cheerfully insists that it is perfectly natural for people to spend interludes in their spiritual lives *not* believing in God.

But the *guru* is very ill. He has so much that he still longs to impart to his boys. He will not be with them for ever – mere months at best. And the disciples have gone to Bodh Gaya without even telling him. Perhaps he is a little wounded? Perhaps he is secretly smarting? Who knows? And perhaps this is why he chooses today, the first of the New Year, his final year, to do what he does.

So the Master is out in the fresh air. He is walking, slowly, gently supported, around the gardens. The devotees are naturally delighted to see him (perhaps he is recovering after all! Perhaps their fervent prayers have finally been answered!) and as soon as he appears among them they swarm towards him. Girish (ever the drama queen) prostrates himself at the *guru*'s feet, loudly incanting his praises. The *guru* instantly falls into ecstasy. The crowd becomes still more jubilant, singing, clapping, chanting his name.

The *guru* returns to partial consciousness and looks around him, his face glowing with love and gratitude. How might he possibly repay their loyalty and faithfulness? He raises his arms, holds out his feeble hands, his eyes filling with tears, and murmurs, 'May you all be illumined!'
The crowd suddenly feels itself being enveloped – surrounded, permeated – by an incredibly warm and comforting hug of ineffable bliss.

The *guru* begins to move among them, barely conscious, touching them, one after the other, with his outstretched fingers. Each person responds differently to the Master's touch because each person *is* different, and the *guru* will give them only what he thinks will send them forward on their spiritual journey. Some begin praying, some speak imaginary languages, some start to sing, some fall to the ground their bodies contorting, some are silent, unable to speak, some wail and weep, some sit quietly and meditate, some dance, some whirl around and scream.

Some – just a couple – the *guru* does not touch. He withdraws his hand. 'Not yet,' he whispers, coldly. Imagine the feeling! To be refused the touch of the *guru*! To be notably excluded – and in public! One of these sorry individuals is Akshay Kumar Sen. Akshay is tiny and dark-skinned. He is not considered attractive. He is not young and plump and beautiful like the *guru*'s favoured boys. He is in his early thirties. He has lived a poor, hard life. But he is clever. He is diligently supporting himself as a tutor in Calcutta.

Akshay is desperate – needy. From his very first sighting of Sri Ramakrishna he is utterly besotted by him, but the *guru*, while unerringly polite, is always slightly cool and distant with Akshay. Many devotees are permitted to touch – even gently massage – the *guru*'s feet, but the Master will not countenance Akshay's touch. When Akshay approaches he swiftly withdraws his feet with an exclamation of disquiet. Poor Akshay. He knows that the *guru* is perfectly capable of giving him the vision of Lord Krishna which he craves more than life itself, but for some reason he refuses to. Akshay tries everything he can think of to persuade the haughty *guru*: he is helpful and humble and obliging. He brings him gifts. The *guru* loves ice – the impoverished Akshay brings him an ice cream. The *guru* turns up his nose and will not touch it. Akshay endures endless snubs and rebuttals at the *guru*'s hands. But every disciple is different. And Ramakrishna – the ever-inscrutable – is crushing Akshay's ego through *in*difference. This is Akshay's path. He will be rejected, ignored, passed over, humiliated. And even today, on this day, when everyone is touched, Akshay is held at bay.

In several written accounts of this landmark occasion, it is made clear that Akshay is rejected. In some, he is seen presenting a flower to the *guru*, even described as standing some distance away and then being genially called over by the *guru* and blessed. But the accounts of him being turned away have a greater ring of legitimacy to them. Sri Ramakrishna is not Jesus Christ. He is not democratic. He will not accept just *any*body. He is complex and discriminating. So let us imagine Akshay being turned away on that special day. And let's ponder his sense of rejection, his feelings of inadequacy, of injustice, let's dwell on his humility, his need, his poverty. Where, we wonder, may this whirlpool of emotions ultimately lead him?

A sour note has certainly been sounded on an otherwise magical day. But does it destroy Akshay's faith in the *guru*? Does it undermine his confidence in Sri Ramakrishna's status as an incarnation? Nope. Not one bit. When the *guru* dies Akshay remains one of his most ardent devotees, and after a while an urge rises within him to pick up a pen and to write about the *guru*. Akshay has no confidence – he is not well-educated, he has not attended the university, he was never a favourite of Ramakrishna's, not comfortably of the inner circle – but he picks up his pen and he begins writing down all his feelings of great love (underpinned, as they are, by this desperate sense of unworthiness, of unfulfilled desire), and creates an extraordinary landmark in the history of Bengali verse – a giant, crazy, stirring, magical, hysterical four-volume love song, a love-*rant* to the *guru*: *Sri Sri Ramakrishna-punthi*.

And perhaps this is how the Master encourages Akshay's *sadhana* – and in so doing, quite coincidentally, inspires his own, great literary monument. Ramakrishna's cruel rejection of this needy devotee only spurs on his ardour, nay, his idealism. Consummation can sometimes – just sometimes – be over-rated. Which of us remember the happy endings? Surely the poems of an unrequited lover are always the most passionate, the most moving, the most fierce, the most agonising, the most heartfelt, the most indelible?

When yearning for God,
Be just like the mother cow
Pursuing her calf.

... Oh, that you were like my
    brother,
Who nursed at my mother's breasts!
If I should find you outside,
I would kiss you;
I would not be despised.
I would lead you and bring you
Into the house of my mother,
She who used to instruct me.
I would cause you to drink of
    spiced wine,
Of the juice of my
    Pomegranate ...

Song of Solomon, 8:1

The Rani. Ah, the glorious Rani – she started off this story, did she not? And now, at this late hour, she must be cordially deputised to end it (before it's even truly begun) . . .

This is the Rani's final scene. But it is two scenes. The Rani can never do anything by halves. She is a creature of many cuts, of many edits, of many versions. All that we can be sure of, is that she is perfect, that she is noble, that she is a creature exquisitely of her time and out of it.

The Rani (the indignity!) has been struck down by chronic dysentery. Her doctors, fearing the worst, ask for her to be moved to more hospitable climes. Hospitable or no, the Rani opts for her Garden House in Kalighat (adjacent to the famous temple), which stands on the banks of a small tributary of the holy Ganga.

Shortly before her death, as is traditional, the Rani is carried down to the banks of the river and partially immersed there. It is late at night and very dark, so many lamps have been lit. In one version of her death scene a violent gust of wind blows them all out.

But the version we are following, the scene we are watching, sees the Rani blinking, owlishly, into the shining lights around her and then suddenly, furiously, impetuously, exclaiming, 'Turn off the lights! Turn them off! I have no need of them! I have no need of artificial illumination now! Turn off the lights!'

Shortly after, embraced in the ebony arms of that coruscating darkness, with a small sigh of relief, a brilliant smile: 'Ah, Mother,' she murmurs. 'My Mother. Have you come?'

An indelible moment, I think you'll all agree . . . (the sound man conspicuously checks his watch). And how fortunate that we [The Cauliflower®] were here to record it! What a *coup*! Later, however (much later), when we anxiously scrutinise the footage, we discover that we have nothing (*nothing!* Not a damn thing!) in the can.

The Divine Mother – we know for an absolute fact, we are *certain* – has come herself, in person, to escort her favourite daughter into the heavenly hereafter. But the film? The *film*?! *Urgh*. Completely blank.

Hmmm . . .
Perhaps, after all, we were just too close to see her.

We have a little sister,
And she has no breasts.
What shall we do for our sister
In the day when she is spoken
      for?
If she is a wall,
We will build upon her
A battlement of silver;
And if she is a door,
We will enclose her with boards of cedar.

I am a wall,
And my breasts, like towers . . .

Song of Solomon, 8:8

Afterword

This novel (if I can call it that) is truly little more than the sum of its many parts. It's a painstakingly constructed, slightly mischievous and occasionally provocative/chaotic mosaic of many other people's thoughts, memories and experiences. I have not lived in the nineteenth century. I have never met Sri Ramakrishna. I am not a practising Hindu. I have never visited Calcutta. If I had, I probably could not have written this book. I wouldn't have been stupid, arrogant, brave, naughty – and possibly even dispassionate – enough.

This novel is a small (even pitiable) attempt to understand how faith works, how a legacy develops, how a spiritual history is written. I have been fascinated by Sri Ramakrishna for much of my life. He's such a perplexing and joyous character. And I felt that his story might benefit from being told again – shared, enjoyed, celebrated (especially now) – but from a slightly new (and, yes, vaguely warped) perspective.

As a ten-year-old child in South Africa I was given a free album about Krishna Consciousness by an eccentric (even magical) stranger in Fordsburg's controversial Oriental Plaza. Thank you, that kind gentleman, whoever you were/are. Because that's basically where my journey began. If yours starts here, then please do have a look at some of the incredible books that have been not only the building blocks but the very joists and mortar of this one.

Nicola Barker

Books

Sri Ramakrishna the Great Master, Swami Saradananda (Jupiter
   Press)
The Gospel of Sri Ramakrishna, Mahendranath Gupta
   (Ramakrishna-Vivekananda Center)
Sri Ramakrishna's disciples are a uniformly charming
bunch, and none more so than Mahendranath Gupta, the
secretive 'M'. This would probably be my number one go-to
book on the *guru*, just because of its honesty and loveliness
and modesty.

They Lived With God, Swami Chetanananda (Advaita
   Ashrama)
Ramakrishna As We Saw Him, Swami Chetanananda (Vedanta
   Society of St Louis)
Swami Chetanananda has scrupulously detailed everything
known about the *guru* in these two wonderful books. My
humble effort owes most of what is good about it to the learned
swami.

A Portrait of Sri Ramakrishna, Akshay Kumar Sen (The
   Ramakrishna Mission Institute of Culture)
The Great Swan: Meetings with Ramakrishna, Lex Hixon
   (Larson)
Lex Hixon's work is both mesmerising and extraordinary.

This is the Isherwood section. Isherwood writes brilliantly
about Ramakrishna, but my favourite book by him – *My Guru
and His Disciple* – is not actually about Ramakrishna, as such,
but about Isherwood's touching relationship with his own *guru*,
the glorious Swami Prabhavananda.
Vedanta for the Western World, Christopher Isherwood (ed.)
   (Unwin Books)

Ramakrishna and his Disciples, Christopher Isherwood (Advaita Ashrama)

My Guru and His Disciple, Christopher Isherwood (University of Minnesota Press)

The Song of God: Bhagavad-Gita, translated by Christopher Isherwood and Swami Prabhavananda (Mentor)

The *Bhagavad-Gita* is an exquisite work of art, and this translation is just superb.

Kali: The Black Goddess of Dakshineswar, Elizabeth U. Harding (Nicolas Hays)

I owe Ms Harding a giant vote of thanks for this brilliant, beautifully written and meticulously researched work.

Offering Flowers, Feeding Skulls, June McDaniel (Oxford University Press)

Not only is this an incredible book on goddess worship, but Ms McDaniel was also immensely kind and helpful to me when I approached her for help during the writing of *The Cauliflower*.

Hinduism: New Essays in the History of Religion, Bardwell L. Smith (ed.) (Leiden/ E.J. Brill)

Transgender Spirituality: Man into Goddess, Sakhi Bhava (self-published)

I truly cannot overstate what a startling and revolutionary little book this is. It's spiritual and philosophical dynamite!

Sri Ramakrishna (1836–1886) and a Nineteenth Century Subaltern: Rani Rashmoni (1793–1861). Creating our Feminist Genealogies, Tapati Bharadwaj (self-published)

Women Writing In India: 600 BC to the Early Twentieth Century, Susie Tharu and K. Lalita (eds.) (Pandora)

Mother Teresa: Come Be My Light, Brian Kolodiejchuk (ed.) (Rider)

Mother Teresa: Her People and Her Work, Desmond Doig (Fount)

Calcutta Diary, Ashok Mitra (Frank Cass)
Calcutta, A Cultural History, Krishna Dutta (Interlink Books)
Calcutta, The City Revealed, Geoffrey Moorhouse (Penguin)
*Scenes and Characteristics of Hindostan with Sketches of Anglo-
Indian Society, Volume 1*, Emma Roberts (Elibron Classics)
Calcutta: Two Years in the City, Amit Chaudhuri (Union Books)
The Birds of Calcutta, Frank Finn (Hardpress)

The Imitation of Christ, Thomas à Kempis (Penguin)
I mention this wonderful book because it was Swami
Vivekananda's favourite.

Films

The Apu Trilogy, Satyajit Ray (Artificial Eye)
The Goddess, Satyajit Ray (Mr Bongo Films)
Calcutta, Louis Malle (Pyramide)

Radio

The Enigma of Sara-la-Kali, Tessa Dunlop (*Heart and Soul*,
BBC World Service)

Music

Night and Daydream, Ananta (Touchstone)